SPECIAL MESSAGE TO READERS

THE ULVERSCROFT FOUNDATION
(registered UK charity number 264873)

was established in 1972 to provide funds for research, diagnosis and treatment of eye diseases. Examples of major projects funded by the Ulverscroft Foundation are:-

- The Children's Eye Unit at Moorfelds Eye Hospital, London
- The Ulverscroft Children's Eye Unit at Great Ormond Street Hospital for Sick Children
- Funding research into eye diseases and treatment at the Department of Ophthalmology, University of Leicester
- The Ulverscroft Vision Research Group, Institute of Child Health
- Twin operating theatres at the Western Ophthalmic Hospital, London
- The Chair of Ophthalmology at the Royal Australian College of Ophthalmologists

You can help further the work of the Foundation by making a donation or leaving a legacy. Every contribution is gratefully received. If you would like to help support the Foundation or require further information, please contact:

THE ULVERSCROFT FOUNDATION
The Green, Bradgate Road, Anstey
Leicester LE7 7FU, England
Tel: (0116) 236 4325

website: www.ulverscroft-foundation.org.uk

FRECKLES

You are the average of the five people you spend the most time with.

When a stranger utters these words to Allegra Bird, nicknamed Freckles, it turns her highly ordered life upside down. As a parking warden, she has left her eccentric father and unconventional childhood behind for a bold new life in the city. But a single encounter leads her to ask the question she's been avoiding for so long: who are the people who made her the way she is? And who are the five people who can shape and determine her future? Just as she once joined the freckles on her skin to mirror the constellations in the night sky, she must now again look for connections.

CECELIA AHERN

FRECKLES

Complete and Unabridged

CHARNWOOD
Leicester

First published in Great Britain in 2021 by
HarperCollins*Publishers*
London

First Charnwood Edition
published 2021
by arrangement with
HarperCollins*Publishers*
London

A catalogue record for this book is available
from the British Library.

ISBN 978–1–4448–4808–3

Published by
Ulverscroft Limited
Anstey, Leicestershire

Printed and bound in Great Britain by
TJ Books Ltd., Padstow, Cornwall

This book is printed on acid-free paper

For Susana Serradas

Prologue

The crunch of a snail under my shoe, in the darkness. The crack of the shell. The squish. The ooze.

It hurts me at the back of my teeth, a shooting pain through a nerve in my gums.

I can't pull my foot up fast enough, I can't rewind, the damage can't be undone. I've hit the squishy interior of the snail's sluggish insides. Flattened and twisted them into the ground. I feel the mush on the sole of my shoe for the next few steps. Carrying a crime scene on a slippery sole. Death on my shoe. Smeared guts. A twist and wipe rids me of it.

It happens walking at night, on rain-slicked ground, when I can't see where I'm stepping and the snail can't see who's stepping. I've always felt bad for the snail, but now I know what it's like. Retribution. Karma. I now know how it feels for my outer shell to be cracked, for my insides to feel exposed.

He stepped on me.

He walked with me for a few steps too, his sole slippy with my mush. I wonder if his soul is slippy with me too. If he felt the crack and ooze of me under his gaze as he spat his hate-filled words and then walked away. My shield taken with him for a few steps before he realised he was still carrying me. A twist of his shoe, like extinguishing a cigarette, and I'm discarded.

The remainders of me on the pathway. Cracked and exposed, an unprotected soft interior I've worked so hard to protect. A leakage of all the parts that were so well-contained. Feelings, thoughts, insecurities all

1

oozing out. A silvery slivery track of emotional entrails.

I didn't see his foot coming. Wonder if I took him by surprise too.

Even though it may feel like it, this is not where it all ends. I'm not dead. I'm crushed and oozing. A smithereened Allegra Bird. You can't fix the broken outer shell. But you can rebuild.

1

When I was thirteen years old I connected the freckles on my arms together, like a join-the-dots puzzle. Right-handed, my left arm would become a web of blue pen lines. After a while it developed into drawing constellations, mapping them out from freckle to freckle until the skin on my arm mirrored the night sky. The Plough — the Big Dipper to some — was my favourite constellation to draw. It was the one I could immediately identify at night, and so when it was lights out in boarding school and silence descended upon the halls, I turned my reading light on low, clenched a blue gel pen, and traced the seven stars from freckle to freckle until my skin resembled a night-map.

Dubhe, Merak, Phecda, Megrez, Alioth, Mizar and Alkaid. I didn't always choose the same freckles, sometimes I liked the challenge of replicating this constellation elsewhere, sometimes on my legs, but crouching over for such a long period of time stung my back. Also it didn't feel natural, like I was forcing these other collections of freckles to become something they weren't. There were the ideal seven freckles, perfectly aligned already on my left arm to specifically be the Plough, and so I eventually gave up on the other freckles and each night, after my morning shower had washed the ink away, I would begin again.

Cassiopeia followed. That was an easy one. Then Crux and Orion. Pegasus was a tricky one with a total of fourteen stars/freckles, but my arms saw more sunlight than the rest of my body, face not included, so

3

it had a higher concentration of melanised cells, perfectly positioned for a fourteen-star constellation.

In the darkness of our boarding school dormitory, in the cubicle beside me, Caroline heavy-breathed as she touched herself thinking nobody knew, and Louise on the other side of me turned pages on the anime comics that she read with a torch. Across from me Margaret worked her way through an entire bag of mini Crunchies before sticking her fingers down her throat and puking them out, Olivia practised kissing against a mirror while Liz and Fiona kissed each other. Catherine sobbed quietly because she was homesick, and Katie wrote hate mail to her mam who had cheated on her dad, and everyone else in the all girls' boarding school immersed themselves in their secrets in the only small space that they could call their own while I mapped my freckles like they were stars.

My private act didn't stay secret for long. I would do it nightly, and blue pen on top of blue pen, night after night, eventually doesn't wash off. The ink lodged itself in the pores in my skin and even a scouring brush, hot water and a highly stressed nun, Sister Lettuce — nicknamed by all of us due to her tendency for beginning every sentence with Let us . . . Let us give thanks and pray. Let us open our books to page seven. Let us do lay-ups because she was also our basketball coach — couldn't do anything to get it off or make me stop. I received odd looks in the shower room, at swimming, when wearing short sleeves. The weird girl with the pen marks on her arm. They're patterns on the celestial sphere, animals, mythological people and creatures, gods and objects, I'd tell them, holding my arm out proud, never ashamed of my designs. The response to that was a lesson in ink poisoning. More

4

trips to the counsellor. Extra laps of the running track. They knew physical health equalled mental well-being and they were trying to busy me with as many activities as they could to distract me from vandalising my skin, but it all felt like punishment to me. Run her in circles. Get that girl away from her skin. But you can't get a person away from their skin. They're in it. They are it. No matter what they said, I couldn't stop. Every time the lights went out, and the silence moved in like a mist from the sea, I felt the familiar longing to connect with my skin.

I wasn't embarrassed about the pen marks. I didn't care if people stared. The only big deal was the commotion they made of it and I certainly wasn't the only girl who had marks on their skin. Jennifer Lannigan cut herself with a blade, tiny little cuts all over her legs. I had a good view of them in English class, the white gap between the top of her grey socks and the end of her grey skirt. We weren't allowed to wear make-up in school but after hours Jennifer wore white make-up, black lipstick, pierced her own lip and listened to angry music by angry men and for some reason her entire package made it acceptable to us that she would do this insane thing to herself.

But I wasn't a goth and drawing on your skin had no psychological explanations that they could find. The dorm supervisor went through my cubicle and removed all my pens, which were returned to me in the morning before class and removed again after study hour. People would watch me around pens like they would a child with scissors. So, pen-less, I kind of found myself in the same camp as Jennifer. I never understood the compulsion to inflict pain on oneself, but it was a means to an end. I took to using the

5

sharpened corner of my ruler to scratch a line from one freckle to the other. I knew better than to scratch the actual freckle, I had been warned on the perils of cutting moles and freckles. I graduated from rulers as I found sharper items: my compass, razor blades ... and pretty soon after, horrified by what she saw on my skin, the supervisor returned my pens to me. But she was too late, I never went back to using ink. I never liked the pain, but blood was more permanent. The hardened scabs between freckles were more distinctive, and not only could I see the constellations but now I could feel them. They stung when the air hit and they throbbed beneath my clothes. There was something comforting about their presence. I wore them like armour.

I don't scratch the surface of my skin any more but at twenty-four years old, the constellations are still visible. When I'm worried or stressed, I catch myself running my finger over the scarred raised skin of my left arm, over and over again, in the correct order, from one star to the next. Joining the dots, solving the mystery, chaining the events.

I'd been called Freckles since the first week of school when I arrived at twelve years old until I left at eighteen. Even now, if I randomly meet someone from school they still call me Freckles, unable to remember my real name, or probably never knew it in the first place. While they never meant any harm, I think I always knew what they really saw of me was skin. Not black or white like most of theirs, so white it reflected the sun. Not a Thurles colour, but a colour they desired and went through bottles and sprays in order to get but came closer to looking tangerine. There were plenty of girls with freckles who didn't

6

inherit the nickname but freckles on darker skin to them was different. It never bothered me, in fact I embraced it because it went beyond a nickname and held a deeper meaning for me.

Pops' skin is as white as snow, so pale in some parts it's almost transparent like tracing paper, with blue lines running beneath. Blue rivers of lead. His hair is greying and thinner now but it was curly red and wild. He has freckles, reddish ones, so many on his face if they joined up he'd be a sunrise. You're lucky they call you Freckles, Allegra, he'd say, all I was ever called was matchstick or, even better, fucking ugly! Then he'd guffaw loudly. Ding-a-ling-a-ling my hair's on fire, ding-a-ling-a-ling, call nine nine nine, he'd sing and I'd join in with him, singing the song he was taunted with. Me and him, ganging up against the memory of them.

I never knew my mam, but I know she was foreign. An exotic beauty studying on Irish shores. Olive-skinned, black-haired and brown-eyed, from Barcelona. The Catalonian Carmencita Casanova. Even her name sounds like a fairy tale. Beauty it seemed, met the Beast.

Pops says I had to get something of him. If I didn't have freckles, he doesn't know how he could have claimed me. He's joking of course, but my freckles were the calling card. When he's the only person I have and have ever had in my whole life, my freckles connect me to him in a way that feels vital. They are my proof. An official stamp from heaven's bureau that bind me to him. The raging mob could not come to our house on horseback, with torches of fire, demanding he hand over the baby the mother didn't want. Look, she's his, she has his freckles, see.

7

I inherited my mam's skin tone but I inherited Pops' freckles. The parent who wanted me. Unlike Mam, who gave me up to have everything, he gave up everything to have me. These freckles are the invisible blue ink-line, the permanent scar that connects me to him, dot to dot, star to star, freckle to freckle. Link them and you link us on and on and on and on.

2

Joining the Gardaí Siochana, the Irish police force, had been my lifelong goal. There was never a Plan B and everyone knew it. Detective Freckles is what they'd called me in our final year.

Ms Meadows the career guidance teacher had tried to push me into doing a business degree. She thought everyone should study business, even the art students who went in with their creative bendy thoughts and came out like they'd had electroconvulsive therapy after being preached to on the advantages of a basic business degree. Something to fall back on, it was always said. Business made me think of a mattress. I was hopeful about my future, I wasn't contemplating failing never mind planning on falling back. She couldn't convince me to change my mind because I saw no other place for me in the world. Turns out I was wrong. My application to the Gardaí was denied. I was stunned. A little winded. Embarrassed. With no mattress to fall back on I did some recalibration and found the next best thing.

I'm a parking warden with Fingal County Council. I wear a uniform, grey pants, white shirt, a high-vis vest and patrol the streets, not unlike a garda. I got close to what I wanted. I work on the side of the law. I like my job, I like my routine, my route, my beat. I like organisation, and order, rules and clarity. The rules are clear and I uphold them rigorously. I like that I'm fulfilling an important role.

My base is Malahide, a suburban village outside

Dublin city, beside the sea. A pretty spot, an affluent area. My home is a studio flat above a gym in the back garden of a mansion on a leafy road bordering Malahide Castle and Gardens.

She, Becky, does something with computers. He, Donnacha, works from home in his art studio, one of those nice garden rooms, doing fine art ceramics. He calls them vessels. They look like bowls to me. Not for cereal, you'd barely get two Weetabix in the base and it doesn't have the depth for enough milk, especially with the Weetabix absorption levels. I read an interview with him in the *Irish Times* culture magazine where he describes them as definitely not bowls, which is a description that brings him great insult, the bane of his professional life. These vessels are receptacles for his message. I didn't read far enough to get the message.

He talks a curious kind of prattle with a faraway look in his eye as if any of his agonising wonderings mean something. He's not a listener, which I thought would be typical of an artist. I thought they were supposed to be sponges absorbing everything around them. I was half-right. He's already so full of shit he can't make room for any more absorption, he's just leaking it all out now on everyone else. Artistic incontinence. And it costs five hundred euro minimum for one of his tiny bowls.

Also five hundred euro is my monthly rent and the catch is that I be available for babysitting duties for their three kids whenever they ask. Usually that's three times a week. Always on a Saturday night.

I wake and turn to look at my iPhone: 6.58 as always. Time to process where I am and what's going on. I find being one step ahead of my phone first thing

10

in the morning is a good start to the day. Two minutes later the alarm rings. Pops won't own a smartphone, thinks we're all being watched. He refused to have me vaccinated, not because of the health dangers, but because he had a theory they were inserting chips into humans' skin. He once brought me to London for a weekend for my birthday and we spent most of the time standing outside the Ecuadorian Embassy calling Julian Assange's name. The police moved us along twice. Julian looked out and waved and Pops felt something monumental passed between them. An understanding between two men who believe in the same cause. Power to the people. Then we saw *Mary Poppins* in the West End.

At 7 a.m., I shower. I eat. I dress. Grey trousers, white shirt, black boots, raincoat in case I need it for those little April showers. In this uniform I'd like to think I could be mistaken for a garda. Sometimes I pretend I am. I don't imitate a garda, that's illegal, but in my head I do, and I speak like I am. That air that they have. The aura. The authority. Your protector and friend when you need them, your foe when they think you're acting the maggot. They choose which one they are at any given moment. It's magic. Even the new fellas with chin-fluff can do that stern disappointed old-before-their-time look. As if they know you and know you can do better and Jesus why did you have to let them down. Sorry, Garda, sorry, I won't do it again. And the girl ones, you wouldn't mess with them, but you'd definitely go on a session with them.

My hair is long, coarse, black, so black it has a blue sheen, like petrol, and takes an hour to blow dry so I only wash it once a week. It goes back in a low bun, cap on and low over my eyes. I wrap the ticket machine over my shoulder. Ready.

I leave the garage, fifty yards from the house, separated by an enormous garden designed by an award-winning landscaper. The pathway from my place weaves through a secret garden, the route I was told to take, towards the side of the house, where I get out through the side pedestrian gate, special code 1916, the year of the Irish Republicans' uprising against the British, chosen by Donnacha McGovern of Ballyjamesduff. If Padraig Pearse could see him now, doing his bit for the Republic. Making bowls in his back garden.

The ground floor that faces me is almost entirely glass. Floor-to-ceiling sliding doors that open up like they're a brasserie in the summertime. Bring the outside in, bring the inside out. You don't know which is the house and which is the garden and then you shake it all about. That kind of designer waffle. I can see into every room. It's like an advertisement for Dyson. White circular futuristic-looking things in each room, either sucking in or pushing air out. What the window wall really does to the house now is reveal the mayhem in the kitchen as Becky rushes around trying to get the three children ready for school before she drives to work, somewhere in the city I think. I call her Goop, to myself. You know, one of those women that has kale and avocados on their weekly shop. Sneezes chia seeds and poops pomegranates.

They feel sorry for me, them in their sprawling mansion, me living in one room above a gym. In their back garden. Wearing a high-vis vest and a lightweight operational safety shoe. I let them feel that. My room is stylish, it's clean and warm and I'd have

12

to pay the same amount of rent just to share a space with three others anywhere else. They would have to lose everything to ever find themselves in my position. That's the way they see it. For me, I kind of left everything behind to gain this. That's the way I see it.

I'm not lonely. Not all the time. And I'm not free. Not all the time. I look after Pops. Doing that from two hundred and fifty miles away isn't always easy but I chose to live here, this distance from him, so that I can be closer to him.

3

I try not to look into the kitchen as I pass but Becky lets out an almighty roar for everyone to hurry the fuck up and impulsively I glance inside and see the kitchen island covered in milk and juice cartons, cereal boxes, lunch boxes, the makings of lunches, children in various states of dress, cartoons blaring on the TV. Becky's not dressed yet, unusual for her; she's in pyjama shorts and a vest with lace trimmings, no bra, her boobs low and swaying. She's lean though, she works out from 6 a.m. to 7 a.m. most mornings in the gym below my bedroom. She's one of those women that women's magazines talk about. The lean-in woman. When I hear that phrase I picture Michael Jackson doing that tilted dance move. Gravity-defying. Then you hear his feet were clicked into the stage and it wasn't real at all.

Donnacha sits on a high stool at the breakfast counter reading his phone as if nothing is happening around him. Time is no obstacle. He'll drop the kids to school and then will dilly-dally in the studio with his bowls. Just as I've safely reached the front of the house, about to walk down the long driveway lined with their expensive cars, where palatial gates protect the house, and wild rabbits scarper as they see me coming, Becky calls my name. I close my eyes and sigh. At first I wonder if I can get away with pretending I haven't heard her but I can't do it. I turn around. She's standing at the front door. Her nipples in her flimsy vest are hard as they hit the morning air.

14

She tries to hide one behind the door frame.

Allegra, she calls, because that's my name. Can you babysit tonight.

It's not a regular babysitting night and I'm not in the mood. It's been a long week and I'm more tired than usual. Spending a night with kids who keep to themselves in their bedrooms or sit motionless with their heads in computer games isn't taxing but it's not the same thing as relaxing on my own. If I tell her that I can't and they see me in my room, then I wouldn't be able to relax either.

I know it's late notice, she adds, giving me an out, but before I get the chance to take it, she points out firmly that it's nearing the first of May. We need to discuss the rent, she says, all business now. I did say we'd evaluate it after the first six months. All assertive and power-stancey, even though she's hiding her hard nipples. It sounds like a threat. The only time I haven't been able to help her out is when I've travelled home to Pops, which I've given her advance notice of. I'm always available, but I don't bother saying that.

About the rent-evaluation thing, I say, sure. But I still can't babysit, I have plans tonight. As soon as I've said it, I know I have to make plans, which is annoying.

Oh Allegra, I wasn't implying, she says with a shocked expression at my accusation that a discussion of my rent was a thinly veiled threat. Not so thin at all, flimsier than her PJs. Really, people are all so transparent I don't know why we bother to fuck.

Have a good night, whatever you're doing, she says before closing the door, wobbly boobs and all.

I can't afford a small increase in rent but I can't afford not to live here either. I haven't done what I

15

came here to do yet.

Maybe I should have said yes to the babysitting.

* * *

To get to the village I walk through Malahide Castle grounds: mature trees and landscaped walkways. Benches with brass plaques in honour of those who walked here, sat there and looked at this and that. Immaculately kept flower beds, no litter in sight. The occasional grey squirrel. Curious robins. Mischievous rabbits. A blackbird doing its morning vocal warm-up. It's not a stressful start. I mostly pass the same people at the same places, at the same time. If I don't it's because they're running late, not me. A man in a business suit, wearing a backpack and enormous headphones. A woman with an alarmingly red face who jogs as though she's falling sideways. The leaning jogger. I don't know how she does it. Stays upright, keeps going. The first few days she used to catch my eye, as if in a hostage situation seeking rescue from her ambition, but now she's zombified, in the zone, staring into the distance and chasing something that keeps her going, an invisible carrot on a stick. Then there's the dog walker and the Great Dane, followed by an old man with a wheelie walking frame accompanied by a younger man who looks like he's probably his son. They both say good morning, every morning without fail. Good morning, he says, good morning, says he, good morning, I say to them both.

My shift begins at 8 a.m. and ends at 6 p.m. It's relatively quiet in the village itself, until the school traffic mayhem kicks in. Before I begin, I go to the bakery on Main Street every morning. The Village Bakery.

16

It's owned and run by Spanner. He always has time for a chat when I'm there, because I'm there earlier than most of the crowd. It gets momentarily busy when the 7.58 Dart arrives and everyone gets off and scrambles into his place for a coffee. He's been there since 5 a.m. baking bread and pastries. You can barely see him over the top of the counter that's filled with a dozen type of breads, twisted and braided, puffed up, polished and decorated in sesame, poppy, and sunflower seeds. They're the kings of the bakery, in prime position above the glass cabinet of cakes. He insists I call him Spanner, even though it's Dublin slang for idiot. He did something stupid one time during his school days and it stuck. Maybe more than one time — I know he served time in prison. Said that's where he learned how to bake. So I told him I once had a nickname too, at school they called me Freckles. And he took it upon himself to start calling me that. I didn't mind. After moving to Dublin it was kind of nice to have something here that was familiar, like somebody here knows me.

Morning, Freckles, the usual, he asks, barely looking up from guiding dough through a machine and folding it over. Danish pastries, he tells me before I even ask. Apple and cinnamon ones, fuckin machine broke this morning. I'll have them ready for lunchtime instead. Good enough for them.

He always talks about customers like they're the enemy, like they'll be the ending of him. I'm a customer but it doesn't insult me, it makes me feel good that he talks to me like I'm not.

He folds the dough over again, into another layer. White and blobby. It reminds me of Tina Rooney's stomach when she came back to school after having a

17

baby, and her flesh had grown around her caesarean scar, doubling over like raw dough. I watched her in the changing room as she lowered her camogie jersey over her head. She'd seemed so exotic at the time. A girl our age who'd had a baby. She only got to see him on the weekend, and her bedroom cubicle was plastered in photographs of the little thing. I don't think any of us had appreciated how hard that was for her. How she was living two completely different lives from one day to the next. She'd told me she slept with a fella at Electric Picnic, the music festival. In her tent. During the Orbital set on the main stage. She didn't know his full name or have his phone number and she was going back the next year to see if she could find him. I wonder if she ever did.

Bleedin Whistles gave me an earful about the pastries, Spanner says, bringing me back in the room. He carries on, not looking at me: I tell ye, the nerve of him, givin out to me about what he gets for breakfast. He should be happy he gets anything at all. He says the last bit louder, over his shoulder, glancing towards the door.

I look outside to homeless Whistles sitting on a flattened piece of cardboard, wrapped in a blanket with a hot coffee in one hand, and biting down on a fruit scone.

He's lucky to have you, I tell Spanner, and he calms a little, wipes his brow, throws a towel over his shoulder and gets me a coffee and waffle.

I don't know where you put those things he says, sprinkling the waffle with icing sugar, before wrapping it in newspaper to hand it to me.

He's right, I eat what I want and my body stays the same. Maybe it's because I walk so much all day every

18

day, on the beat, maybe it's because of my mam's genes. She was a dancer, apparently. Or wanted to be one. That's how she met Pops, she was doing performing arts, he was a music professor. Maybe she got what she wanted for a while at least between wanting to be and not being. I hope for her she was. You wouldn't want to give up something for everything and end up with nothing. Quite unfair on the something.

Two euro twenty for a coffee and pastry, a morning special. Less than half of what you'd pay in Insomnia or Starbucks down the road. A real bakery competing against those commercial chain fuckers, don't get him started. I'm in here at 5 a.m. every morning . . . Spanner's mostly cheery though, he's a good start to my day, the best and fullest conversation I have with anyone most days. He steps round the counter and reaches for his cigarettes in the front pocket of his apron and stands outside.

I sit on a high stool up facing the window, looking out to the village Main Street that's slowly coming alive. The florist is moving her display out onto the pavement. The toy shop is being unlocked, new flowers, rabbits and eggs hand-painted on the window in preparation for Easter. The optician is still closed, the off-licence, the stationery shop, the solicitors. The coffee shops are opening. Spanner beats them to it every morning.

Across the road in The Hot Drop, she puts a chalkboard out front advertising a special omelette and carrot cake. She's slowly but surely putting more cakes on the menu. It used to be just toasted sambos. I wonder why she'd bother, his are the best. Spanner eyes it, narrow slits. She waves nervously, he nods his head slightly, while inhaling, eyes squinted, smoke drifting in.

Friday night, Spanner says, blowing smoke out the side of his mouth, speaking as if he's had a stroke. Are you going out.

Yeah, I say, continuing the lie I began with Becky.

I've committed to it, now I just need to find somewhere to go. I ask him about his weekend.

He looks up and down the road, like a 1950s burglar casing a joint.

I'm going to see Chloe.

Chloe the mother of his daughter, Chloe the woman who won't let him see his daughter, Chloe the weight watcher's cheat, the solpadeine addict, Chloe the monster. He sucks the cigarette, his cheeks concave.

I have to go see her, and end this. I just need her to listen, face to face, one on one, no one getting in the middle and confusing everything with their opinions. Her sisters.

He rolls his eyes.

Ye know what I mean, Freckles. She'll be at a christening party at the Pilot so if I just happen to be there, no reason why I wouldn't be, I've drank there before, me mate Duffer lives around the corner so I'll go out with him, few pints, all very above board, and she'll have no choice but to speak to me.

I've never seen anyone drink tobacco in like him, long and hard, inhaling practically a quarter of it before flicking it. The cigarette goes flying across the path of a woman, a local pharmacist I recognise who drives a blue Fiat that she parks at the Castle car park. Startled, she yelps a little as the cigarette just misses her, and looks at him angrily, then, frightened by his size and demeanour, a baker not to be messed with, continues on. Whistles whistles negatively about half the fag being wasted, then shuffles over to the still-lit cigarette in the gutter and brings it back to his cardboard seat.

Ye rat, Spanner says to him, but gives him a fresh cigarette before coming back inside.

You should be careful, Spanner, I warn him, concerned. The last time you saw Chloe you had an argument with her sisters.

The three ugly sisters, he says. Faces on them like busted cabbages.

And she threatened you with a restraining order.

She couldn't even spell it, he laughs. It'll be grand. It's my right to see Ariana. I'll do anything. If bein nice is the last resort, then I'll be nice. I can play that game.

The commuters from the 7.58 Dart start to mill on to the Main Street from the train station. Soon the small space in the bakery will be crowded and Spanner will be single-handedly serving coffees, cakes and sandwiches as fast as he can. I finish up my coffee, and take my last mouthful of waffle, wipe the icing sugar from my mouth, discard the napkin and I'm gone.

Move on now, Whistles, Spanner shouts at him. You'll put everyone off their food and not one of them ever gives you a cent.

Whistles slowly stands, grabs his stuff, his cardboard seat and shuffles off around the corner and down Old Street. The breeze blows his tuneless song in my direction.

The first jobs of the day are the local schools. Not enough space, too many cars. Tired, stressed-out parents, pulling in where they shouldn't be, parking where they shouldn't be parking, cardigans and coats hiding pyjamas, trainers with business attire, hassled heads sweating to drop off before they leg it to work, bed-headed kids with school bags bigger than themselves being shouted at to hurry up and hop out. Would someone for the love of God take their kids from them so they can go and do all the things. I get abuse from the same double-parked stress-heads every morning. Not the kids' faults. Not my fault. Nobody's fault. But I've still got to patrol it.

First I eye up the free space outside the hair salon that will be filled within the next half-hour with a silver three series 2016 BMW. I glance inside the small salon, lights off, empty and closed until 9 a.m. While I'm looking in the window, a car pulls into the available space outside the salon. I turn around and eye the driver, a man, who's switching off the engine and undoing his seat belt. He looks at me the entire time. He opens the door, puts one foot out on the pavement and stares at me.

Can I not park here, he asks.

I shake my head and even though I'm not imitating a garda, I am being one in my head. Gardaí don't always have to give reasons.

He rolls his eyes, pulls his leg back into the car, and as he's securing his seat belt and starting the engine he looks around at the signage, confused and irritated.

I stand there until he drives away.

It's only 8 a.m. Pay-and-display begins at 8.30 a.m. No legal reason why he can't park here.

But she always parks here.

Every day.

It's her spot.

And I protect it.

4

9 a.m. to noon it's mostly parking offences. Cars in loading bays preventing van deliveries, causing mayhem on small village roads. Parking tickets for cars left over from the night before, drinkers getting taxis home and not getting back to their cars in time the next morning to pay their parking fees. Busier with that today than any other weekday, with Thursday night being a popular night out. Parking is free on Sundays. They can do what they like then.

I'm kept busy.

I walk by the silver BMW outside the hair salon. In her spot. You're welcome. Parking all paid up. Business pay-and-display in the correct place on the dashboard. Correct vehicle for the correct disc. Good woman. Most people forget to alert the council to their change of vehicle. Which is an offence that they get ticketed for. The BMW is all legal. Six hundred euro for that annual disc. She's doing well. Her own little hair salon. Only has six seats inside but it's always busy. Two shampooing stations, three chairs before a mirror. And a little desk and chair at the window for nails. Shellac and gel. She's always there. I notice when her car's not there, wonder if she's okay, or the family, but I assume I'd know from the look on her staff's face if something terrible had happened. Her parking credentials are always above board, but still I check. No one is infallible. Disc in the dashboard, a booster seat in the back.

That captures my attention for a moment.

At noon I walk down James's Terrace, a cul de sac of terraced Georgian houses, now all businesses, facing the tennis courts. I admire the view ahead of me, right across to Donabate, fishing boats, sailing boats, blue, yellows, browns and green, reminds me of home. Home is a marina town too, not exactly like this, but the sea air is something to connect me, and it's as close as Dublin gets to home for me. Cities make me feel claustrophobic and this suburban village has given me more breathing room.

Home is Valentia Island, Kerry, but boarding school was Thurles. I went home most weekends. Pops worked in Limerick University, a professor of music until he semi-retired a while back. He plays cello and piano, taught them on the weekend and during summers in our house, but his main job and obsession was talking about music. I could imagine his lectures, him full of joie to vivre about his favourite subject. That's why he called me Allegra, Italian for fun and lively, but really from the musical description allegro, a piece of music that is played in a fast and lively way. The best instrument of all was Pops' humming. He could, and can, hum the entire four minutes thirteen seconds of *Marriage of Figaro*.

He worked in Limerick Monday to Friday while I was at boarding school and I would catch a train to Limerick on a Friday evening. He'd collect me from the station and drive us home to Knightstown, Valentia Island together. It should have taken three hours to get home but took dangerously less with him behind the wheel, a speed limit being just another way for the government to control us. As soon as I saw home on Friday night, that moment when the bridge from Portmagee brought us from the mainland to the island, that's when I felt peace envelop me. I was as excited, if not more, to be home than to see Pops. It's home, isn't it. The seemingly invisible things that go right to your soul. The feel of my bed, the pillow just right, the ticking of the grandfather clock in the hall, the way a patch on the wall looks at a certain time of day when the light catches it. When you're happy, even the things you hate can become the things you love. Pops playing Classic FM too loud. The smell of burned toast, until you have to eat the burned toast. The way the boiler roared every time the tap was running. The sliding of the shower curtain rings against the rail. The sheep in the field behind us on Nessie's farm. The crackle of the coal in the fire. The sound of his shovel scraping the concrete in the coal shed out the back. The tap tap tap, three times, always three, against his boiled egg. Sometimes I ache for home. Not here by the sea when I'm reminded of it, mostly I ache when I see nothing around me that reminds me of it at all.

Apart from the yellows of the sand and island I see another familiar yellow. The canary yellow Ferrari is parked outside number eight James's Terrace. I'm guessing in advance that there's no paid parking disc in the windscreen, as there hasn't been for two weeks running. I check all the cars leading up to it but I can't really concentrate. I need to get to the yellow car before someone gets in it and drives away, before I get to issue the ticket. I'd feel cheated. I give up on the other cars and go straight for the yellow sports car.

No disc in the windscreen. No ticket either. I scan the registration. No online parking paid. It's the second week the car has been parked here, in the same place, more or less, and I've given it a ticket every single day. Each fine has cost the owner forty euro, which increases by fifty per cent after twenty-eight days and if it's not paid a further twenty-eight days later then court proceedings are initiated. Forty euro every day for two weeks isn't cheap. It's practically my month's rent. I don't feel bad for the owner. I feel angry. Agitated. Like I'm being deliberately mocked.

Whoever drives this car must be a wanker anyway. He'd have to be. A yellow Ferrari. Or it could be a woman. One who leaned in a little too fucking much, fell over and banged her head. I issue the ticket, bag it, and tuck it beneath the windscreen wiper.

For lunch I sit on the bench down the lane behind the tennis club and scout club overlooking the sea. The tide is out and the muddy stones are revealed, a few plastic bottles, a trainer, a baby-soother peer up unnaturally from the slippery seaweed bed. But even in the ugly there's pretty. I take out my lunch box from my backpack. Cheese sandwich on granary bread, a Granny Smith apple, a handful of walnuts and a flask of hot tea. More or less the same thing every day and always in the same place, if the weather is relatively good. During bad weather I stand under the protection of the public toilets' roof. Rainy days are usually busier days, nobody wants to run to a pay-and-display machine and back to their car in the rain. Cars will pull into loading bays and double park, hazards on, to get in and out of the weather quicker. But my rule book is the same in all weathers.

Sometimes Paddy joins me for lunch. Paddy's a parking warden too and we split the zones in this area between us. Paddy's overweight, with psoriasis and flakes of dandruff all over his shoulders, and he doesn't always hit the zones by the right times. I'm happy most days when he doesn't arrive. He spends the entire time talking about food, how he prepared it, and cooked it, in painstaking detail. Maybe a true foodie would appreciate his conversation but it feels odd to hear about twenty-four-hour simmering and marinades when he's scoffing an egg mayonnaise sandwich and cheese and onion Tayto crisps from the petrol station.

I hear someone curse loudly, and a car door slam. I look back and see yellow Ferrari fella reading his parking ticket. So that's what he looks like. Surprisingly young. My cheese sandwich covers my mouth, hiding my smirk. I don't usually enjoy this kind of thing, ticketing cars isn't personal, it's a duty, but the car being what it is and all that. He's tall, skinny, man-child, in his twenties. Wearing a red cap. It looks like a MAGA cap but when I get a better look I see it has a Ferrari symbol. Even more of a wanker. He shoves the ticket in his pocket, his movements all huffy puffy, irritated and angry, and opens the car door.

I chuckle.

There's no possible way he could have heard me, I was quiet, the cheese sandwich was my soundproofing, and we're too far apart, separated by a road, but as though he senses he's been watched, he looks around and sees me.

The sandwich feels like a brick in my mouth. I try to swallow it but remember too late that I haven't chewed it yet. I choke, cough and look away from him to dislodge the food from my throat. Finally it loosens and I spit into a tissue but some crumbs are still left there, tickling. I wash it down with tea and when I look back at him, he's still staring. He doesn't look concerned, more like he was hoping he'd witness me choke to death. He glares at me, sits into the car, bangs the door and speeds off. The noise of the engine turns a few heads.

My heart is pounding.

I was right. Wanker.

5

After lunch I patrol the coast road. Parking here is used by a lot of people getting the train into work, as though it's a park-and-go area. At least at first it is; they quickly learn their lesson though. They think they'll get away with paying the maximum three hours, get a train into the city, leave their car there the entire day and return at 6 p.m. Maybe they get away with it with Paddy, but not me. I don't reward half-assed attempts, a mere gesture of a down-payment. You pay for the hours you use, no special treatment, not even if you walk with a limp.

As I'm making my way back towards the village, I see the yellow Ferrari a few spots down from where it was earlier, and I feel a tingle of excitement. It's like chess. He's made his next move. I could technically finish for the evening; it's 5.55 p.m. The pay and display ends at 6 p.m. Nobody could pay for exactly five minutes even if they tried, ten minutes is the minimum, and though I'm a stickler for the rules I don't expect people to overpay either. Money is no laughing matter. I look around and make sure the driver isn't in sight or watching. I lower my cap over my eyes, and hurry to the car. I glance at the windscreen, my heart pounding.

He has paid. For the first time ever. My tickets have worked. I broke him down. Suspect interrogation a success. However, it was up at 5.05 p.m. He'd paid the three euro for the maximum of three hours at 2.05, and it irritates me that he thought by doing so he'd get the final hour for free. That's not how it works.

Before I issue a new ticket, I scan his reg to make sure he hasn't paid online. Nope.

I tut and shake my head. This guy doesn't do himself any favours. If he'd kept his earlier parking fine on the windscreen I wouldn't be able to issue him another. There's clearly no thought given to helping himself.

I issue the fine.

And then I very quickly walk away.

★ ★ ★

When I've finished my day's work I can't go home. I told Becky that I'd be out and there's not many places I can go to in a parking warden uniform on a Friday evening. I buy fish and chips from a takeaway and go to Malahide Castle grounds and watch a gang of teenagers with suspiciously full backpacks searching for a secret drinking spot.

It starts to get dark at nine-ish and I can't stay out much longer, they're locking up the castle grounds and I'm bored, I'm cold and frankly I don't want my Friday night to be ruined on account of my refusing to babysit. I guess if they've found someone else to do it then it will be safe for me to go back by now.

It's nine-thirty when I get back to the house. I see the kids flashing by various windows, but no parents so I don't know if Becky and Donnacha stayed in or got another babysitter. I keep my head down anyway, hoping they won't see me and say oh look you're back early, can we go out now. I'm cold and tired, I want a shower and my pyjamas.

I know something isn't right as soon as I step inside

the gym. The lights are off but it feels like someone is in the building. I don't close the door behind me just in case it's an intruder and I have to run. I'm not that scared, I assume it's Donnacha. There's a door to his office off the gym and a spiral staircase that leads to my studio flat. His office is beneath my room and is used for viewing porn and wanking. Possibly also for invoicing and accounts.

There's nobody in the office and the sound is coming from upstairs, my bedroom. I briefly wonder if I've left my TV on, but I know that I didn't. It sounds too real. Breathy and grunty and groany and sighy. Somebody is having sex in my room. Preferably two bodies. Discovering one would be even more awkward.

First thought, it's Becky and Donnacha. If I wouldn't babysit for them, they're going to punish me by coming all over my sheets while I'm out, disgusting spoiled over-privileged folk they are. Can you be over-privileged, or is just privileged enough. I'm not sure. Second thought, it's Donnacha. Maybe Becky went out anyway and he had to stay in. Maybe he's decided to have some fun without his wife. Lean-in wife in insecure cheating husband shocker. I wonder with a shudder how often he's used my place.

I tread lightly on the spiral staircase, my lightweight boots despite their design are heavy and clumpy for sleuthing. My phone's ready in my hand. The door to my room is slightly ajar, which is a silly mistake to make so I guess it's deliberate. Not to be caught, no one wants that, but so they could hear if somebody enters. But you'd never hear an intruder with sex that loud. I've arrived at the right time. I hold the phone up and film, which is everybody's go-to now when something violent, dangerous or peculiar happens.

31

Film now, think later. We've lost our gumption. Our compassion. Our instincts to react. The instinct now is to film now, think and feel later.

A hairy, muscular bum pounds away between a pair of bronzed lithe legs up in the air, her thighs held in place, impressively wide, by her own manicured fingernails. Shellac or gel, I can't tell. Wonderful flexibility and how kind of her to hold herself open for him. A gentlewoman in the sack. I recognise those nails, those legs. It is Becky.

Ah. And so this must be Donnacha's ass. Nice to meet you.

Now that I've discovered my landlords, I'm a little less smug at having caught them, and more disgusted. It's their property but it's my personal space and this is a violation. If I could issue them a ticket, I would. I'd smack it against his hairy arse, hoping the sticky bit would burn like hell when he pulls it off. I lower my phone and go back downstairs quietly, and wait for them to finish, which they do, loudly and with great gusto. So proud of their clever selves. Then I go right back up the steps again, this time as normal, just a pair of heavy tired feet after a hard day's work. I've given them time to at least disentangle themselves so I hope they've covered up. I push the door open, making sure I register surprise on my face that first my door is unlocked and secondly my discovery.

Jesus, Allegra, I thought you were out tonight, Becky says, which I think is an amusing defence. How dare I intrude. She's wrapped in a blanket, my turquoise fleece blanket. On her sweaty naked body. Her face is red and flustered, probably mostly from the sex and not as much shame as I think is necessary. To my own surprise, my response is of genuine shock because the

32

ass doesn't belong to Donnacha. The man that's not Donnacha is less bothered about me than Becky is, in fact not bothered at all. He takes his time making a move, an amused expression on his face. He bends over to pick up his clothes, hairy asshole and ball sack in my face.

Could you give us a minute please, she asks, irritated by my presence, as if I don't have the social cop-on to leave and give them privacy. I step outside and go back downstairs to the gym. I sit on the rower. Rock back and forth gently, thinking.

The man who's not Donnacha passes me by, dressed in an expensive suit, still smirking. His aftershave almost chokes me. And then Becky arrives with my bed sheets and duvet cover all bundled messily under her arm. The assertive tone again. Allegra, I would appreciate it if you could keep this to yourself. There are . . . things . . . not everything is as it . . . it's private, she finally says firmly, her decision made not to go any further.

Sure, I tell her, rocking back and forward on the rower. So about the rent, I say, would you like to talk about that now or another time.

She can't believe I've said it. She just can't. As if my words in that tone, in this moment are worse than what I just walked in on her doing. She looks at me differently. With dislike. Disgust. Loser. Weirdo. The rent stays as it is she says, giving me a firm look, and all is understood. Loud and clear. The rent stays the same, and I say nothing about the hairy ass that didn't belong to Donnacha. Not that I would have anyway. I'll wash these, she adds about the bed sheets, walking self-consciously from the gym, probably still tender.

I make up a new bed, throw my favourite fleece

blanket to the corner of the room. I have to open the window wide to get rid of the smell of his aftershave but it's so heavy it feels like it has sunk into every fibre of the room. I finally get in to bed, feeling so cold from an entire day outside and evening hanging out in the park, but too tired now to take a shower.

I watch the video of them a few times. I filmed first and now I'm trying to figure out how I feel about it.

6

I wake to the sound of the children screaming in the garden. It's 10 a.m. on a Saturday and I'm glad I've managed to switch off the Monday-to-Friday internal alarm clock and sleep so late. I would have assumed, considering what I discovered in my bedroom last night, that Becky would be treating me more kindly. Breakfast in bed, no noisy children under my window, a reduced rent. Perhaps she's trying to get rid of me. Six-year-old Cillín is the loudest. I bet he's wearing his princess dress now. I can hear the tone in his voice, the character he becomes when he's wearing dresses. I sit up and glimpse outside. Yes. Purple Rapunzel dress, a long blonde wig and a Viking helmet. Atop the playhouse waving his sword in the air, announcing the impending head-severing of his brothers.

I throw the covers off and knock over two empty bottles of wine on the floor. One red, one white. I couldn't make up my mind which one to open so I recall, at 2 a.m.-ish after *Cliffhanger* ended and *Tootsie* began, the red wine was opened. I feel a little groggy, events of last night like a mirage now and I'd wonder if they happened at all if I didn't have the footage in my phone to confirm it.

I usually babysit every Saturday night but I don't know if Becky will bother now after her extracurricular activities, perhaps she will have to, her husband deserves a turn after all. I'm sure all will become clear soon enough. Anyway I can't sit around, my Saturdays are filled. I shower and shave myself all over and moisturise. I dress. High-waisted blue skinny jeans, ripped at the knees, black military boots and an army green parka jacket coat. I soften the look with a blush-pink sweater. I say good morning to the kids, pretend to die as Cillín stabs me with his sword. As he runs away laughing I see the sparkling princess shoes beneath the dress. I deliberately look into the house to find Becky. I'm curious what a domestic scene looks like after you've been fucking another man. I survey the kitchen, it all looks normal. Business as usual. My my she is good. Donnacha must still be in bed after his night out. Maybe he was with someone else as well. Maybe that's the agreement. Maybe not. I don't judge but I wonder. The kitchen sliding doors are open. I catch Becky's eye.

I'm staying in tonight she calls, her voice drifting through the open sliding doors. I take that to mean I'm off the hook with babysitting tonight. I suppose she was quite active last night, who can blame her.

I hop on the number 42 bus on Malahide road, and ride it all the way into the city, almost the last stop. I get off on Talbot Street and walk the few minutes to Foley Street, once Montgomery Street, nicknamed Monto, that was in its heyday from 1860s to the 1920s the biggest red-light district in Europe. I head straight to Montgomery Gallery, an art gallery celebrating nouveau Irish painters, sculptors and creatives, see Jasper, one half of the husband-wife owners, serving a customer, and climb their wooden paint-splattered steps to their second floor. It's just an empty room. Stripped back, walls peeled of paper, floors unvarnished, everything back to its bare-boned essentials in a cool vibey edgy way that stops it from being a desolate house. It is a vessel for holding stuff,

36

just like Donnacha's work but far more useful. They sell his bowls but I've never mentioned him to them or this place to him. Wouldn't want him showing up when I'm here. Two large windows mean light fills the room. The floor creaks. It feels like the room is lopsided. It's used for exhibitions, parties, launches, displays and today for a live art class featuring moi.

There's a changing screen in the corner. Tongue-in-cheek images of naughty cherubs fondling themselves. It's Genevieve and Jasper's kind of humour. Exhibitions and gatherings go on into the early hours of the morning, filled with their artist friends, anything can happen. I have witnessed this.

Genevieve greets me upstairs. Her look is so austere it's in stark contrast to the inner fluidity that I know is there. A blunt black bob with fringe, black squared thick-rimmed glasses, red lipstick, always red lipstick. A military-style jacket, gold buttons, done up to the top, high-neck, a military-style belt cinching in her waist. Beneath her jacket, two enormous boobs protrude. She wears a black cashmere skirt, to the ankle, and military-style boots. No skin on show. She doesn't seem to notice or care that the boots bang and scrape across the creaky wooden floors, Genevieve is not here on this earth to be silent. The room is so old the floor is tilted. I've gotten a kick out of watching new artists' easels and stools roll across the floor, towards me. The horror on their face as their paints almost crash into the naked woman. They need to ground those easels in a crack in the floorboards, root their feet to the floor.

I shiver. The windows are wide open.

Sorry, Genevieve says, setting up the stools and easels. It was a wild night last night, I'm trying to get rid of the smoke.

I sniff the air, tell her I don't smell anything. Such a blank canvas now but I can imagine it hours earlier, with heaving bodies, sweat and whatever else. Not unlike my bedroom last night. She lifts her nose to the air to see if I'm telling the truth. Okay I'll close them now, she says, banging over the floors to get to the windows, and I can imagine her in a previous life, grabbing a rifle, dropping to her knees and sniper-shooting soldiers below. In reality she slides the windows shut. We have twelve today, she says, no drop-ins. Drop-ins aren't allowed after the last time when a drop-in decided to drop his hand down the front of his trousers while watching me, instead of painting. Genevieve, no-nonsense, had practically dragged him out of the building by his cock. We smile at one another at the memory.

You can't blame the man, I say. It was her nipples! I imitate his conciliatory wails as he was cast out, both loving and loathing my nipples for his undoing.

You do have great nipples, she says, her eyes fleeting down briefly to my chest.

It's a compliment. She's seen her fair share of tits.

I move behind the screen and remove my clothes. The floor is ice cold and goosebumps rise on my skin. I'll need to get warmer for the sitting, though they'll appreciate the hardened nipples and areola. They don't go for beauty, they want detail. Character. I massage oil onto my skin, wanting to glow. I'm not excessively vain but there are certain standards I set myself and dry skin, sock marks and goosebumps aren't it. Not the details I want to give them. Genevieve prefers for me to take my seat on the small podium after everybody has arrived. She says there's

38

no point in me freezing my tits off for other people's tardiness. I don't actually disrobe until I'm seated but I know what she means. A little bit of respect for this slab of meat please.

Finally everyone has taken their places, just one stool is missing a bottom but Genevieve waits for no one and we begin. I don't look at their faces until after I've removed the robe and I'm comfortable in a position. The patterned silk robe hangs down the wooden chair I sit on, art deco in style, hard on my ass but at least the silk softens it a little. I survey the audience. Some familiar faces, some eyes meet mine in acknowledgement, others run over me as though I'm a fruit bowl. Looking for shadows and angles. Creases and blemishes. Detail and character.

The new eyes run their gazes across the obvious place on my body that attracts attention. My left arm. Still scarred from my adolescence of scratching con-stellations into my skin, connecting freckle to freckle. I think this is why Genevieve keeps asking me back. An interesting feature, apparent self-harm. A real task for the student; do they ignore it or tackle it. Some appear to make it more obvious than it is, garish and ugly, deep trenches in my skin, while making the rest of me appear as this injured frail bird. Others paint or draw them as mere traces, scratches, or there are those who paint me as a brave warrior. Nobody sees them as constellations. Of course there are those who don't see them at all, and spend longer highlighting freckles and moles, or dimples in my thighs. I find that though I am the person naked in the centre of a room, the artists reveal so much more about them-selves than I do. I'm detached, in my own zone. But at the same time feeling a little bit special beneath their

gaze. I am a puzzle they have to solve. They are painting my shell, while their insides are oozing out on to
the canvas, tattle-tales to their secrets. Artist incontinence. I may be naked but they're revealing their
souls. That's what I like most about posing nude for
artists, the fact that while they think I'm on show, I'm
watching them.

That and the fifteen euro an hour that I receive in
cash.

The door opens softly and somebody steps inside.
I'm not so poised that I don't break my position to
look. Somebody tuts at my movement. They can fuck
right off.

Sorry, the tardy young man says.

He's tall and lean, wears a denim shirt with jeans,
Converse, looks studenty. His face blushes at disturbing the session.

Okay okay, Genevieve says, irritated. James, is it,
start time is one p.m., okay, you won't be late next
time, if there is a next time. You can sit over there.

There's never truly any comfortable position while
posing nude, something will always start to hurt at
some point but at the beginning of the session I'd
chosen to angle my body in the direction of the empty
stool James is heading to, my legs parted ever so
slightly, not because I'm shy of the others seeing but
because I found the thought of a tardy artist being
faced with an eye full of vagina amusing. I have to get
my kicks somehow.

James crosses the room, the tilted floor creaking
with his every step and he sits on the stool, gets his
equipment ready, knocking things over in a cringing
Hugh Grant way as he self-consciously sets up. This
could be the opening scene of a romantic comedy,

40

this could be the beginning of a new relationship for me. Well grandchildren, I met your granddad when he painted me nude. He thought he was saving me but it was really I who saved him and look at us now, all this time later. I'm laughing on the inside. He looks up at my body, and quickly away again. I wait for him to look at my face. He doesn't. He continues his prep. Genevieve explains some housekeeping rules and he steals glances at my body while he listens, scratching his nose, fidgeting.

After the two-hour class, the paintings, sketches, whatever material they've used, are revealed.

James has focused entirely on my sex. Enormous erect brown nipples, exaggerated areolae, and a raging crimson fleshiness between my legs. I'm a compilation of interlapping pigments on his canvas; burnt sienna, dark yellow ochre, carbon black smoke. There are no distinguishable features on my face, just a blur of sketches, criss-crossing. I try not to laugh. He, with the clearest view of the scars linking my freckles, has chosen not to include this peculiarity in his painting at all. I don't think he has omitted them out of kindness, and I don't think he ran out of time to paint my face. My take on James is that no matter what woman he looks at, all he sees is sex.

Some men. Not all men. Tut tut.

But babysitting is off tonight and I've nothing else to do, so I sleep with him anyway. Maybe we're more erotique noire than romantic comedy. But the idea of our dalliance as being anything remotely romantic at least makes me laugh.

7

Monday morning. Wake at 6.58. Up at 7.00. Dress in grey and high-vis. Pass the dapper suited businessman with headphones. The leaning tower jogging woman. The Great Dane dog walker. The old man with the wheelie walking frame and the younger version of him. Good morning he says, good morning says he, good morning I say to them both. I reach the Village Bakery at 7.45. Spanner looks up quickly as the bell rings and straight back to his work again.

Howya, Freckles. The usual.

He turns his back to me to first pour batter into the waffle machine and then operate the coffee machine. Broad back to me, white T-shirt, muscular shoulders and tattoos down his arms. I've never tried to figure out what's on them, there are so many, blue in colour, and all running into each other. He operates the coffee machine, arms everywhere, as it hisses and slurps and he twists and bangs, like an old nutty professor. He turns to me with my coffee in his hand. It didn't go quite to plan, Freckles, he says, placing the coffee cup on the counter and seeing to the waffle.

I think at first he's messed up my coffee but it's grand, so I look back up at him. There's a fine black ring around his right eye that's slightly closed.

Turns out Chloe has a new fella and if she thinks this fella is going to live with my little Ariana and see her whenever the feck he wants to, when I'm the da, then she has another thing comin and I told her so. Simple as that.

42

He hands me the waffle. He's forgotten the icing sugar.

Freckles, he says, he was a skinny little muppet, with the flat head on him, five years younger than her. He could be a paedo for all I know, all I asked was for him to be Garda vetted. He could be preying on Chloe because she has a little one, a da has to be careful, mindful of perverts. Paedos are everywhere. Manky bastards, the lot of them.

You said all this to her, I ask, while pouring sugar into my tea. Two sachets. I wonder if I can sprinkle some over my waffle while he's not looking. It's not the same as icing sugar though. If he'd stop talking about his woes, I'd have my icing sugar. I care about his life, but not to the detriment of my day.

I said it to him meself he says, moving his neck around, rolling his shoulders as though gearing up for another fight, proud as a peacock. He punches the air with his pointed finger and says, you, I says to him, better not be a fuckin paedo.

So he gave you the black eye.

I wasn't expecting it, to be walloped at a christening. Came out of nowhere. Bleedin muppet. And then all the sisters jump in. You don't be starting on him, cluck cluck cluck, like a bunch of hens. I should get a restraining order on him.

Probably not wise, I remind him, if he's living in the same house as Ariana. You want to be able to get near her.

Yeah well . . . He throws the dishcloth over his shoulder and comes around the counter reaching for his cigarettes in his apron and going to the front door.

I'm sorry, Spanner, I know you were really trying, I say, watching him drinking in the tobacco, his black right eye squinted shut even more to stop the smoke from getting in.

Shouldn't you get a solicitor, Spanner, I say. You have rights.

The cost of paying a wanker solicitor, Spanner says straightening up, when I'm well able to sort this out myself, there's no point.

Whistles, sitting on his cardboard box, wrapped in a grubby blanket, looks away with an amused expression. He might be down and out but he knows better. Whistles goes for the still-lit smoke that Spanner has flicked down the pathway. He's left more of it than usual. He hasn't flicked it as far as usual. A kindness.

I glance down at my waffle. I can't do this any more, I can't be what I'm not.

Spanner, I say, you forgot the icing sugar. I hand the waffle back to him as he makes his way to the counter.

★   ★   ★

I walk away from the school area, leaving the insults and murderous glares well behind, glad the rain has stayed off again. It's easier to work without droplets blurring the windscreens, distorting tickets and discs or condensation and frost making tickets unreadable. Paddy may often be lazy when it comes to checking details but I know people display old parking tickets thinking they'll get away with it. It's not enough to just witness a white ticket on a dash; the numbers count.

Though my mornings move like clockwork, I don't have a fixed route. I used to when I started, until I moved faster than usual one morning and arrived at a zone a few minutes earlier than usual and caught a car illegally parked.

I do this every day the driver says, you don't usually get here until ten.

Biggest mistake he ever made telling me that. I realised then that people in the village were watching my movements, and I don't want to be predictable. Got to keep them on their toes. It doesn't give me a feeling of absolute power, as some of them spit at me, it just reveals them for the absolute idiots they are. All that messing around to avoid paying one euro for an hour's parking. It may be just one euro for them, but all those euro add up for the council. They'd miss us if we were gone. Paddy told me that in training.

Without us, he said, it'd be pandemonium around here.

I find myself walking directly to James's Terrace. I'd like to tell myself it's for the comforting view of the sea but I know it's because of the yellow Ferrari. I'm curious, oddly drawn in that direction. Even though the aim is to see the car, I'm still surprised to see it parked there at this early hour. I thought someone like him would have the kind of job where they stay in bed until noon. It's not just the model, but the yellow that specifically makes me think that.

It's lonely on the empty road at this hour. A few other cars dot the street but these quieter side streets don't get busy until after nine. It could be sitting there since last night but I don't think someone would leave a car like this on its own overnight. Maybe if they were drunk enough.

The garda cars are parked in their special positions. I don't even glance at their windscreens, it would be an insult to them if I did. I tip my hat at a young female

45

garda through the window, thinking that could have been me, wondering which part of my application let me down, knowing it must have been the interview. You and me aren't like other people, Pops had said one time when I was frustrated by yet another confusion over an interaction with somebody. Hearing him say it was both harsh and a relief. I knew he was right. Still is. There's something about my timing. Like the icing sugar and Spanner. Human interaction is often like a dance I can't catch the rhythm to.

I don't approach the car yet. I stand back and survey the building it's parked outside. Number eight. It'd been under intense refurbishment for the past year, for as long as I've been working here, with a skip outside and work vans taking up all of the spaces for other businesses. White vans and delivery trucks caused congestion and issues with parking for nearby businesses. I had to hear about their woes and ticket them.

It's a Georgian row. Number eight has four floors including a basement. High ceilings, huge windows, fancy cornicing, overlooking the tennis club, the sea to the left, detailed plasterwork on the ceilings. A nightmare to dust, especially now with no servants. The Ferrari doesn't fit with the building somehow. Classic and tasteful versus ostentatious and garish. The building was bought for two million euro, I'd looked it up online, dying to know what was inside and saw pictures of the property when it was on the market. Like most of the row it had been broken up into businesses per room and per floor. It had a hair salon on one floor, an internet café, acupuncturist and nail bar on the top floor, a Chinese restaurant in the basement. It was grotty and old. They had to rip it all

46

out, modernise it, new plumbing, new heating, new everything. A building like that would be a money pit, who knows what the final spend was.

The skip and the builders are gone now, for the past two weeks it looks as if whatever business is inside there has begun, and it's just one, with a shiny gold plaque reading Cockadoodledoo Inc. What the fuck. I dip my cap low again over my eyes, place my hands in my pockets and take on my patrol walk.

My heart is pounding. I don't know why exactly, I never fear issuing tickets. I'm a warden, and it's my right, but maybe I can admit that leaving a ticket yesterday with only five minutes to go until the end of business was unfair. Still. It was legal. It was my job. I go directly to the car, conscious of the large office windows overlooking me. Heart thumping, maybe I'm scared, maybe it's excitement, but it's different to anything I've felt before on the job.

The big reveal. I look at the windscreen. Nothing. I can't believe it. After two tickets yesterday he hasn't bothered to pay today.

No pay and display on the dashboard.

No new disc or permit on the window that businesses can purchase for ease, for all-day, all-year parking.

I scan the reg. He hasn't paid online either. Or used the app. It couldn't be made any easier for him.

He's egging me on, that's what this is. It's a taunt. Well, the next move is mine.

You're usually supposed to give the customer fifteen minutes' grace between replacing their pay and displays. Gives them time to get to the meter and back to the car, a bit of a gentlemen's agreement. I abide by it. But there's no fifteen minutes between the last time yellow Ferrari bought the first ticket. He didn't buy one, period. Pay and display begins in this area at 8 a.m. It's now almost 9 a.m. As far as I'm concerned he's had enough grace. More time than I'd ever give anyone else.

I'm about to input the information into my ticket machine when a sudden chafing sound behind me gives me a fright.

There you are, says Paddy, breathless.

Jesus, Paddy, I jump, startled, heart pounding at feeling caught. It was his protective rain gear, the sound of the fabric as his thighs brushed against each other.

He looks at the car and whistles. He walks up and down beside it, looking in the windows nosily. A Lamborghini, is it, he practically presses his face up against the glass, hands shielding the light, leaving fingerprints and breath marks on the clean window.

Ferrari, I correct him, uncomfortably, looking up at the building. I see a figure at the window, great big curly blond hair on his head. He looks out at us and then disappears. Terrific, the lookout tower has given me away. I need to be quick.

Did you not get my message, Paddy asks, face still nosily pushed up against the driver window. I texted you last night saying I'd take this zone today.

No I didn't, I say, distracted.

Another person has come to the window, two young guys now. They look like they're in a boy band. None of them my Ferrari fella.

I'll take over here, Paddy says.

No, I've got this, I say abruptly. I log the location, the zone, FCM, and the offence. I take a photo. I issue the ticket. Paddy's talking but I'm not listening to a word he says. I'm conscious of hearing a door open from the building beside me.

Hey, a guy calls.

I don't look up, I pull the ticket from the machine, wrap it in plastic to protect it from the rain and elements. My fingers are shaking as I do it, my heart is pounding, Paddy is oblivious to it all. I place it under the windscreen wipers and actually step away, feeling breathless, slightly dizzy. Done.

What's going on, the fella from yesterday asks.

Paddy looks at me.

No pay and display, unfortunately, I say politely but firmly.

I've been here since six o'clock this morning, it's free parking, I don't need a ticket until nine. I've got ten minutes, he says, looking at me as if I'm a piece of shit on his wanker Prada trainer.

I point at the signage. Pay and display begins at eight in this zone. I feel the quiver in my voice and it surprises me. This whole thing has the adrenaline pumping around my body. I put the ticket machine strap over my shoulder like it's my gun in its holster.

He stares at me. He's wearing the red cap. The Ferrari one. It's down low, like I wear mine and his eyes are barely visible but I can see them enough to know they're filled with utter hatred. It's difficult to hate a person you don't know, but I can feel it emanating from him to me. I swallow.

This is some car you have here, Paddy says lightly. Whose is it.

I look at Paddy, surprised.

It's mine, the guy snaps. Why else would I be standing here asking about the parking fine.

Excuse me, Paddy says offended and all sensitive,

49

fixing his cap. Thought it was your boss's. He looks past him to the building.

I am the boss, the guy says, and there it is, that privileged white male whine that I deplore so very much. Poor little rich guy got a parking fine because he couldn't bother to check the rules and put a euro in the parking meter. Now the whole world is out to get him. Boo fucking hoo. It's probably the worst thing that will ever happen in his week.

He lifts the wiper and grabs the ticket. He lets go of the wiper and it smacks against the glass. He glances at it briefly but he doesn't need to read it to know what it says exactly, he already received two just like it on Friday a few hours apart, and one every other day for the past two weeks.

Have you a vendetta against me, he asks.

I shake my head, no vendetta, I say, just doing my job.

What's your problem, he asks again, more angry, as if he didn't hear my answer. He steps closer to me. Shoulders square and wide. I'm tall but he's taller.

I don't have a problem, I say, sidestepping the situation now, I don't like it. It's too tense, he's too angry and his aggression levels are rising. I should move but I can't. I'm stuck, frozen on the spot.

You power-tripping fucking wannabe garda, he growls suddenly.

I look at him in surprise. Part of that sentence is correct.

Now now, Paddy says. Come now, Allegra.

But I'm stuck where I'm standing. This is like a road accident, I must slow down to see clearly, all the grotesque details that my mind doesn't need to see. The blood and guts. I've trained for this moment, for the moment someone gets aggressive. A week of intensive training on the meanings of kerbside stripes and squiggles and also on conflict management. I'm supposed to stand side-on and be prepared to walk away but my training goes out the window. I'm stuck to the spot, head-on, staring at him like a deer caught in the headlights. Waiting for more.

They say you're the average of the five people you spend the most time with, he says, glaring at me, nostrils flaring like a wolf. Doesn't say a lot about the company you keep, does it. That's one, he points in Paddy's direction. I wonder who the other four losers are in your life.

He slides the parking ticket from the plastic slip and proceeds to rip it up into pieces. They flutter to the ground, a confetti storm. He takes the steps in twos back into his office and slams the door.

My heart is pounding. It's in my actual ears. Like there's been an explosion and my ears are ringing.

Jesus Christ, Paddy says, giving a wheezy nervous laugh and moving to me as quickly as his chafing legs will allow him. The inner legs of his trousers have risen to the line of his socks and are all bunched and gathered around his crotch.

I look at the bits of paper on the ground. The parking fine in smithereens.

It takes a while for the blood to rush out of my head and back around my body, for my heartbeat to calm, for the panicky feeling to subside, and when it does my body is left shaking.

She's still standing out there, I hear somebody say loudly, followed with a laugh. A mocking laugh. It has drifted out of a window from the office where a few of them have gathered to watch me, smiles on

51

their faces. The two familiar lads and a few new faces. When I look at them, they disperse.

I'm going to avoid this terrace for the time being, Paddy says. You take St Margaret's and everything west. Okay, he asks, when I don't respond.

I nod.

I wouldn't let him get away with that, Paddy says, or he'll think he can rip up every fine he gets and he won't have to pay, but we'll leave it for the time being. Let him cool down. I'll come back later and check on it. I'll ticket him if he hasn't learned his lesson.

I still can't move my feet. My legs are shaking.

You didn't take him to heart did you, he asks, watching me.

No, I finally speak, and it comes out all croaky and choked.

I didn't even know what he was talking about.

And that's true.

When he was saying it, none of it made sense. Just a bunch of angry words too ridiculous and drawn out to be an insult. But that's why I had to think about it more, I had to re-hear his words over and over in my head for the rest of the day, and well into the night, to make sense of them.

His insult was like a song that you don't like when you hear it first, but grows on you the more you hear it. It's an insult that didn't really hurt the first time I heard it. The words were too complicated to be powerful. Not an easy F you. But the more I hear his words, the more they grow on me. And they hurt more each time. Like the wooden horse of Troy, his words innocently passed through my boundaries, and then bam, deceived, all the troops jumped out, hitting me hard, one after the other, spearing me again and

52

again and again.

The cleverest kind of insult.

And so that's how he leaves me. A slushy, mushed snail, crushed by the sole of his trainer, by the strength of his words. Shattered. Flattened. Forcefield down. Antennae up.

8

I have a turbulent night's sleep. The same dream on a loop. It's exhausting. I'm doing the same thing over and over, trying to solve the same problem. I keep finding myself in a toilet cubicle with no walls or door, everyone can see me. So very busy in my dreams that I wake late on Tuesday morning.

It's 7.34 a.m. My iPhone shows that I turned the alarm off at 7 a.m. but I don't remember. This has never happened to me before. In shock, and feeling shaky from being knocked off my usual routine, I shower quickly. The water barely washes over me and the soapy shower gel sits on my skin when I step out of the shower. I'm still damp when I dress. I'm feeling panicked and hassled. It's thirty minutes of a difference and the day feels off. The light is different, as are the sounds. The birds are quieter. I've missed their performance. I've lost my time to do what I usually do. I'm a few steps behind. In a contradictory twist I stop moving for a second to try and catch up with myself. I'm out of sync.

There was such order in boarding school, everything accounted for, no minute wasted: 7.30 a.m. rising followed by breakfast and study; 9 a.m. school; 1.05 p.m. lunch; 1.50 p.m. school; 3.40 p.m. games/other activities/cuppa; 4.30–6.30 p.m. dinner; 6.30–7.30 p.m. recreation; 7–9 p.m. study; 8.55 p.m. night prayer; 9–9.30 p.m. night cuppa and recreation; 9.30–10.15 p.m. lights out. Freckles. Constellations. A regimental life was the very opposite to living with Pops, a free

54

spirit who seemed to exist on his own time, who made the world bend around him. I thought life was normal with Pops, but something clicked in me when I reached boarding school. The routine, the discipline, the knowing what was around the next corner settled me. Never bored or suffocated me, the way it did some of the other girls.

I leave home late. Head down, I ignore the action in the house. Once in Malahide Castle grounds I pass by the man in the suit with the headphones. He's far further than he'd usually be. I'm way behind. I walk faster. I don't pass the leaning jogger, and I expect to at some stage. The man walking the Great Dane is nowhere in sight. How could that be, did he take another route. Where is the old man and his son, and did the earth fall off its axis this morning. It's Wednesday. No. It's Tuesday. I'm confused. What kind of hex has Ferrari fella put on me.

I arrive at the bakery at 8.15, by which time it's crowded and I can't get inside the door. Spanner doesn't even see me because I'm faced with a line of backs. I'm late. My shift may have begun but I have a routine to keep to. I feel shut out of the party, staring in at the steamed-up windows like a child who hasn't been invited. I walk away, unsure of where to go. I've been there every morning for three months. Where to now.

Feeling disoriented, a little dizzy, I keep walking. I feel like everyone is looking at me because I don't know where I'm going. I stop and start. Turn around and then go back the way I came, before going back the other way again as my mind runs through the possible places to go. I'm like an ant whose line has been broken. It's his fault. I join the line in Insomnia and examine the counter of unfamiliar muffins and cakes. I hear Spanner giving out about them. They don't have Belgian waffles. Only packaged Stroopwafels by the till. I can't decide on anything so I leave. Outside I meet Donnacha.

Good morning, Allegra.

His jeep is right out front. The engine is running, the hazards are on and the kids are active inside. He's parked on double yellow lines. The keys dangle from the ignition. I wonder how he will react to me telling him to move. I haven't seen him since I caught Becky out. I wonder if he suspects anything, if I need to watch what I say. I'm more concerned about his parking.

I saw a fox last night in the garden, he begins.

My eyes wander as he talks. The kids are screaming in the car, I can hear them from here and he keeps talking about them being nocturnal hunters. Solitary hunters. Scavengers, not a threat to dogs or cats so Barley and Rye should be fine.

A nimble snout of flood, licks over stepping stones and goes uprooting, he says.

Ah he's spewing poetry already and so early in the morning.

Heaney. The hedgehog and the fox, he says.

Oh. Right. We studied his stuff, I say. Something about potatoes.

That was 'Digging,' he says.

Right. I don't remember. It was a while ago.

It's about work, ritual and the desire to craft, he says.

One of those deep looks at me, like I know what the hell. I can't do this today. Not with how my head is.

I just thought it was about potatoes, I kind of

56

mumble.

You know the hedgehog was Hume, and the fox was Trimble.

He takes my non-answer, my lack of eye contact and my general air of disinterest as encouragement to continue.

John Hume. SDLP. David Trimble. Ulster Unionist. Hesitant progress with assured movement.

Right, I say, feeling sweat breaking out on my back. Prickling against my shirt.

I look at the car again.

Isn't it dangerous to leave the keys in the ignition when the kids are in the car, I say.

It takes him a moment to adjust to the subject change, and when he does he shrugs lightly. No they won't touch it.

I don't mean the kids, I mean somebody could jump in and drive off.

He laughs. Whoever it is would drive them right back, believe me. Maybe you'll keep an eye out for it.

For what.

For the fox. See if he visits again. I was trying to figure out which way he came in, he says. And around and around again he goes.

I eye the car, irritation prickling, my skin feels itchy, my nose is too.

Donnacha, I interrupt him, you know I'm a parking warden and you're parked on double yellow lines.

I'm not parked, my hazards are on. I'm only going to be a minute.

He doesn't know the meaning of a minute. I feel like everybody is staring at me, this warden not doing her job properly. Burn her at the stake for inefficiency. A garda car drives by, and my heartbeat quickens. I don't want them to see me not doing my job properly. I make my expression more stern. Maybe they'll think I'm lecturing Donnacha. I'm on the case.

Your car is illegally parked here, I say, and you're putting me in a very difficult situation. And your wife is shagging somebody else. I don't say the last bit aloud. But I could. And I might. If he doesn't let me go. Release me from his snare. It's on the tip of my tongue.

Okay, okay, he says.

I have to leave before I blurt it out. I take a left down Townyard Lane so I don't feel his eyes on my back. I'm trembling. It's Ferrari fella's fault. He's made me fall apart. At the seams. Stuffing hanging out. I started off on the wrong foot, and can't find a natural rhythm. I feel jumpy. The heeby-jeebies. As I approach the hair salon I notice that the BMW isn't parked outside. Confused, I look around to see if she's parked it somewhere else but there's no sign of it. I cross the road quickly not paying attention to the traffic and almost get run over. Where is she. What's wrong with her. Why didn't she go to work today. With a car horn ringing in my ear I jog up to the window of the salon and look inside. She's right there, at the window, doing nails. This I'm glad of and I relax a little, but where's her damn car, and what the hell is going on.

I walk up and down the street a few times, checking every single car for her parking disc. Maybe she bought a new car, maybe she drove in another car, and if that's the case, I hope she's transferred the new vehicle details to her disc or I'll have to ticket her. But there's nothing that belongs to her or her business. I stare through the window, confused. She looks up briefly and catches my eye again. She smiles, all professional, always on the lookout for new customers. I turn around and walk away quickly, heart pounding at the connection.

I stop at the head of James's Terrace and look down the street. My heart is pumping, pounding. I don't know if I want to see the Ferrari or not. I feel weary as I make my way down past the cars, an impending sense of doom, and somebody runs out of number eight — not him, it's the curly-haired lad. Dressed casually, fashionably preened and polished in a T-shirt and jeans, so unbusinesslike for an office environment. I wonder what they do in there, apart from ruin people's existences. He looks at me, grinning, as he runs down the steps. Digging for money in his pocket, he hurries to the pay-and-display machine, then to the Ferrari. He opens the door, places the ticket on the dashboard, winks at me as if he's beaten me in a game I have no desire to play, or do I, and runs back inside.

Ah, he's been promoted to a parking angel.

I'm glad Ferrari fella has paid, or at least sent out one of his footmen, but only paying because he sees me coming isn't the point at all. This is not a cat-and-mouse game, this is not about me, you're supposed to pay for all the hours. I'm agitated again.

I need a break. I haven't had coffee or breakfast but maybe I should take an early lunch. I walk by the office, looking straight ahead, down the steps to the coast road. I head for my bench but it starts to rain and I have to divert immediately. It's bucketing down, big thick cold raindrops. Wet rain, as we'd say. I hurry to the public toilets on the corner, beside the tennis club. Pretty flower boxes outside, and hanging baskets. Standing, I eat my cheese sandwich, making sure my back is to number eight. Look at her eating her lunch by the skanky toilets in the rain, I imagine the male models say, as they place their Prada trainers on their desks and lean back to drink cappuccinos with half almond milk half llama milk.

For distraction I watch the windows of the garda station, bright strip lighting peeking through vertical office blinds, wondering what they're working on, wondering if my parking tickets will ever help them solve a case.

It rains for the remainder of the afternoon, a grey day made greyer, dirtier and cold. A cold wind picks up, sending the promise of spring away and plunging us back into winter again. By the time I'm finished for the day I arrive home freezing. My feet are numb and my fingers are so cold I can barely wrap them around my door key. I could do with babysitting tonight, the kids would be a nice distraction. Usually Becky and Donnacha go out on Tuesdays, but the house is quiet. I walk across the flagged stone pathway through the secret garden to the gym.

The rain has enticed worms and snails outside up from their hiding places.

I feel a crunch underfoot. I twist my shoe to wipe the snail's slush off.

★   ★   ★

I stand in the shower for a long time. It takes a while for the heat to soak through my skin and reach my bones. The mist and steam are so thick I can't see through the glass, and I'm finding it hard to breathe. I've heat rashes all over my skin, and yet I turn the temperature higher.

Later I can't sleep. My mind is too busy, it won't settle. It won't focus on one thought for long enough, it keeps jumping back and forth, to nonsense. To five people.

I hear a sound outside. A crash, a bang. It sounds like the wheelie bin. It's windy but not so much that it would send a wheelie bin flying. The McGovern family wheelie bins are gathered together in an area nearer to the house. Sectioned off behind khaki painted fencing. Two green bins for recycling, a brown bin for food and a purple for home refuse. I have one of each outside the garage for my own use. I'm meticulous with my recycling. Everything must be separated, food cleaned out of plastic before binning, labels peeled off. All rules must be obeyed. It pains me to see what other families do after all my hard work. To think that their crap will be bunged in with mine. I picture that plastic swirl in the sea. The bang has come from right outside my window. I look outside but don't see anything. There's a security light that comes on with motion sensors but I switched it off because the tree outside my window kept setting it off every time it swayed.

I pull on my lounge pants again, throw a sweater on and hurry downstairs. The lights are off in the office and gym. I'm alone in the building. I open the door and look outside and come face to face with a fox. He looks up at me and doesn't blink. He has toppled the green bin. Bad idea, my friend, no food in there, though he may have sniffed out the remnants of food from the packaging. My heart's pounding as we take part in a staring match. I daren't breathe. Or blink. His tail is hugely bushy, white at the tip. Not too dissimilar to a dog but its tail gives it away.

61

Madra rua, the red fox.

We stare at each other, I don't know for how long, probably not as long as it feels. His stare isn't threatening, but is he dangerous. Maybe if you're a chicken. Are you a chicken, Allegra. Bok bok bok. Are you going to let what that man said break you down, knock you off your axis. Are you, Allegra. He called you a loser. He thinks that the five people you spend the most time with are losers and that you're a loser and maybe you are because look how you've reacted, Allegra. Or should I call you Freckles. Who are you since you arrived here. Allegra or Freckles. Come on, make up your mind.

I step back inside and close the door on the fox, heart pounding in my chest.

Bok bok bok.

Beneath the duvet I realise I'm running the finger-tips of my right hand across the skin on my left arm. I've been tracing the scarred raised skin near my bicep over and over as though wearing a path. I don't need to look at which constellation I'm focused on because I know by feel. Cassiopeia. A five-star constellation. I still remember the star names; Segin, Ruchbach, Navi, Shedar, Caph. As I run my fingers over each star I think about the words Ferrari fella said to me.

Five people. Five stars. Freckle to freckle. Star to freckle. Person to star. Person to freckle. Over and over again until I fall asleep.

9

I'm looking at the dashboard of the Ferrari. It ran out of pay-and-display juice thirty minutes ago. I'm momentarily pleased, not because I can ticket him again, but because I can see he has again made an effort. Then I'm angry with myself for dropping my standards. To simply make an effort is not acceptable.

I take the four steps up to number eight. The steps have been cleaned and polished, restored, unlike all the others in the terrace which are uneven, chipped and broken over time. There's not a sign of my mucusy slime from when he stepped on me, crushed me with his words. The Georgian door is black, shiny, with a grand gold knob and a large gold 8 above it. To the right-hand side there is just one buzzer along with the company name Cockadoodledoo Inc. I press it, step back and clear my throat.

It takes a while and as I consider leaving, the door is finally pulled open by a woman, probably my age, who, while tall, only fills a quarter of the height of the door. She looks like a miniature person, a doll in a doll's house. I'm startled by a loud deep male cheer, as though a football team has scored a goal. She barely reacts and as soon as I realise the cheer was not at my expense, as far as I can tell anyway, I settle.

The sour-faced beauty stares out at me. Hiya, she says.

She's long-legged, brunette with tight black jeans, ripped strategically at the thighs, high-heeled sandals, a check shirt, one half tucked into the waistline of her

63

high-rise jeans, buttons open halfway, sleeves rolled up. A sexy meshy vest or bodysuit beneath. Effortlessly cool. Messily sexy. It's all so crisp and clean. A lot of eyebrows on her face. Thick caterpillars, skilfully pruned and brushed. Hooped earrings. Big lips. Lots of lips. Skin so clear it's almost not real. Not one blemish, not one freckle or hair. It looks as though it's been scraped clean, a new packet of butter when the lid is peeled off, the ground after a fresh snow. The whites of her eyes so white, her eyes the kind of amber that reminds me of Pops' cello bow resin. The new female species. Kendall Jenner's body with Kylie Jenner's face. Or wearing her make-up line at least.

Hello, I say, I'm a parking warden for Fingal County Council. I would like to speak with the owner of the yellow Ferrari.

I stand a little straighter than I usually would. I'm taller than her. I don't know why that should make me feel better but it does. I look past her, down the long corridor, to where the shouting is coming from. It's all greys and whites. Walls, cornicing, wooden panelling, like something out of an interiors magazine. A cat wanders down the hall towards us. Grey and white, as if it was dipped to match the interiors.

Rooster's in a meeting, she says, bending down to pick up the cat, air kisses it so that her glossy lips don't stick to the fluff. Her nails are the long pointy kind that could do some damage. Fake ones, painted a blush colour. There's another cheer, from down the hall.

Rooster, I ask.

Rooster owns the Ferrari, she says.

I'm very disappointed. Not by the name. That's a gift. What better name for the wanker owner of a tosspot car. I thought this would be the perfect opportunity to talk to him again. Come face to face with the fox. Ask him more about the five people, the hex, the curse he placed on me. What does it mean and why does it bother me so. But I shouldn't waste the trip entirely.

I raise the manila envelope in the air.

I want to leave this for him, I tell her.

Yeah sure, what's it about, she asks.

She struggles to keep the cat in her hands. Her pointy nails look like they're going to pierce it and send it flying around the room. The cat frees itself and finally leaps out of her arms towards me. It lands on the doormat, then darts backwards away from me as if I'm the threat. Contrary fecker.

It's in relation to his parking, I say. I noticed that he parks here every day and that he has a business. I pause. Is this a business, I ask.

She narrows her amber eyes. Well, yeah, of course.

I wanted to give him this paperwork, I say, handing the envelope to her. It's an application for a special parking permit. The annual fee is six hundred euro, which can be paid at once or monthly. It means he'll get a disc on the dashboard and he won't have to worry about pay-and-display parking or fines.

I give her a small smile when I mention the fines but she doesn't seem to get it. Any of it.

Hold on, she says, confused. Are you a sales person.

No, I sigh, I'm a parking warden. I say it slowly and clearly.

She looks me up and down, there's another cheer from the back of the building, a final one, and the voices get louder as a group of young men file out of a room in the back and down the corridor. They all look similar. Jeans, trainers, T-shirts, caps, hair, facial hair. Moisturised and smelling good. What's the collective noun for boy-banders. A bunch. A gaggle. A bouquet. A dazzle.

The parking angel sees me.

Shit, is it up, he asks, looking at a large-faced watch with a pink strap on his wrist.

Yes, I begin, but I'm —

Rooster's in a meeting, he interrupts me. Has been for the past three hours so he can't top it up. I asked you to do it, he looks at her.

I didn't know, she shrugs. Anyway she's, like, selling parking permits.

No, I'm —

Just take it from her, Parking Angel says, with a limp dismissive flick of his hand in my direction and disappears into the office, the one he watches out for me from the window like he's on the night's watch guarding the wall. Lads criss-cross the hall from one room to another, the cat, and a small dog too. They look at me, interested at first, then away again, uninterested. I give up.

Okay. Bye.

I turn around and walk down the steps. I should check the remainder of cars on the street but I can't be bothered sticking around. They got lucky today. I feel hot around my eyes. I hear a snigger and the door closes. I decide to take an early lunch. That way Paddy can't join me and I won't have to talk about what happened, relive the episode.

There's someone sitting on my bench.

Fuck.

I say it out loud.

The elderly couple sitting on it look at me. The man

is leaning forward, holding onto a cane, wheezing as he breaths heavily.

Do you think you'll be here long, I ask them.

They both look at me.

Alive or on the bench, he asks.

On the bench, I say.

He needs a rest, she says, defensively.

Do I need a ticket, he asks, eyes twinkling, and I smile.

I'll let you off this time.

I recalibrate. Everything off again today.

I sit on a low stone wall overlooking the marina. I've never sat here before and I feel like a dog, circling it a few times before choosing how to sit. Before me is a boat slipway leading down into silky water. Calm and mirror-like on this fine day. A man stands in the centre of the slipway, hands in his pockets staring out. I watch him for a while, then the island across the way. Now and then I see a few dots moving as golfers traverse the golf course on the island.

I've just bitten into my cheese sandwich when a foot and leg appears over the wall beside me, quickly joined by a full body. I recognise the trainers first. Prada.

Mind if I join you, he asks. He stands, waiting to be welcomed.

Sure.

He sits.

Thanks for these, he says, the envelope and the loose pages in his hand. I just got out of a meeting. I'm guessing they're from you.

I thought it would be easier for you than to keep running out and topping up the machine. Most businesses around here use parking permits.

Yeah makes sense. Thanks.

I take another bite of my sandwich. I can feel him staring at me, chewing becomes unrhythmical and unnatural. I should have spoken instead of eating. That timing thing again. Swallow.

Look, you can pay for parking whatever way you want, I say, but if you don't, I have to ticket you, it's my job, it's not personal. I don't have a vendetta against you. I ticket lots of cars. Most of the time I don't know the owners.

Though I do have a very good memory for who owns what around here, but I don't bother telling him that.

Look, I'm very sorry about the other day, he says, about ripping up the ticket and saying what I said. It was extremely disrespectful, really out of character, I don't usually, I mean I never blow up like that, and I didn't mean it.

Yes you did.

Well I did at the time, but it wasn't . . . I'm sorry anyway.

He cowered immediately. Maybe chickens can scare foxes, maybe snails can crush people.

Tell me more about it, I say.

Well, he says and thinks. I'd had a bad day. And I'd gotten a parking ticket every single day for two weeks. And I was stressed, very stressed, you know, new business, office politics . . . Why are you smiling.

I meant tell me more about what you said to me. You are the average of the five people you spend the most time with, I say. I say it loud and clearly as I've been saying it to myself since he uttered the words. The hex. The curse. The Trojan horse.

Oh that. No. Really. I didn't mean it.

68

He seems embarrassed. About insulting me or over how he insulted me, I don't know which. Kind of a dorky insult when you think about it. Still, I need it broken down for me more.

Okay, I say, but what does it mean.

You are the average of the five people you spend the most time with is a business expression, he explains. An inspirational quote. Jim Rohn said it. He's a motivational speaker. It means the people you spend the most time with shape who you are.

He looks up at me then, finally, to see if he still has me. He has. He's had me since he said the words to me. Not in a *Jerry Maguire* way, he has done the very opposite of completing me, but the phrase has triggered me.

According to research, he says, the people you regularly associate yourself with determine as much as ninety-five per cent of your success or failure in life. They determine the conversations you have. They affect the attitudes and behaviours you're regularly exposed to. Eventually you start to think like they think and behave like they behave. I'm taking some business classes and I'd just read it, I suppose it was fresh in my mind, when I saw you, and . . . you know, just blurted it out.

You thought that I was surrounded by losers, I say. That the five people I spend the most time with must have been nothing, to be able to group together and make me so nothing. You called Paddy a loser. My colleague. As you ripped up the ticket in my face, you weren't intending to inspire me.

Clever, really. Sly old fox. I look out to the fisherman on the slipway.

Like I said, I'm sorry.

69

Stop saying sorry, I say. We're past that. I need to figure it out.

Figure what out.

My five people. I mean if everyone was to pick five people wouldn't it just be their husband or wife, and kids, or parents or —

No, you see it can't be family, he says, smiling.

Why not.

Because then everybody's five people would only be their families.

Mine would only be one.

Oh.

But continue.

When you look outside of the family group there are other influential people in your life who are having an effect on you that you may not have considered.

I open my container of walnuts and offer it to him. He shakes his head.

I don't think you should read into it so much. What I said to you was stupid. A bit of a random thing to say. It was just on my mind.

Yeah, true but it's like an earworm.

What's that.

You know one of those things that you can't get out of your head, like a song, that goes round and round. I keep thinking of it.

Yeah it is a bit like that. Probably why I passed it on. It was in my head too.

Could one family member be acceptable for your one of five, I ask.

I guess it could be if they're extremely influential.

He is. Pops.

Is that your granddad or your —

My dad.

70

Okay. Yeah. He shrugs.

So four more, I think aloud. Is it the people you literally spend the most time with, whether you like them or not, or could it be people who . . . I pause. People who you haven't even met.

People you haven't met, he says, thinking aloud. Like, what do you mean, people who inspire you, he asks, reaching into my container for a walnut and popping it in his mouth while thinking. He looks out at the sea. Mmm that's nice, usually I hate walnuts.

They're candied.

I don't know, he says, you're overthinking this. I know it's hard to reduce all the people you know down to five. You could be inspired by the idea and actions of someone . . . let's say Oprah, but she can't be on your list . . . you need to have interactions with the five. They need to intersect with your life.

He stares at me.

I stare back.

He'd be quite handsome if he wasn't such a cock.

Explain it to me again, I say, because I still don't really get the parameters for how one goes about becoming five.

Five people, he says slowly, this time with a broad grin and revealing perfect teeth, that you spend the most time with. That's it. He stares at me, smiling.

What's so funny.

Your face. You seem so confused.

I am, I say. You make it sound so simple. The five people. Whoever they are. They make me who I am. Forever. Just because I happen to spend time with them. That's it. Nothing to do with me or how I was raised, or the decisions I make or my genes or anything like that. It all comes down to these five people.

71

Yes but no, he twists his body towards me, hands flying as he talks again. Big fancy watch on his slim wrist. Blond arm hairs on sallow skin. You are who you are, obviously, but that's the beauty of it. The second part of the quote is, choose wisely. You get to choose. You get to choose your five people and that means you get to choose who shapes who you are, and therefore get to choose who you are. Let's say you were putting a team together for basketball, wouldn't you choose the best five people for the team, who are all skilled in specific areas. You've got the point guard, the shooting guard, the small forward, the power forward and the centre.

I don't play basketball.

Not the point. He rolls his eyes. The project is you. Who do you need on your team, to be who you want to be.

Well now it's inspiring, I say. Why didn't you just say that before you ripped up the ticket.

We laugh.

Truce, he asks, holding his hand out. I nod.

What's your name, he asks.

Allegra Bird, I say.

His hands are soft. Softer than mine.

Allegra Bird. Cool name.

Comes from allegro. Means to play music lively. Pops is a music professor.

He's one of your five.

He's my number one. Do they need to be in order.

He laughs, a fantastic sound that makes me smile, amidst my utter spinning head of confusion.

Some people call me Freckles, I say, quite unnecessarily, but I can't think of anything else to say.

Freckles, he says, smiling and he studies my face. I

72

feel self-conscious. As though he's mapping them out. Cute.

Well, Allegra aka Freckles, I'm Tristan.

I thought your name was Rooster.

No, Rooster's my YouTube name.

Why do you have a YouTube name.

Because . . . how do you know I'm Rooster if you didn't know I was a YouTuber.

Your secretary told me. I gave her the envelope that you have in your hand, I say, confused. He must be a bit mental if he's forgotten what brought him here to me in the first place.

He's frowning, looking at the envelope.

I found this on the floor by the door, he says, I thought you'd put it through the letterbox.

No. Your posse said you were in a meeting.

Yeah. I was.

Which do you prefer, I say, Rooster or Tristan.

Who do I prefer to be, he asks, or the name.

I hadn't thought of that really but I tell him both.

I prefer being Rooster. But you can call me Tristan. What about you, which do you prefer, Allegra or Freckles.

I look at him. And he's done it again. Another trigger.

Pops calls me Allegra. I have freckles because of Pops. But I don't say either of those things. I just shrug and we part, both needing to get back to work.

10

I'm going home for Easter and I couldn't be happier. It's good Friday morning and I sit on the 06.20 train from Dublin to Killarney, watching the country racing by. The village was quiet for the week with the kids off school, and the difference no school made to the traffic. Most people cleared out for the two weeks. The streets were relatively empty, lots of parking spaces, there wasn't a whole lot for me to do, no one to argue with every morning. I amused myself on Ash Wednesday by counting the amount of grey splodges on foreheads. Singed brains. As a little girl I'd thought somebody's head had been on fire, was relieved for them they'd managed to put it out.

I'm not religious. Neither is Pops, though he's technically Church of Ireland. Despite going to a Catholic boarding school I didn't have to take part in any religious studies. I wasn't the only one. A few Protestants, three Hindus and a Muslim. And a girl who'd moved over from Malaysia to study in Ireland while her parents stayed behind in Malaysia. She said she was an atheist and I had no religion so whenever religious things were happening we were always put together and given other work to do. Essays, worksheets, pointless errands, that kind of thing. Once we were brought outside on a sunny day to tie-dye our T-shirts while the others were stuck inside learning about transubstantiation. People were jealous of our non-religious cult.

I still liked Sister Lettuce even though I wasn't into

her religion. She was young, in her thirties and really believed in her cause. I think she thought she had to single-handedly make up for all the hateful things the decrepit nuns did in the past. She tried with all of us, to hear our problems, to show us she cared, to fix them.

I take my gold notepad out of my bag and place it on the table and start working on my list. From the age of five to eleven my five people were my best friend from Valentia, Marion, Cara, Marie, Laura and Pops. In secondary school it was Marion, Sister Lettuce, Bobby my boyfriend for a year but obsessed over for longer than that so much so that he shaped my dreams and thoughts, Viv who was my closest school friend, and Pops. After school when I didn't get into the Gardaí and all the way up to now, it was Marion, my boyfriend Jamie, Cyclops, my aunt Pauline, and Pops. Always Pops.

It's been months since I've been home and I'm looking forward to catching up with them. With most of them anyway.

It's 10.20 when I step off the train at Killarney station. The drivetime to Valentia Island is an hour and twenty minutes, or one hour if Pops is driving. It's not easy to get back home, my part of the world is badly serviced by public transport. Valentia Island is a small island, eleven kilometres in length and three kilometres in width and it's not that far away but accessibility-wise I sometimes feel like I'm trying to get to Australia.

Even if I were to hitch a ride to Portmagee, I'd still need a car to get over the Maurice O'Neill Memorial Bridge, which links the mainland to Valentia Island, and then to Knightstown, which is the town at the furthest point from the bridge entrance. There's a car ferry from Reenard's Point that runs directly to Knightstown, a five-minute journey. But it only operates from April to October during the busier season and if you're not at Reenard's Point by 10 p.m., then you've missed the last ferry. I worked on the car ferry after school, it was the job I left to become a parking warden. From April to October anyway, the rest of the months I worked in the gift shop of Skellig Experience, a museum showcasing the story of the island. Thanks to a sixth-century monastic site, the place has been declared a UNESCO World Heritage site offshore. They needed more staff when *Star Wars Episode VII: The Force Awakens* was released.

Tom Breen is usually the man to rely on to get from Cahirciveen to home. He's the local taxi but he plays a lot of golf and isn't always helpful when he answers the phone from the fourth hole on Kinsale and asks if you can wait a few hours. And he's slow. As much as Pops' driving terrorises me, Tom Breen's driving makes me feel murderous.

I survey the train station car park. Pops isn't here.

I ring him.

Allegra my love, he says, I'm at the house, I couldn't drive to you.

Are you okay, I ask.

I'm fine, but the car is not.

I look around the car park and wonder what my options are. Buses to Cahirciveen don't run on a Saturday and even if they did, I'd have to call Tom Breen and oh God, I think I'd walk home faster. And when did this car trouble happen. He could have told me earlier. It would have taken him an hour to get here, he should have left the house an hour ago. Why didn't

76

he call or text, why am I finding out now by ringing him.

I fight my irritation while weaving through the cars and trying to figure out how to get out of Killarney.

But don't you be worrying, he says, I've arranged a lift for you.

My stomach drops. I see a familiar car enter the car park and hope to God it's not here for me. Tom Breen's car.

Pops, you didn't call Tom Breen, did you.

It's not Tom, he says.

Good, he must be here for someone else I think with relief, but then wonder who Pops has arranged to meet me. My uncle Mossie perhaps, or my aunt Pauline, though she'd be busy with her B&B and wouldn't have time to collect me. She won't be happy at a last-minute request such as this, much as she loves me.

Tom's car is creeping through the car park. I turn away and walk in the other direction just in case he accosts me and insists I share with someone else. It drives slowly towards me and crawls after me like a stalker.

Tom wasn't available, Pops says, at such short notice, he was out golfing but he said he'd send his son Jamie.

His son Jamie, as if I've never heard of Jamie in my life. Jamie who was my boyfriend for three years. On my list of five. I just wrote it on the train, I can't deny it. But he was the one I wasn't looking forward to seeing quite so much.

Jamie. Fuck.

I stop walking and the car stops. I look in, Jamie looks back at me. Neither of us smile. I left Valentia

Island behind, I left Jamie behind. Not on good terms. And now I'll be stuck in a car for an hour and twenty minutes with him.

He gets out of the car and opens the boot for my luggage but I tell him I'd prefer to keep it with me and he slams it closed and gets back into the car. I take a deep breath and briefly wonder if I have any other options, but I know I don't, and avoiding this could make things even worse, so I sit inside, in the back, behind the passenger seat, which feels odd as he and I would always sit side by side.

I hope you drive faster than your dad, I joke. We all know his dad crawls, we both laughed about it, it drove Jamie insane. But maybe I forget to add warmth to my voice and he doesn't realise it was supposed to be playful. Or he does and he doesn't want to pretend everything's okay when it's not, because he looks at me in the mirror and says, I hope you're not a perv like your dad.

He locks the door, turns the radio up loud and drives.

Faster than his dad.

11

Your dad is a perv.

I'd heard it before. When I was in secondary school. I must have been twelve years old.

She came out with it one day, Katie Sullivan, after I'd tackled her in camogie training and then went on to score. She'd always been a bad sport, hot-tempered and vicious. Mostly it came out in kicks, scratches, pulls and even a bite. Not me. Opposing teams usually. I wasn't expecting her to say it. I laughed at first. It seemed like such an odd, random insult to choose and her anger was funny. Flared nostrils, red face, a vein down the centre of her forehead, cartoon character angry. She had issues. This is the same girl who wrote hate mail to her mam for cheating on her dad. I heard a rumour she'd flirted dangerously with her mam's new boyfriend and then accused him of coming on to her. She was twisted. Made of anger.

My image of a pervert didn't match up to my Pops. Some dirty-haired old greaseball in a soiled trench coat flashing people in parks. That's what made the accusation so funny. But nobody else laughed. I remember that. That was almost worse. They didn't know that she was just making it up to embarrass me, to hurt me in the same way as me tackling her, and winning, had made her feel.

It's true, she'd shouted as she was being taken off the court by Sister Lettuce. Just ask Carmencita. I'd laughed again, nervously this time. But the name shut me up. Stunned me. Made my body shake on

79

the inside. Because that was my mam's name and no one but me, Pops, Aunt Pauline, Uncle Mossie and my two cousins, knew about Carmencita. I thought maybe she'd read the name in one of my notebooks where I'd doodled it once or twice, but it seemed unlikely that, even if she had, she'd be able to link the name with my mam.

After the shock of what she'd said died down I wanted to ask her more, but she'd received such severe punishment for what she said she was afraid to even look at me. She was suspended from the camogie team for the rest of the season, which was a punishment for the whole school because she was our star player. I got the blame then, from everyone on the team. The girls used to crowd around me and tell me to forgive Katie. Convince me that she hadn't hurt my feelings at all. As if I had any control or power over her punishment.

Of course I assumed what she'd said wasn't true, why would I actually believe it, but I did want to know what she knew and how. Katie travelled on the same train as me to Limerick on Friday evenings, where Pops met me. When she was alone one day I built up the courage to sit beside her on the carriage and ask her, Why did you say that about my Pops.

★   ★   ★

Jamie Peter, JP, flies along the country roads as fast as he can through Saturday-morning traffic with his music blaring. I feel a little sick from all the jerking and try to lower my window but he has it locked and I can't bring myself to break the tense silence even though I can't breathe and need air. He pulls into

80

a service station and gets out without a word. The music finally stops. I let out a slow breath. I use the opportunity to buy a few things for Pops, like bread, milk, bacon, porridge, juice, pears, the basics he never seems to have. I don't know what he survives on. Ham, tomatoes and cartons of vegetable soup.

Jamie is behind me as I'm paying and I feel his eyes boring into me. There's an awkward moment, another one, when I've finished paying and I don't know whether to wait for him in the shop or not. I wait but it's more of a linger at the paperback stand. He pays and leaves and I follow him, wishing I hadn't bothered waiting at all. He doesn't turn the radio back on when we get back in the car and I wonder if he's going to say something but we sit in silence. I zone him out, trying to pretend he's just another taxi driver, lower the window, which is now unlocked, close my eyes and breathe in the air. Almost home.

When I open my eyes he's watching me in the rearview mirror. Caught, he has no choice but to speak.

So how's the Big Smoke, he asks. Busy, I suppose.

There's an air of bitterness to his tone. Sometimes there's a feeling with people left behind that others have departed for something greater. That we must be looking down our noses at everyone and everything when we return. An inferiority complex which doesn't sit well because the island is far superior to Dublin and any city in the world. If he could see where I live now, above a garage in a suburb I don't think it would quite match up to the ideas he may have of me single-handedly managing Dublin city traffic. I'm not sure if I want him to know the truth.

Yeah. It's okay, I tell him, eventually deciding that okay is neither too braggy or too whingey. Is this your new job or are you just filling in.

I took over the business in January. Dad retired.

Seriously, I ask. I thought you said you'd never join the family business.

I didn't join, he says. I'm in charge now. Dad had a heart attack in February.

I had no idea, Pops didn't tell me. I'm sorry, Jamie.

He's grand now, he says. It was a rough few weeks.

Again that tone that seems angry with me for not knowing, for not contacting him.

He's never been happier though, he says, he's playing golf practically every day. Is dropping shots and winning tournaments.

Do you like it, I ask.

What.

Driving.

I've always liked driving.

Not what I meant but we did go for long drives all the time. Just me and him. It was the thing we did, to get away. Knightstown is a small place, so is Valentia Island. We'd go driving for hours, pull over, have sex in the car — not this car, he shared a Volkswagen Beetle with his sister. He hated that it wasn't manly, his sister got to choose it, but he used it more than she did. I wonder if he's thinking about the same thing now. I study him. He wasn't a bad boyfriend, he was a good one. We were together for almost four years. And then I left.

I was the first person he had sex with. He wasn't mine. That happened when I was away on a sun holiday with Pops at fifteen. He kept putting me in a kids' club that I was too old for while he explored the island that I'd no interest in seeing because I was fifteen and eternally cranky. So I ended up helping

82

the kids' club teachers. We'd do the kids' club morning dance on stage by the pool at 11 a.m. to welcome children, dancing with Geluk the mascot, a giant blue fish with skinny yellow legs.

Sometimes I could see when Geluk had a phone in his pocket, one time as he was doing 'Agadoo' at the kids disco, I could see a packet of cigarettes against the bright yellow spandex. I asked Geluk for a cigarette one day and that was that. I slept with Geluk, who was really Luuk from Amsterdam. Anyway it wasn't when Jamie and I were going out that I popped his cherry, that happened earlier, when I was sixteen. We were friends for years, then it became serious between us when I was nineteen until I left for Dublin.

I study his profile. His acne has disappeared. His roaring angry spots and nasty whiteheads have faded from his face and only a trace can be seen on his neck. He must have finally found the right cream after trying something new every week. He's better dressed, less scruffy, a new haircut. Tom Breen is more than a taxi company. To really make a business he acted as chauffeur, driving rich American golfers from course to course around the country. I can't imagine Jamie acting like the tour guide, pointing out places to Americans, pretending to care about old ruins and repeating the stories his dad could tell in his sleep. Maybe he's good at it. But other than that, he's the same old Jamie. I find myself smiling fondly at him. He catches me in the mirror.

What, he asks.

Nothing.

What.

Just remembering things.

We hold each other's stare in the mirror.

Killarney to Killorglin, and then the N70 to Cahir-civeen. He turns off for Reenard's Point.

It's April, I say, as if just realising.

Yep.

Car ferry season. Jamie and I were deck attendants for years during the season. I loved that job. I loved both the feeling of coming home and leaving the island. Watching it disappear behind me, so I could see it in its full glory, but never leaving it behind completely, just getting a hint of what it would be like, before coming back in again. Two of my favourite feelings every ten minutes from morning to night. It never got boring, something always happened, at least one incident a day.

Is it busy yet, I ask him.

Yeah. Easter.

Right about now everyone starts working two or three jobs until November. Tourist season starts, you've got to make hay while the sun shines because it will be dead, dull and quiet from November on.

Remember the time the bull got stuck when the tractor was unloading, I say. In the middle of summer, holding up the traffic on both sides.

I grin as I recall Jamie running around with the farmer trying to catch a bull who went wild on the ferry. It had taken a few brave men from the line of cars to volunteer and surround the bull, guide it back to the box, reattach it to the jeep. While I stood back and almost peed myself laughing.

Remember the time I organised the Easter egg hunt on the ferry for you, he says, and I can hear the smile in his voice without needing to even look at him.

Thirty Cadbury's Creme Eggs. I was nearly sick, I say.

84

You still a chocaholic, he asks.

I'm into waffles now.

Birds Eye.

Belgian. A fella at the local bakery makes them fresh every morning, I tell him, and he makes a face as if that's so fancy and I've changed with my other island fancy ways.

We join the queue of cars at Reenard's Point. Not too many in front. Maybe ten, we'll make the next trip. The ferry is coming towards us, drifts in on calm waters. I feel butterflies in my stomach. Home. I open my seat belt and move to the middle, between the front seats, like an excited child. Closer to Jamie.

You seem happy to be home, he says.

I am. Even I hear the relief in my voice.

Dublin not what you thought, he asks.

I shrug.

Did you do what you set out to do.

Yes and no.

What's that supposed to mean, he asks. He turns to look at me.

All of a sudden I feel emotional, like I'm going to cry. If it was the old me and Jamie I'd tell him about Becky, all over my sheets, invading my space. And I'd tell him about Tristan and how he'd ripped up the ticket and called me a loser. And we'd slag them both and I'd feel better after it. And I might even tell him what else is on my mind. About the quote about the five people. How it's lingering in my head and what does that mean. Why can't I let it go. And you know, maybe I will tell him. Because he's looking at me like he cares.

A car beeps from behind and startled, Jamie jumps into action. The car in front is on the ferry, we're holding everything up. A fella I don't know is wildly waving us on. Jamie and I used to guide the cars onto the ferry. It's drive on, drive off, not complicated. Only room for two rows. Then we'd take turns to handle the money. Eight euro one-way. Twelve euro round-trip. It hasn't changed. It hasn't even been a year, what was I expecting. As soon as Jamie has parked, I get out of the car. I stand at the chain, and watch Reenard's Point getting further away, then when we're halfway across to the island, I move to the far end and watch as we get closer to Knightstown pier. A perfectly clear day, on the other side of the island Skellig Rock in all its glory would be in sight, endless breathtaking views, views that I grew up with but never grew tired of. The Royal Valentia Hotel dominates the pier, the white building there since the 1800s, the red clock tower in its prominent position, the town clock, a meeting place for pretty much everything.

Pops' grandparents moved to Valentia Island to work on the transatlantic cable station that opened in the late 1800s. I was reminded throughout my childhood of how, when the cable was pulled ashore from Valentia to a tiny fishing village in Newfoundland called Heart's Content, my grandfather was responsible for the first successful message from Queen Victoria to the US president after the treaty of peace was signed between Austria and Prussia. Only the wealthy could afford to use the cable at one dollar per letter, payable in gold. The island was a prosperous place then, between the cable station and the slate quarry, but too much competition from satellites saw the cable station close in 1966. Out of work, Pops' family left the island to move to what we call the other island. Ireland. When I was born, Pops came home.

As we near the pier, those who left their cars to breathe it in get back inside to prepare to leave the ferry. I tear myself away and get back in the taxi feeling a rush of exhilaration.

Wish I felt like that coming home, he remarks gently.

I've always liked this part, even doing it ten times a day.

I know. I remember. That's why I'm surprised you left.

I had to.

He grunts then starts the engine and follows the car in front. Two more minutes and I'll be out of the car.

I'm sorry I left, Jamie, I say.

He looks at me in surprise and says, I understand why you did. I did at the time. I'm not sorry you left, he says, I'm sorry how you left. No warning. Just, you know.

Yeah.

I'd stuff planned.

What kind of stuff.

Stuff for us.

I didn't know.

He looks away angry, jaw tightening. And you didn't ask me to come with you, he says. I'd have come with you.

You hate Dublin, I say. You hate Dublin people.

I loved you.

I don't say anything. It's not a surprise. He said it all the time. Wasn't afraid of it. And wasn't embarrassed to say it. He was always too good for me. Loved me more than I loved him. He said it all the time, as if trying to convince me. I believed him, but every time he said it, I felt a little less for him. Like one of those fellas outside restaurants on holidays. Come in come in, I do you good price. The more of a good price they do, the louder they call, the fancier their gestures, the less you want to go in. You hear the desperation. Assume the food must be crap. You'll go somewhere else. To the busy popular one where the fella barely looks at you when you enter and makes you wait for a table.

He pulls up outside the house and I get out. He does too but leaves the engine running, one foot in the car, the other out, leaning against the roof.

Look I'm only here until Monday but do you want to meet for a drink over the weekend, I ask and look at him. I should have some fun while I'm here. Maybe that can make up for the way I left.

I'm going out with Marion, he says, out of nowhere. Well not nowhere, it was from somewhere to him but nowhere to me. Plucked from his arsehole, it feels like. I've a good mind to shove it back in there.

Marion. My best friend. Marion and Jamie, two of my five. Pops my third, but really my first.

Marion and I were in the same Montessori together, we went to separate schools because I had to board, but we remained best friends. I haven't heard from her in a while, she was supposed to come to Dublin a few months after I moved but we couldn't make it work for different reasons. Life being irritating. Phone calls turned to text messages. Text messages became less common, but she's still my best friend.

I can't help it: I smile. It's a nervous smile. The one I do if I hear terrible news like someone has died, and I can't take the pressure of my face having to be serious, the pressure of how I'm supposed to act. If I

88

was a doctor I'd smile when giving a cancer diagnosis. If I was a pallbearer, I'd smile all the way up the church aisle. At a play, I laugh at the quiet awkward bits. I'm that person. No synchronicity at all between events and my expression. Non-verbal malfunction, maybe that's what the Garda interview report said. Maybe they couldn't have me showing up to a victim's family house at three in the morning with a grin on my gob. Sorry lads, you lost your daughter.

Jamie's angered by my smile. He was angry anyway, insulted maybe, that's why he told me about him and Marion. To hurt me. I'm not laughing at him, but if he remembered me the way he always knew me, inside out, better than most, he'd remember that I'm grinning at him foolishly now because I'm feeling awkward, nervous, scared by what he's told me. But this is what happens when you come apart, the secret bits you knew about each other dissolve into nothing. Like the most important parts that made up a person are no longer relevant. The spell that was cast on us was broken when I left the island. He doesn't remember me. Not the way he should.

She's eight weeks pregnant, he adds, then gets into the car and drives off, leaving me standing outside the house, at the side of the road with a broad smile at a time of despair.

12

The front door is unlocked as it always is. I'm greeted by a smell of damp, of moss, of burned toast, of something stale and left behind and something new and indistinguishable. There are homely scents hidden amidst the new smells, nice comforting ones. They come and go as I breathe in. I drop the bags in the hallway and hurry to the front room, the TV room, where I'm guessing Pops is waiting. The front room feels cold and dark. Pops struggles to get up from his armchair. It's a burgundy-coloured leather chair and a footrest pops out from the bottom when you push it back. We picked out the entire suite from Corcoran's in Killarney before I went away. A little going-away ritual, it felt like. The room still smells of new leather, which is welcoming over that stale indistinguishable smell.

Don't get up, don't get up, I say, going to him for a hug but he stands anyway, rises above me, a tall man, not as tall as he was, not as anything as he was, and I'm taken aback. I hide my worry in a hug, glad he can't see my face, wondering why I couldn't get this face right for Jamie and use the smile for now. How long is it since I've seen him, I try to remember. Three months, probably, much longer than I should have waited but I was holding out for Easter and couldn't take more holidays. I should have come home a few weekends. He feels thinner in my arms, his face is narrow, gaunt, his eyes darker and hollow. His hair is orange in places but grey, a lot more grey. He hasn't shaved and I hate to say it but something smells dirty, something stale left behind on his clothes. Or maybe that's him, the stale thing that I left behind. Selfishly maybe, maybe not. There's a stain on his sweater and down his trousers. Something claggy that's gripping the material and won't let go.

What's wrong with the car, I ask, trying to divert my attention from his face, feeling a little stunned by his appearance.

Ah don't mind that, he waves me away. Come and have a look, he says, leading me through to the hall, to the kitchen that looks out over fields beyond, none of the land ours but nice to look at all the same. I want to show you something, he says, struggling to unlock the back door that has never been locked. I found it here this morning, bleating away at my back door, it must have wandered away from its mother, and why isn't this key turning for feck sake — this is, ah, it wasn't locked that's why, well that's not very safe, is it, they could've come in through the back, the thieves and good-for-nothings, but never from the front or they'd be seen. It's what they're doing now, only in the back doors. Laurence had his tools stolen there last month. Silly fecker shouldn't have had them sitting out, but they came in the back. Okay just out here, you'll love it, Allegra, a sweet little thing.

He heads out to the garden, making a whish-a-whish-a-whish sound. He wanders around the garden whish-a-whishing while I remain on the doorstep. Even though the weather is fine, it's clear and sunny, actual heat in the air, there's parts of the land that are soggy and boggy all year round, where the sun never hits and the grass never grew properly and he's slushing around in it in his old trainers, mud splashing up his calves in thick splodges, on top of the dried splodges from the last time he was out whish-a-whishing. He's pressed two fingers of his right hand together, rubbing together, as if he has something more than thick fingers to offer. I watch him until I realise there's a creature he's calling and then I look around too, waiting for its appearance.

Is it a cat, I ask.

Whish-a-whish-a-whish.

Pops, is it a cat.

Come here, little one, it's okay, don't be scared now. Whish-a-whish-a-whish, he turns in my direction and I see his face is thunderous that it's not going his way.

Pops, if you tell me—

Whish-a-whish-a-whish—

What it is then—

Whish-a-whish-a-whish—

I can help you—

Feck it anyway. It's gone, he says, straightening up. He's breathing heavily, panting. He won't meet my eye. It was a little lamb. It's lambing season you know.

Yeah, I saw them all the way down.

Must have wandered off from its mother, came in here yesterday. I'd been feeding it and minding it, he says, wandering around and searching again, stepping in more muck. His shoes are encased in it now, mummified forever, to be unearthed thousands of years on by the next species, the orthofoot with the abzorb heel to prevent shocks to the body when walking, the celebrated shoe of mankind. It will be studied in museums by future beings, the foot of my father.

Pops, you're getting dirty.

I didn't leave it for a second all day. Whish-a-whish-a-whish.

One last attempt.

I swallow, feeling a rising panic in my chest, a swirling in my stomach. I hear the tremble in my voice. His behaviour is unsettling.

It probably went back to Nessie's farm, I say. So what's up with your car, I ask.

He stops circling the garden and looks up at me.

I couldn't drive because of the rats. Come on, he says, with a wave of his hand as though he's a farmer leading a herd, though Pops doesn't have a farming bone in his body.

Rats. I follow him. First lambs, now rats. Pops, your shoes, I warn him as he treads mud into the cheap linoleum kitchen floor, all through the house and out to the front garden. He lifts the bonnet of the car and stares into it. He looks at a bunch of wires and I think I look at him the same way. Something wrong with the wiring.

Look.

I don't know what I'm looking at.

The engine.

Well I know that.

Well then, you know more than you're letting on. I tried to drive this and smoke came out of the engine. Gerry came over and said rats had made a nest and eaten all the wires. It's completely gone. He can't fix it.

Rats, I ask.

That's what he said. They nibbled through the wires.

Does your insurance cover it.

No, they say they need proof that rats ate the wires. I told them I'd bring one in as a witness to testify to his acts, but how good are they with plea deals.

93

Jesus. I lean in closer. That's disgusting. So did they do that damage overnight or were you driving around with them in there.

I don't know. I suppose if they'd been in there when I was driving, I'd have burned them out, but there's no dead ones in there that I can see. But it doesn't explain what they're doing in the piano.

There's rats in the piano, I call after him, wide-eyed. As disgusted as I am, I'm relieved he's not losing it after all. If Gerry was a witness to this then it means he hasn't made it up. But it leaves the lamb open for investigation. Detective Freckles.

No, not rats, he says as I join him in the music room. I'd say these are mice. House mice.

He has a beautiful baby grand piano. Throughout my youth he taught classes here, individual classes for children and adults, hour after hour on a Saturday. I would play outside or upstairs in my room or watch TV while listening to wrong notes and slow playing while he patiently guided them. Always so patient.

He holds a finger up for me to listen.

I listen.

The room is silent, I don't hear anything. Just a creak in the floorboards as I shift my weight.

Sshh, he says, annoyed by my disturbance.

He looks into thin air, ear cocked. Something triggers his head to move. He looks at me hopefully. Did I hear that.

I, I clear my throat, I didn't hear anything.

He stares at the piano. Well it's not playing right, he says.

Maybe it needs to be tuned. Play me something.

He sits down. His fingers move gently over the keys as he thinks of what to play, as they try to find their

94

place. Mozart's Piano Concerto number twenty-three, second movement, he says, more to himself, and he starts to play. I've heard him play this piece before many times. It's beautiful, heartbreaking, but haunting. He once bought me a ceramic ballet dancer that played this music when it spun around. You would have to twist it, wind it up, and it would start playing fast but then slow down. Sometimes during the night it would let out a sudden tune, giving me a fright, and as it twisted all by itself I would hide under the covers, avoiding the cold stare of the ballet dancer's blue eyes. It's beautiful when Pops plays it, but it always haunted me.

He plays one dud note and he bangs his hands down on the keys. Loudly, dramatically. The deep notes echo for a moment.

Mice, he says, pushing the stool back and standing. I'll lay another trap. He opens the top. That'll stop them.

He leaves the room, the smell of his BO staying in the room with me.

★ ★ ★

Katie is on the train. She's sitting alone, nobody else beside her. I deliberately followed her into this carriage and watched the empty seat beside her for twenty minutes, anxiously. It's been about two weeks since she said what she said to me about Pops being a perv and I haven't been able to get it out of my head, it has kept me awake late into the night doing more scrapes of my skin from freckle to freckle than usual, and to top it off I'm under pressure from girls at school to win back our star player. Something bad

95

was said to me and I'm the one who's supposed to be apologising for it. Sometimes it would be easier to be a human if there weren't other humans. I finally build up the courage to sit beside her, and when I do, she looks at me with such fear on her face. I've never seen her look like that before and I wonder if her fear is because she's afraid of me, or because of Pops.

Her eyes widen and she looks around as if trying to catch somebody's eye for help. What do you want, she asks angrily.

I want to know what you meant about my Pops.

Your Pops, she rolls her eyes. Freckles, I shouldn't have said anything. I said sorry already, okay. I got mad and it came out and it shouldn't have.

If you tell me, then I'll tell Sister Lettuce that I forgive you and to let you back on the team.

She sits up at the mention of that. We're getting closer to Limerick station, I want her to hurry up.

It's just something I heard, she says finally.

From who.

My cousin Stephanie. She recognised your dad when he was picking you up from the station a few weeks ago. She said, That's Mr Bird, he's a perv. He slept with a girl in my class. Bird the perv. They had a song. Bird Bird Bird, Bird is the perv.

My heart hammers. I ready myself. But she just stops talking. Go on, I say.

Well that's it. He was a teacher, she was a student. That's gross. They were out one night in a pub and other lecturers and professors were there, and him and her got talking and when my cousin was leaving her friend wouldn't go with her, so they figured she was in safe hands and left her. Anyway they slept together. She told my cousin after that she totally regretted it.

96

Then no one heard from her for months before the finals, she just disappeared. That's all I know, she says with a shrug.

Do you know where the student is now, I ask.

How the hell would I know.

I mean, is your cousin still friends with her.

No it was, like, a million years ago, Freckles. Before you were born, not last weekend. Don't freak out about it.

She hasn't put two and two together. That Carmencita is my mother. That the Spanish-sounding name matches my Spanish-looking skin, my Spanish hair. But all she sees is the freckles that match my Pops.

And it wasn't Limerick University, she adds, it was in Dublin. Stephanie was in college with her there. She says he shouldn't be allowed to teach in Limerick. That she should do something about it. It's like the priests, they all get moved around to different places. Look, it's all I know, okay.

The train pulls into the station and she stands up, cocky again. Puts her bag on her back. You can think whatever you want, but my cousin isn't a liar. Your Pops is a perv teacher who slept with a student, which is frankly totally gross but whatever. You'll get me back on the team now. I told you what you wanted.

I follow her off the train, and out through the station. Pops usually waits outside in the car, but this time he's in the station, at a vending machine.

Ah Allegra, there you are my love, and who is this.

I didn't know Katie had stopped beside me and she's staring at him like he's a disgusting piece of filth, all the twisted hatred back in her previously scared little shit face. I hate her.

This is Katie. From school.

Nice to meet you Katie from school, Pops says with a chuckle.

Katie gives him a look as though he's the most disgusting thing she's ever seen and she hurries away as quickly as she can.

Interesting girl, did I say something wrong, he asks as he watches her leave, then turns his attention back to the vending machine. I watch him as he puts the coins in the slot, carefully counting them out, enters the number. I watch his fingers, his hands, the hands that Katie thinks are disgusting, the hands that reared me and that I see move over the piano keys and cello so beautifully.

She's not my friend I say finally.

Pops looks at me over the rim of his glasses, concerned.

Is that so, well then consider her disinvited to any future gatherings. Here, I got you salt and vinegar Pringles for the car, you better share them with me.

He kisses me on the top of my head and wraps his arm around my shoulder, guides me to the car.

Katie told me nothing that I didn't already know. I knew Pops was a lecturer at the university and I knew my mam was a student. We discuss everything openly in our household. He wasn't her teacher though, but I didn't bother saying that. I don't think it would have made a difference. I also know he's no pervert but the surprising thing that I learned in all of this was about myself.

I had wanted to find out where my mam is.

★ ★ ★

98

Pops and I have been sitting in the TV room all afternoon since the mice incident. He hasn't budged once. I cleaned the mud off the floor and then joined him. He's watching nature documentaries, a constant stream of one after the other. It's what I was looking forward to, chilling out with easy company but after the welcoming scene, I'm not chilled. I'm tense. I'm watching him. Maybe he's spent too much time alone. Maybe this is what happens to a person when they're isolated for so long. Three months since I've visited but still, he has his work, his colleagues.

I think I'll have a drink, I say finally, keeping an eye on the clock until it turns 5 p.m. An acceptable hour to start drinking.

He perks up. Time for a home brew.

I wasn't thinking of tea, Pops. I need something stronger.

Oh no, it's not a tea. It's much better brew than that. It's in the hot press, he jumps up, divilment in his eyes.

The hot press, I ask. Oh God what now.

He pulls open the storage space, and there on the slatted shelving built around the hot water system, among his towels and clothes that are drying, are large plastic buckets and the pungent smell of alcohol and gone-off cheese.

There it is, my own barrel of beer, he says, lifting a bucket out. It's been bubbling away in here for a few weeks.

I look inside. Sugar, soapy beer fermented in a plastic bucket among the bedlinen, towels and underwear, heat, gases and liquid.

We sit in the conservatory in the back of the house, drinking the beer, watching the land, feeling calmed

99

by the glimpse of cows and sheep in the farmland behind.

I can't believe you're brewing beer in your hot press, I say, giggling, taking a sip. It tastes rancid. Like dirty socks and melting plastic.

You'll get used to it, he says, noticing my reaction. First batch exploded all over my clothes and bed-sheets.

I feel a wash of relief. So that explains the smell from him. Maybe he's okay after all. My worries get lost in a beer fog.

Good to have you home, love.

Good to be home, Pops.

We sit together, occasionally a gentle chat, but mostly in peaceful and comfortable silence, watching the sunset, and much later into the night watching the stars, until the two buckets are gone and I haven't a worry in the world.

★   ★   ★

I wake during the night to banging. Pops is in the music room, in his baggy boxer shorts and a white vest. He's leaning over the opened piano, as if study-ing the engine of a car.

Pops, what are you doing.

They're in here.

What are.

The mice. He presses down on a key over and over again, the same one.

He's not joking. I feel like I'm at a tea party with the Mad Hatter, only it's nothing I wished it would be. It's real for a start. And it's Pops. Nonsensical mutterings. I wonder if he's even awake, or if he's sleepwalking.

100

He has a dazed, sleepy look about him as though he's not really here.

Pops, just go back to bed. It's late. We can look into it in the morning. Call pest control.

I can hear them scrambling, he mutters, then wanders back to his room.

★ ★ ★

As soon as I wake, which is 10 a.m., I rise and leave the house in search of food. Despite my light shop yesterday the fridge is empty of a suitable breakfast and I'm hungry. My head is pounding, not from the hunger, but from the bad home-brewed lager and lack of sleep. I was awake for hours after Pops' night-time escapade and somehow succeeded in eventually falling asleep to birdsong. Usually I'd take Pops' car, but I can't on account of the rat-infestation story. I'm tempted to try to start the car anyway, to see if it's true, but I don't want to risk it. My second mission is to visit Gerry and question him about the car and the rats. Detective Freckles. If Pops has concocted that, I really do have a problem on my hands.

Pops has always been exciting and dramatic. Eccentric is perhaps the word. He doesn't measure himself against anybody else's behaviour or expectation, and that's good, he has always been free to think independently, uniquely, I think interestingly, and share it without embarrassment. But this behaviour is different. Rats in the engine, mice in the piano is not a new interesting theory, it's muddled nonsense.

Our house is a ten-minute walk from Main Street and the morning is bright but foggy, the mist hanging over the island. It will lift, like a magician's silk hanky, the beauty of the island will be revealed in one great ta-da. The air is light and it makes me wetter than I thought. Soft rain, we call it. I don't mind, I like walking in the rain, this kind of invisible rain, it's always made me feel free. It cools my pounding head, sizzles the frying brain, even though it frizzes my hair.

There's already a line of cars at the port awaiting the ferry which is returning to shore, probably the first outing of the day, and it's already filled with cars. Tourist season. Every business person's favourite time of year. The island is busy for the Easter weekend and outside the Royal Valentia Hotel preparations are underway for a Hardman half-marathon and 10k run.

I purchase enough food at the foodstore for today and tomorrow's Easter Sunday dinner. We're not religious but we like to eat and support any occasion that is marked with food. Pops has purchased the lamb directly from Nessie, the farmer who lives behind us, and I wonder if that's where his dear little lamb friend disappeared to. If there was a lamb at all. Shopping totes in hand, I continue the short walk to Gerry's garage. Problem is, his business is at his home, where his daughter Marion lives. Marion who has recently opened a hair salon and gotten pregnant by my ex-boyfriend and first love. I'd rather stay away from her, but I need to see about Pops and, with a bit of luck, I won't encounter her.

I walk up the driveway. House to the right, business to the left. Cars in various states of life parked up, some rusted and without wheels that look like they're there for the long haul. You wouldn't know Gerry has money; he acts and talks like he couldn't pay attention, but Pops always says he's so tight he'd peel an orange in his pocket. Everything looks the same; it's

102

the same house I played at most days growing up. Where I had sleepovers. Marion and I loved having adventures around the cars. Ducking low, weaving in and out with walkie-talkies on a new adventure, sitting behind the steering wheels in imaginary high-speed car chases, tumbling across the bonnets as we're struck. There's probably even a few of the same cars we played in, still not crushed. All's the same apart from the sign out front — Marion's hair salon. She did it. Her dream.

I avoid the house and make my way to the barn that's the garage. Two little Westies come down to meet me. Ham and Cheese or Peanut-Butter and Jelly or something like that. They don't remember me either and yap at my heels, whacking their heads against my swinging bags as they try to jump up on me. The garage shutters are down, which is disappointing. I should have known he wouldn't work over an Easter break.

I see a figure at the downstairs window of Marion's house. Shite I've been spotted. I turn around and meander through the rusted cars towards the exit, dogs yapping giving me away.

Allegra Bird, is that you, I hear Marion's voice and I want to settle in the soil and die like the rust-bucket cars. Lay down my roots, give up, and not have to face her. In truth I stopped loving Jamie long before I left to go to the other island, if it was really love at all, but I still hate her and him right now for even daring.

Rhubarb, away, she says, voice nearing me. Custard, get out of there.

Marion comes towards me down the porch and makes her way through the maze of cars. I step out of my hiding place, feeling foolish.

Oh Marion. Hi.

What the hell are you doing.

Her cardigan is wrapped tight around her, held by her arms across her stomach. I see a baby bump where there isn't one, there couldn't be any yet, she's only eight weeks, it's probably the size of a tab of e. Cyclops used to get them for us, he took them when he was DJ-ing, supplied them too. They never did much for me; mild euphoria, I suppose, but Jamie used to experience higher pleasure from physical touch so he loved it. If anything it gave me moments of clear focus and some of those moments, while I had my hand down Jamie's pants, I was plotting and planning on leaving Valentia. Focused on my next goal. I never deserved him.

JP told me you were home. For the Easter break, is it, she asks.

I can't stop looking at her stomach, I wonder if they talked about me. They must have. Even if it wasn't malicious, they must have poured their hearts out. Pillow talk, quiet whispers of the things about me that bothered them. I know I used to do that with Jamie about Marion. I wonder if he told her the things I'd said. Innocent things really, but hurtful if you ever heard them about yourself. Stuff you'd mull over and wonder about changing your personality to fix. Lying in bed with two of us. I feel hot and angry, my heart pounding. Connecting over their shared frustration of me. How dare they. There's so much that I could say to her, and I don't want to say any of it. It couldn't make anything better.

I wish you'd told me you were coming back, she says.

She shifts from foot to foot. Cold. Awkward. The

104

mist has thickened now, is spraying our faces. Pummelling around us dramatically before it takes off. I feel droplets drip down my forehead. My hair must truly be a sight now. Too thick for this island. It was made for the Catalonian sun and mountains. She looks back at the house, checks to see if we're safe, maybe if she's safe, then back at me.

Look, JP told me he told you about us, and about, you know. I could've killed him. It's too early. We've told no one yet, you know anything could happen and then there'd have been no point in telling you at all.

Oh right yeah, like a miscarriage, I say, and she bristles. Again there's so much I want to ask her but I can't be bothered. I don't want to sound desperate, I don't want to hear the bitterness that will drip from my words when I know I'm not entitled. My ex-boyfriend and my best friend. Ex-best friend now probably. We haven't talked for months. When did the texts end. She was supposed to visit. Something came up. She never did. Maybe it was Jamie's knob that came up. But I didn't invite her again. I don't know why I didn't do that. I wasn't planning on staying in Dublin for so long . . . well, yes maybe this long, but not permanently. My friends were supposed to be here when I got back, whenever that would be. Not screwing each other and making a baby. Just here, like on pause. Him on the car ferry, or working behind the bar in the hotel, her at the community hospital and doing hair nixers when she could.

We didn't plan it, Allegra, she says. It was an accident. Me and Cyclops broke up. He's changed, gone weird from the drugs. Like even more weird than usual. He's concocting his own shit now. It was just me and JP. We missed you. I mean, I missed you.

I can't help but picture her corned-beef thighs wrapped around his skinny waist. She was always bottom heavy, pear-shaped and pear-like with her pale skin with purple and blue spots, pockmarked with cellulite. She hated wearing a bathing suit. Always wore little shorts over it. A red rash from shaving her bikini line every day because she was allergic to the wax. I wonder what he thought of those legs when he saw them for the first time. Her pocked pear legs.

She keeps talking.

We got along better than I thought. Never really got to know each other properly before. When it was the four of us, you know, anyway JP encouraged me to stop being so afraid of doing the things that I wanted. The salon was his idea. I mean it was mine, but I'd never have done it without him.

She looks back at the house again. I don't know why she keeps doing it, maybe she's got a client sitting there with bleach burning through to her skull. It's in the front room, I can see some equipment set up, they've also knocked the front wall and added a new patio door, for direct entrance to her business. Just a room in her parents' house. The room we watched cartoons in. Hardly a business. Even with her cheap signs plastered all over the island I wonder who would go to her, past the scrap metal in the junkyard, to get their hair done. Well, maybe I would have.

I did it, she says proudly, with a huge grin that reveals her deep dimples, and a twist of fear that's cute. And maybe it'll be easier to work from home with the baby and all, she adds.

All that information and all I can wonder is why she's called him JP. Only his mother calls him JP. All his friends call him Jamie. It's twisted.

Most people have to leave the island to make things happen. Most of the people we grew up with are gone. *Decimated with emigration* a Wi-Fi ad for the Aran Islands says in its efforts to lure people back. I left. But not Marion. She stays here, opens a hair salon, has a baby. Dream made. By her. In the place I thought I had to leave to accomplish.

So did you see her, she asks, changing the subject. Allegra, say something, she says, smile gone now.

Her hair is soaking wet now, flat on her head, beads of water cling to the bits of wool on her cardigan. She's shivering. I picture her e-tab-sized baby with goosebumps. Probably the size of a goosebump.

I came here looking for your dad, I finally say.

She looks at me in surprise. Then hurt. Then disgust. A sprinkling of hate. I do feel stupid but she should know me by now. I never say the right thing. I know I don't say the right thing and I used to tell her that. I used to tell her all the stupid things I'd say to other people during sleep-overs in her house and she'd either laugh and say it was harmless or she'd be patient and tell me how to say it better the next time, but it's like she's forgotten all those pep talks, just like Jamie, she's forgotten who I am. The acceptance and patience that comes with friendship is gone. You've got to earn that shit. I'm past earning it. She turns on her heel and walks off, Rhurbarb and Custard at her heels, their chins high as if in a pompous huff. Away from the car graveyard and into the house. I'm not sure whether she's going to pass the message on to her dad or not. Would it be foolish to wait.

I pace up and down beside a green Mazda with a battered side door, kicking a stone here and there. The shopping bags are starting to get heavy, maybe I should be off, maybe I'm getting this all wrong. The door opens and out comes her dad Gerry in a shirt and trousers. No work gear.

I wait by the cars and try to read his face but I'm not good at that so whatever this expression is I'm not sure what it means. He could be about to punch me or kiss me. I doubt Marion would have told him anything, if she did, she'd have to explain about the pregnancy and she wouldn't have after the miscarriage fear. And she wouldn't have told him that quickly, and he wouldn't be walking to me like this if he'd just heard.

Allegra, he says.

I've come to you about Pops, Gerry.

All right, is he.

You tell me. He said that you told him he's got rats living in his car.

Yeah, he says, and I'm relieved.

I let out a breath I didn't know I was holding in.

They climbed in the exhaust and nested in the electrics, he says, chewed through the wires. Lucky he wasn't driving when the fire started and that it happened on ignition.

So you've seen this before, I ask.

Not a lot. I've seen it around the yard here, but it's frequent enough in cars that aren't being driven for a while.

How long is a while, I ask.

He looks around the yard for inspiration and says, months.

But Pops is driving every day.

He gives me an odd look. He steps back with one foot so that he's standing diagonally. Just like in my conflict resolution training. He thinks I'm about to get aggressive, he's preparing to leave. I don't get it.

I wouldn't know about that now, he says.

Okay not every day probably but most days surely, I say, he has the organ-playing at Mass and the cello at funerals. And there's the music lessons in Killarney. And the choir. I trail off because he's looking at me now in a way that tells me to shut up. I put the shopping bags down. I can barely bend my fingers, the fabric has been digging into them. What is it, Gerry, tell me. And I ready myself for what now.

I don't know now exactly, but he's not doing the churches any more.

The Masses or the funerals, I ask.

Neither. And not the teaching either. And he hasn't shown up at choir for some time.

What, why.

You're best off asking —

If he'd tell me I wouldn't bother being here, Gerry.

He speaks to the ground, my feet really as he says, Something to do with an incident with the woman who works there. Is it Majella, he asks, looking up for a second to check my face at the mention of her name.

I don't know, I say. What woman. Where.

A church administrator in Cahirciveen. Seems your dad was more taken with her than he had a right to be.

I hold my hand up to stop him from saying more, even though he probably wasn't going to. That's long enough of a sentence for him. And it makes sense now as to why Jamie said Pops was a perv. He wasn't just bringing up old insults to hurt me. It was something new. Recent.

How long ago was this, I ask.

109

A month or two, I suppose. I heard about it way back. Not from him.

I pick the bags up again, feeling sick.

Okay thanks, Gerry.

Now, Allegra, will you come in.

No. No thanks, I say. I'm walking away and I remember the other thing I wanted to ask him, and turn around. He's still looking at me. What about the mice, I ask.

He rolls his eyes. The flippin mice. He asked me to look in the piano. Called me over twice, in the middle of the night. Do I look like pest control, I says to him. Anyway I laid traps for him.

He shakes his head and shrugs.

I don't know what to tell you, Allegra. Maybe it's the stress. Can do strange things to a man.

I walk away.

13

I settle into the armchair in the conservatory at home. I've changed out of my wet clothes, into an old tracksuit I left behind here, it feels comforting against my skin again. Something old and familiar. Pops is in the back garden whish-a-whishing for the lamb. The sun has come out again, the day is bright and beautiful but the grass is wet after the rainfall. He's getting muddy and he won't listen to me. I have everything of his in the washing machine that I could find, particularly the beer-soaked towels and bed-sheets. The washing machine is going, the lamb is in the oven, the saucepans are bubbling on the hob. It's all systems go.

I used to call this room the star room. It was added to the house when I was ten or so, I thought it was so glamorous and magical; a conservatory, a room of glass that was inside but felt like we were outside. When it was brand new we used to sit in there all the time, inhaling the fresh paint, eating every meal on our laps, and looking out at Nessie's fields beyond. And of course at night at the weekend when I was home from boarding school. I didn't scratch my skin here, no, Pops would have seen and intervened. That occurred upstairs in my bedroom with the door closed. The star room was and still is for night gazing at the band of the Milky Way, the Andromeda Galaxy, star clusters and nebulae. Pops uses a telescope but I've always preferred the naked eye. Where we are, southwest Kerry, was recently named one of only three gold-tier International Dark Sky Reserves on earth alongside the Grand Canyon and the African Savanah. We'll be able to see Jupiter tonight, an app on my phone tells me.

The fingertips from my right hand move gently over my scars. Five-star constellation. Five people. The phrase comes back to haunt me.

Pops comes inside, takes his shoes off, as I've warned him to do.

No sign of the little lamb, he says.

Was her fleece as white as snow, I ask.

It was, smarty-pants, and I hope that's not her in the oven. He looks at me. He sees me at my arm.

Five, I say, the number of the human being. Four limbs and the head that controls the limbs. Five digits on a hand, five toes on a foot.

He sits down, interested. Five, he says, joining in. Five senses; sight, hearing, smell, taste, touch. Five, he continues, the number of Mercury.

Leo is the fifth astrological sign in the zodiac, I add. We both think. He gets there first.

Five vowels in the English alphabet, he says.

High five, I say holding up my hand, a gesture of celebration.

He high-fives me.

Five lines in a limerick, he says, five arms on a star-fish, an earthworm has five hearts.

I laugh. Five team members on a basketball team.

Five musicians in a quintet, he counters.

Five Olympic rings symbolising the five continents.

He sucks in air. Nice, Allegra.

I'm on a roll. Five was Coco Chanel's favourite number. She always launched her collection on the fifth day of the fifth month.

112

I didn't know that, he says, sitting back and thinking. For dinner, he says finally, I will eat five potatoes.

I smile.

I notice Pops watching my fingers moving over the w-shaped scar on my arm. I name the stars aloud as I move from freckle to freckle. Segin, Ruchbach, Navi, Shedar, Caph.

Which one is that, he asks.

Cassiopeia, I say. The seated queen. In Greek mythology she was the Queen of Aethiopia. She was the mother of Andromeda, who boasted that she and her daughter were more beautiful than the gods of the sea. As punishment for her vanity she was chained to her throne in the sky by Poseidon.

Harsh, he says. He leans forward, elbows on his knee. He looks away from my arm. Maybe it's distressing him to see me distressed. He knows I am when my finger traces my scars but at least it's better than making new scars.

Are you going to tell me why we are discussing the number five, he asks.

I stop rubbing my skin. This fella, I say with a sigh.

He smiles. A-ha!

No not like that. He was rude to me. I gave him a parking ticket and he lost his temper. He said to me, You are the average of the five people you spend the most time with.

And this was rude, he asks, confused.

He didn't mean it in a good way, Pops. Called me a loser, ripped it up in my face.

Ah. That's Dublin for you, he says and goes silent.

So what do you think, I say.

I'd say the fella who said that to you is an odd sort. We're all odd sorts.

113

True. You are the average of the, what now, he asks.

The five people you spend the most time with, I say.

He mulls it over. That's an interesting one, he says. A game of law of averages.

The oven beeps, the lamb is ready. I take the lamb out. It fills the kitchen with even more delicious smells. The skin is bubbling, the juices run to the bottom of the tray. Perfect for gravy. Sprigs of rosemary and shards of softened garlic protrude from the punctured meat. I leave it to rest. I empty the water from the new potatoes, the steam giving my face a treatment, slather them with Kerrygold butter. I mix the mint sauce into the green peas, carve the meat and immediately eat the delicately tender parts that fall off.

What do you mean law of averages, Pops, I ask.

A kind of a mumbo jumbo Murphy's law that has no mathematical principle whatsoever.

He sees my face fall and backtracks.

No that's cynical of me. I can tell you're serious about this, Allegra, I'm sorry. Perhaps it's more along the lines of the laws of attraction, the power of your thoughts to manifest your desires, he says. That the environment we live in affects the person we are, the characteristics we portray and the way we behave.

Yes, Pops. That's it, I say, stirring the gravy and watching him intently. That's what he meant when he said it to me. That I was surrounded by . . . by losers, which makes me a loser.

Pops shakes his head and carries the bowl of vegetables to the table. Why would you entertain a philosophy such as this, he asks.

I have to. It's in my head.

He ponders this. He loves a good crossword puzzle. Who are your five, he asks, going for more of his

114

home brew.

No not that, please, I say with a wince, still feeling it in my head. I bought red wine.

He examines the label and searches a drawer for a bottle-opener.

It's a twist cap, I say. Then, I don't know. I mean, I did know. But now I'm not so sure. I pour the juices from the tray into the pot of gravy and stir.

Probably why it's at you, so. Let me have a go at guessing, he says, sitting down. Pouring the wine and sipping. Marion of course. Jamie, even though . . . Cyclops, Pauline and, maybe me.

He asks that with such hope I want to squeeze him to death in a hug but I'm carrying the gravy. Absolutely you, I say. You are my one sure thing. I place the gravy down on the table. We sit.

Allegra, this is delicious. He raises his hands in the air ceremoniously. And I'm glad he's back to being him again. So how did I do, with your five.

Bang on.

Do I win a prize.

Jamie and Marion are having a baby, I say.

Together, he asks.

I nod but I don't look at him. I might cry if I do.

Ah well. Would have been a shocking coincidence if not. I slice the lamb, the buttery potato, scoop the mint peas on to my fork. I haven't heard from Cyclops since I left this island, I say, before putting it all into my mouth.

I see him driving around in a van with a speaker on the top, dressed as a monster, Pops says.

Chewbacca, I say with a hollow laugh. DJ Chewy. From *Star Wars*. He takes people out on a boat to Skellig Rock dressed as Chewy so they can see the

Jedi hideaway.

More of that *Star Wars* nonsense.

It's giving people work. Bringing tourists. We need them.

It's turning us into Disney World is what it's doing. We'll have a McDonald's before you know it.

What does it matter if they're here for puffins or *Star Wars*.

He grunts a nothing response.

I've fallen out of touch with Pauline, I say. She visited me in Dublin twice, but only for the day and we barely had time to do anything before she was going back to the train station.

She's keeping her distance, I suppose, letting you get on with it.

She hasn't called me since she visited. We haven't texted each other.

Takes two to tango, he says. What about in Dublin, he says.

I push my food around the plate, because I have a horrible feeling in the pit of my stomach and a lump in my throat and I feel like I'm going to cry at the realisation that I don't have five people, not in Dublin and not here. I could have pretended in Dublin, that they were still mine and I was trying to despite the niggling, but here it's obvious. That's why the phrase hurt me. Because some deep primal instinct inside of me knew, faster than my head did, that I don't have five people.

It's clearing up now, he says, looking outside, changing the subject.

Yeah.

Turning out to be a nice day.

I clear my throat. There was a marathon on this

morning. A 10k, to Chapeltown and loops around.

Pops looks out at the weather as if imagining the journey for the poor sods, then spears a potato, runs it around the peas trying to pick up the mint sauce and puts the entire thing into his mouth. It's a baby potato, he has a big mouth.

Delicious dinner, Allegra, thank you, he says as soon as he's swallowed it.

You're welcome. Happy Easter, Pops, I say, feeling happy and sad at the same time. Devastated not to have five people. Elated and feeling blessed to have one.

Happy Easter, he says with a grin, whatever that means.

We clink our wine glasses together.

Gerry told me your car hasn't been working for weeks.

You met Gerry.

This morning.

In town, he asks.

He was home.

Pops fishes through the sea of gravy with his fork for a clove of roasted garlic, squeezes it out of its skin and eats it whole.

You went to see Marion, he asks, licking his greasy fingers.

I went to see Gerry.

What did he say.

That your car has been out of action for weeks. Maybe months.

He keeps eating.

You haven't been going to work, I say.

I'm retired.

Semi. You're the busiest retired person I've ever

117

met.

You're too young to know retired people.

The music school, the funerals, the Mass, the choir. You haven't been working for months, Pops.

He bangs his knife and fork down against the plate and it gives me a fright.

I hold my breath.

You can't look at a woman sideways without being labelled a pervert.

My heart is pounding. What happened, I ask.

Nothing! That's the point!

Something happened or you wouldn't have lost your job.

That's what Gerry told you, is it. Well he's wrong. He can have his bloody mousetraps back because, like him, they're faulty. He thumps his thick closed fist down on the table, rattling the cutlery and tableware. I didn't lose the job, he says. I talked with Father David and it was discussed between us that I go of my own accord. I was not fired.

I look at this man. This fading man. His spritely joie de vivre gone. Slithering down his face and off his bones like his skin. He catches his breath then sits back in his chair.

Majella, he says. She works in the church. Office administrator. Lets me know the funeral times, the songs the families favour. We always got along well. Always had a joke and a laugh, he says, while I try to hide my horror at what might come next. I asked her if she'd like to come over and try my home brew — this is a few months back, you'd been gone a few weeks, and it would have been nice to have the company. It's just as well she didn't because the early stuff was bad, even worse than it is now — and she said no, and then

I leave it at that and the next day I'm preparing for the funeral, no sign of Majella, and Father David tells me to come in to his office for a chat and he says to me that Majella is very upset. And there you have it.

I don't get it. That's it, I ask.

That's it.

You didn't touch her.

I didn't touch her, he says. I reached out and patted her leg.

Ah for Christ's sake, Pops, you can't leave that out, you have to tell me everything.

How the blazes hell do I tell you everything that I consider nothing. If I didn't consider it nothing then I'd tell you because I'd know it was something. I don't know what else I might have done. I might have scratched my eyebrow the wrong way and she didn't like it.

Scratching your eyebrow and touching her leg are not the same thing.

I didn't molest her fecking leg. I didn't hump it like a dog. I patted it. Like that, he says, patting the table. One pat, he says. We were sitting down, as far apart as you and I were, no table between us, and I lean across and do that.

I feel Pops' hand on my leg under the table, one tap.

There, he says. Sorry, your honour. Lock me up for touching a leg. I didn't maul her backside or anything like that. A gentle hand on her leg, was all, not a sleazy feeling her up.

How old is Majella.

I don't know. Forty something. Single, has a daughter. Divorced. Lonely like me. I thought we could have a drink, that's all, I'll know not to ask again. And I'll

119

not lay my finger on a fecking thing for as long as I live.

He goes quiet and I can tell he's embarrassed. I'm embarrassed for him. He admitted he was lonely. I'm not sure if he's more embarrassed about admitting that or about how he had to leave his job. Though I know he meant no harm, I can see Majella's point of view. A hand on her leg. An old man's hand on her leg, the unwelcome hand of an old man on her leg. She was probably being nice to him and it backfired.

Women never used to be so prickly, he says. Are you like that, Allegra.

I think of the men I've slept with over my lifetime, after the art classes, just last week, and prickly isn't a word I'd use to describe myself. Nor is fussy. But I don't go into that with him, he wouldn't understand any of that.

Instead I say, It's called autonomy, Pops.

But all she had to say was no and that was that. She didn't have to run off and tell Father David.

She was letting you know her boundaries.

We were in a church, Christ of almighty. He covers his face with his hands and shakes his head and I can tell he's embarrassed. I tapped her knee, Allegra, I was letting her know it was okay, not to be embarrassed, that everything was grand.

That was her boundary.

He looks down at his dinner plate. A bit of lamb fat left on the side, mint sauce mixed with gravy scraped around and starting to harden. A lone pea that never made it.

We sit in silence.

I'll try and sort the car insurance for you, I say finally, my mind whirring with all the things I need to do for Pops before and after I leave. Round and round, just like the washing machine of his clothes and underwear going on behind me. Give me the details and I'll take care of it. If I can't, Gerry might be able to get it scrapped for cash. No point having it sitting there when you can't use it.

He grunts a response.

Does Pauline know, I ask.

About what.

Any of it.

No.

I'm going to tell her to drop in now and then. You're not looking after yourself.

Who could after being accused of a thing like that. You know how people talk. It's disgusting. Don't you dare call Pauline. She's busy with the Mussel House, especially this week, April tourists, and she's only across the water if I need her.

You can't get to her, you've no car.

There's a car ferry, you're allowed to walk on it last time I checked. And we have a bridge too, a new invention, did you hear that.

What if there's an emergency.

He doesn't answer. It's like talking to a teenager.

I mean, frankly, Pops, the world is a safer place without you on the road, but you can't be stuck in here. He laughs at that. Would you consider trying again with teaching at home, I ask.

Music is in his bones. Talking about it, teaching it, playing it, it's the cartilage that holds him together.

That's if you can get the mice out, I add, more as a joke to myself.

Though I shudder to think of anyone letting their child in here for lessons, the house has become so run

121

down in just a few months. A teacher whose clothes smell of beer from his own brewery upstairs in the hot press, a man accused of being handsy with the church administrator. An eccentric who thinks there's mice inside the piano, because it doesn't sound right. Because he's probably hitting the wrong keys. Because his fingers are more gnarled than usual. With brown spots that aren't freckles. Because maybe he has arthritis and he doesn't know it, or he knows it and he won't tell me or admit it to himself and would prefer to blame mice for the piano sounding off instead.

And who would come to music lessons, everyone's leaving here, he says.

That's not true. They're attracting more people from the other island, stressed-out people with mortgages they can't pay. I tell him what Jamie told me. People dreaming of island living. Of isolation and nature because it's cool now.

He smiles. Island living, he says thoughtfully, moving the words around his mouth like it's a hard toffee. That's an oxymoron.

Maybe you could stay with Pauline, I suggest.

I'd be in her way.

You're her brother.

That's why I'd be in her way. She has the businesses. Her grandchildren. I've heaped enough on her.

We both know what he means.

Mossie might need help at the mussel farm, I try again.

I'm too old for the physical work.

So you can work behind the bar in the Mussel House. Shacking oysters and pulling pints for fancy people coming off their fancy yachts. She always needs extra help for the summer. You'd work for free just to be kept busy, I know you, and imagine the stories you could tell them. You could hold fort every day with new faces. Fresh blood hanging on your every word.

It's shucking oysters, he says, but his eyes are smiling at the thought.

You could even brew your own beer. Mussels in craft beer, there's a new one for the menu. What do you think, I ask.

Ah no.

Think about it.

I will.

I know he won't.

Your life's not over, Pops, I say. Don't be sitting here as if it is.

Yeah.

I'm sorry you're lonely.

You might be too, I think, he says.

I look down.

Five people, ha, he says.

Yeah. Who are yours.

He doesn't ignore me, but he doesn't answer. He's lost in thought. It's gotten in on him too. Or I think it has, until he raises his right hand in the air like he's offering a high five.

Bach, he says lowering his thumb. Mozart. He lowers his forefinger. Handel, Beethoven. And you. His fist stays in the air.

I'm in good company.

Don't be feeling down on yourself, Allegra, he says. You had your five. You had them. But you gave them up to find your one.

You are my one, I say quickly, breath almost taken away by his words. I'm never giving you up.

He takes my hand across the table.

123

I'd tell you to come home but I know you want to be in Dublin. Just say the word and I can be there in a jiffy. Or Pauline, if you don't want me there. You might think she's not around but she's ready, you know, on call, for when you need her. In case it doesn't work out.

I can't entertain that thought. I can't give up everything for something only to not get that something. Wouldn't be fair on the everything.

There's apple pie for dessert, I say, standing and collecting our plates.

I scrape the scraps of food into the bin, my back turned to him, before putting them in the dishwasher. I can feel his eyes bearing into me. I don't want to talk about this any more. I don't want him to ask. But he does.

Have you talked to her yet, he asks.

I shake my head.

I'll have mine with ice cream, he says gently.

14

My last night in Valentia. By 9 p.m. Pops is snoozing in his armchair and I feel antsy. Especially after our conversation about my five, or my lack thereof.

Will we go out for a few drinks, Pops. No no I'm fine here.

It's a bank holiday, there'll be a great atmosphere. Probably a live session in the Royal or the Ring Lyne. But no, he's not having any of it. The man who lives for music doesn't want to hear any music but insists that I go out, enjoy myself. I call Cyclops. I don't know if he has the same number but I'm guessing Cyclops will never change it if it risks losing business.

He answers straight away with a yo.

It's me, Allegra.

Freckles, he says and I smile.

Out of Jamie, Marion and Cyclops, he'd been the only one to call me by my school nickname when I came home on the weekends. It angered Marion. She hated other people claiming me with a stupid name when she's known me the longest. Jamie could never remember it. Maybe Cyclops did and does because he understands what it's like to not just have a nickname but to be your nickname.

Cyclops is so named because of his surname. *Ó Súilleabháin* is Irish for O'Sullivan, but it sounds exactly like *súil amháin* which translates to one eye. He's from a family of six brothers and they're all called the same. Huge broad big brothers they seem to own the name better than my friend, strapping big

125

GAA players, his eldest brother played for the Kerry senior team and is named the Cyclops. That's it, he's the ultimate Cyclops. Then there's Goosey Cyclops, so named because he's a bird plucker. His dad is Chief Cyclops because of his thirty-year involvement in local and county football. Then there's Nixie Cyclops, because his name is Nicholas. Inky Cyclops, because he published a book of poetry and writes for the local paper, and Chops Cyclops the sheep farmer. Someone once told me my Cyclops friend was the runt of the pack. We were on the sidelines watching him get pummelled by everyone. He wasn't a good footballer, not like his brothers. He tried because he had to, couldn't let his dad and the locals down, but cars and music were always his thing. Customising his cars into these muppet mobiles with underglow lights attached to the chassis, illuminating the ground beneath. That's how he got with Marion, he kept asking her dad to do the modifications. He calls himself Chewy Cyclops, because he's DJ Chewy, but unlike his brothers it hasn't quite stuck, it's a name he gave to himself and that's not how it's supposed to work. You earn it. People give it to you, like a badge of honour. Locals call him Cyclops *óg*, which is young Cyclops or kind of like saying junior.

So you heard the news, he says, and I know he means Marion and Jamie. Dirty rats, he says. Fancy meeting up, drowning our sorrows, or celebrating, whichever you want.

Both, I say and that's cool with him, he'll be over within the hour, he has a set tonight, he'll drive us there.

He shows up all proud of himself in a van, with speakers on the top. DJ Chewy decorates the side panels with an image of decks, music notes and a Chewbacca that looks more like a rabid monkey, with a line about bringing the wild to the Wild Atlantic Way. Some smart arse had messed with the word wild.

Bringing the dildo to the Wild Atlantic Way, I read.

Ignore that bit. It's a Sharpie, taking me ages to get it off. Is the Pops in there, I'll go say hi, he's a laugh. Heard about what happened with the church administrator, she can go fuck herself. He shouldn't let them get to him.

No need, he's asleep, I say, circling the van. I thought that the Chewy thing was more for tourists. Why not DJ Cyclops, I ask. Doesn't that carry a better reputation.

The big bro wouldn't let me. His eldest boy's name is DJ.

Oh. I get inside the van. So where are we going.

The syndicate rooms.

It's in Tralee, an hour and a half away but I don't care, I'm glad to get out and away, take my mind off things. Cyclops lights a smoke, starts up the engine and gets straight to the point. So what do you think of Jamie and Marion, he asks.

I don't know if he knows about the baby yet, probably not, I'm sure neither Jamie or Marion would want him to know that. Who knows what he'd do. I don't know, I tell him honestly, it feels weird but I suppose they can do what they like.

It was going on behind my back, he says. When I was gigging around the place, they were at it. Manky rancid bastards.

I study his profile. He looks skinnier than ever. He was always thin but this is unhealthy. His face is skeletal. Pale. A blue white.

You look like shit, I say.

Not you too. Mam keeps throwing Kimberley Mikados at me whenever I'm at the house. And I hate Mikados. Maybe a cherry Bakewell or something but who ever said marshmallow and jam was a good idea.

I like Mikados.

You would. You eat like a five-year-old at a birthday party.

Maybe stop eating cherry Bakewells and start eating iron, I suggest.

What's that in.

Meat, veg.

He makes a face.

You look anaemic, I say, studying him.

I don't puke my food out.

Not what it means. So you moved out of home, I say.

Got a sweet retro caravan in Portmagee with a lad named Tinny. Just not really eating.

Because of Marion, I ask.

Fuck no. I couldn't give a shit what she does. I'm so busy, business is out the door. I have a boat tour business now, you hear about that, he asks. I nod. Yeah out on the sea by day, doing music by night, it's non-stop. Anyway, I hope they're stuck together forever, those two. No vision, not like you and me. You and me always had dreams.

Did I, I ask.

I never thought of myself as a dreamer. I'm pragmatic. Practical.

You always wanted to be a garda, he says. Always. From the second I met you.

I never considered it a dream. I never thought of stuff in wispy ways like that. It was a job I really wanted. And Marion always wanted to have a hair salon, why is her dream any less than mine.

Instead I just say, I didn't get in.

You moved to Dublin, didn't you, he says. You're doing stuff. Not driving your da's taxi or playing hair salon in your ma and da's house. You and I are doing our own thing, paving our own way. Next generation of this island, making a name for ourselves.

I don't know. I look out the window and watch the mountains racing by. He drives even faster than Pops. It's making me feel sick.

Who's Tinny, I ask.

A lad from Cahirciveen. Broke up with his wife, has tinnitus in his ear. He's grand, we're never home at the same time. Just as well, there's only the one bed. So did you do what you went to Dublin to do, he asks, passing the smoke to me.

No. Not yet.

The syndicate rooms are heaving on the bank holiday Sunday. Cyclops' set begins at 11 p.m. and I watch him set up, avail himself of the free drinks he's given by the staff that he doesn't drink and instead passes to me. He impresses me with his sobriety, he really is taking this seriously, but then I figure out he's on other stuff. He starts off with fun Nineties dance music, then it gets hardcore. Strobe lights and smoke, sweat and drunken girls in short skirts and enormous heels falling all over the equipment to get to him and request Beyoncé, which he doesn't play. It's fun to watch. My head is spinning, I get up to dance a few times, feeling happy and free, dancing with total strangers, girls who become my best buds for the length of a song. Cyclops passes me a pill at one stage and I don't know what the hell it is but I take it.

I suddenly go from my happy alcoholic high to feeling woozy and lethargic. The ground moves beneath me and I need to get out of there. I tear myself away from the DJ box, down a pint of water then go outside and stand by the bouncers.

Okay love, one asks and I nod, feeling safe beside him, while breathing in fresh cold air along with his overbearing aftershave. I feel like I could sleep right here, right now.

Last orders at 2 a.m. Music stops at 2.30 and I rest my head against the DJ box while Cyclops packs up his gear. I can feel people laughing at me as they tidy up around me, but I don't care, I can't keep my eyes open.

Come on, Freckles, Cyclops finally says, let's get you home.

I allow him to pull me up and open my eyes. When I do, he's staring right at me, intensely, nose to nose. Uh oh.

Feels good, doesn't it, he says, the buzz.

What the hell did you give me.

I call it Jetlag. Developed it with some lads.

You made this. Jesus, Cyclops, you could go to prison forever. What the hell is in it.

Ssh, I won't tell. Cool though, isn't it.

I preferred being drunk, I feel like I'm going to fall asleep. But isn't that the best feeling, right before you go asleep, all woozy and sleepy and cosy. He shimmies his body beside me. I don't like how he feels against me. Sharp corners, a bag of bones. Wrong.

When I'm in bed, yeah, not when I'm out.

So let's go to bed. They've rooms here. His hands are tight around my waist.

No, no, no, I back away, loosening his grip. Not a

good idea.

Why not, he says. Jamie and Marion are probably pounding away at each other now, laughing at us.

He said that to hurt me, to make me feel vengeful. I may feel like I just got off a flight to Australia and left my soul at the stop-off in Singapore, but I know what he's doing. You just want to get back at them, Cyclops, I say.

So, don't you, he asks. Isn't that why you called me.

No. I called you because you're my friend.

He laughs. Freckles, I haven't heard from you since you left.

I don't recall you ringing me either.

Because we're not friends, he says playfully, prodding me in the side with his finger to emphasise each point.

I step back.

Look, I really don't care what they do, I say. Jamie and I were already broken up. He didn't do anything wrong. I need to concentrate on my own life. I grab my bag, I'm ready to leave now. I shouldn't have come. He's right. Cyclops and I were never friends without Jamie and Marion, it was the four of us but only because of two of us. Marion and I brought Jamie and Cyclops into the fold. Marion's right, the fact that she and Jamie felt something for each other without me and Cyclops around is something special. Outside in the car park, I wait by the van for him while he's paid. The bouncers are still at the door. A girl is puking behind a car. Her friend holds her shoes and pats her back distractedly while staring into the distance. A fella is on his own, friends dispersed, head in his hands as if his life has fallen apart.

I don't care what you say but I know you do care,

Cyclops sings, tauntingly, joining me at the van, carrying his equipment, continuing where we left off. You and Jamie were serious. He was going to marry you, he told me that.

We were never going to get married. Never.

Well he had it all planned, had the ring and everything, and then you just left.

He didn't have the ring, I say, annoyed.

Okay, maybe he didn't, he laughs, but he was serious about you.

He opens the back of the van, puts his stuff inside. It smells of fish. Rotting fish.

Jesus, I cover my nose and step away.

My boat stuff is in there. Well, can I tempt you.

What, in there.

He shrugs. Easier than getting a room and I don't want to spend the cash I just made. Come on, he says, coming over to me again, hands on my waist, pulling me close to him. Just a quick one, I'll give you another pill.

Fuck no, Cyclops. Come on, let's go home.

He bangs the van doors shut angrily. Jesus, you've no problem fucking everyone else you see, Allegra, but not me. How many of my brothers. Two or three.

One, I say, but really it's two. Inky, too, secretly. He used to write me poems. And I don't sleep with everyone I see, thank you very much. I feel the tremble of insult in my voice.

Obviously not, he says, then gets into the van and starts the engine before I've even got in. I'd gladly take any other way to get home right now, but he's all that I have. Him, his fishy Chewbacca van and his Jetlag pills, and the damn stuff has worn off now. I'm wide awake, wary of him pulling over and trying it on

132

again. So I turn my body away from him, rest my head against the cold window and pretend to be asleep as he speeds home, music blaring, chain-smoking, not another word from him the entire journey home.

Jamie gone. Marion gone. Cyclops gone. Another one off my list.

★ ★ ★

Easter is over. Bank holiday Monday, it's time to return to Dublin and I've mixed feelings about it. I'm programmed to hate leaving home. Maybe the newborn in me, deep down, remembers the abandonment after the umbilical cord was snipped. Maybe it's really because I don't know what I'm going back to. And I still haven't done what I moved there to do. I left with fireworks. I was sent off on my trip of exploration with good grace and hope but the people I left behind rarely hear from me and I haven't delivered. Nothing to report. They moved on and I got a bit stuck.

I'm concerned about Pops. About leaving him and about staying with him. He was up when I got home at 4 a.m. checking the piano and the grandfather clock, searching for the mice. I sat up listening to him go from the shed in the back garden down the hall to the clock, back and forth, back and forth for tools and mousetraps.

I will be glad to leave this mayhem.

I will be scared to leave this mayhem.

He's always been unique. He drove too fast but was always late for everything. Let me sleep until noon and fed me ice cream at midnight. Woke me in the middle of the night to show me a spider lacing its web across

133

a window in the moonlight, or at sunrise for a walk on the beach to examine crabs and lift rocks to discover creatures. He would set up his own crab race, on a rock, where we would choose our own crab and cheer them on, then we'd walk back to our house sideways, hands nipping in the air, like crabs, to the amusement of passers-by. He was so good at showing me wonderment, the beneath the surface of everything, he didn't want to hear me say yuck or shy away from touching something from the natural world.

You see, Allegra, the world is right here, beneath your fingertips. You just have to turn over a rock or two and all is revealed. Nothing is ever just as it seems. There is always more but it's up to you to discover it.

But without his guidance, everything was exactly as it seemed to me. Alone, I'd turn over a rock and find nothing, just pebbles and pools. I could walk for an hour on a beach and never see one crab. He was my eyes, but not just that, he was my imagination.

Leaving him and attending boarding school at five years old was like landing on a different planet. Oh so this is how other people live. I didn't have to feel upset about turning over rocks and not finding anything moving beneath, I was with people who stepped on and over rocks, who would never think of what was underneath. People like me. I felt settled at boarding school. Discipline. Schedules. Order and routine.

When I finished school and didn't get accepted to the Gardaí, instead of going to Tipperary for training in Templemore college as I'd planned, a continued life of structure and regimental living, I returned home. The island I missed became ordinary again. Most of the kids my age were gone to university or moved to Cork or Limerick or Dublin or even Australia and

America for work. The ones who stayed had reason to. What was my reason. I was staying because I failed. I didn't know what else I wanted to do.

Until I was flicking through the newspaper one day and it became clear.

★ ★ ★

I have no intention of asking Jamie to drive me to the train station, and after last night Cyclops is a definite no, ever again. The buses won't work for me. I call my aunt Pauline who I know has enough to do on a bank holiday Monday with holidaymakers eating in the Mussel House, especially on a day like this where the sun is splitting the rocks and it feels like the middle of August. She would have dropped everything for me before, and that was probably unfair at the time too, but she doesn't now. She sends my cousin Dara, which is an interesting and disappointing choice as he and I have never been close. He's always been rude to Pops, a sneery kind of cynical sarcastic attitude. His brother John I would have been happy to see but she didn't send John. I wonder if she sent Dara for a reason.

We make polite-ish chit-chat the entire way, about his weird kids and his weird wife, and his weird life, in the weird snidey way that he talks. He does itty-bitty jobs, different things depending on the season, helping out on farms during lambing season, driving lorries whenever a guy he knows needs lorries driven, cutting hay during hay harvest season, working behind the bar at a different bar every year. But never does he work with the family, not helping Mossie out at the mussel farm, or Pauline at the Mussel House or B&B.

I've always thought he can't stand his family, yet he's always around them, he wants to be away from them but can't leave. He wants to do better than them but hasn't the skills or mindset, and so he keeps his distance when he's right beside them. He's unhinged, you can see it in his eyes. I tell him about Dublin and my job, and he makes sarcastic jokes in response to just about everything I say, and I can't wait to get out of the car, to end this charade and wipe his greasy sarcasm and bitterness from my skin.

It's as we're nearing the station, driving through Killarney that I start to feel more confident. End is in sight. When he pulls into the car park I'm ready, I don't want this to be a wasted trip, so I open the door, feel the fresh air on my skin, feel the freedom from him isn't far from me and ask him, Dara, what did you do with her for those two weeks. Where did you go.

He smirks as if he was expecting the question and I immediately wish I hadn't asked.

That's for her to know and for you to find out, he says.

And I know then that I will. I'm not coming home again, I'm not setting one foot on that island until I've done what I was supposed to do.

15

I'm on the 17.39 train from Killarney to Dublin. It will get me there for 21.02, and then the 21.33 to Malahide, so with hours ahead of me and a needy mind that needs company, I put my headphones on and search YouTube for Rooster. I'm expecting to have to trawl through copious amounts of non-Rooster-related content but I'm surprised to discover dozens, possibly hundreds of videos of a teenager named Rooster, who looks like Tristan. Tristan from ten years old all the way up until two years ago. Rooster is playing video games and commenting through them, hands moving in the same annoying over-the-top way when they're not on the controls. I leave one video to enter another and find the same thing. Rooster is visible in the top corner of the screen, while the video game he plays is the larger screen. Talking talking talking in an annoying accent. I watch him grow up. All on his own YouTube account. He begins his introduction with a Rooster call. A Cockadoodledoo production. The brass plaque on number eight suddenly makes sense. His calling card. A link encourages you to get new merch. I click on it and it brings me to a website with branded mugs, hoodies and stationery. A sophisticated Rooster.com complete with links to videos — Cockadoodledoo Inc.

As I watch the teenager excitedly playing, I remember that this is who Tristan said he preferred to be. A confident kid, a bit annoying, precocious, he talks too much, doesn't take a breath, does silly voices. Playacts on a computer game all by himself. The website advertises that new games are coming soon, created by Rooster.

My phone is hot in my hand so I put it away. I have been down the Rooster wormhole for almost two hours and I'm halfway to Dublin.

Not exactly parting words, but over shared buttery scrambled eggs, thick-cut maple rashers and Valentia black pudding, Pops said he'd been thinking about it. The five people theory.

The theory I imagine, Allegra, he says, is that if you surround yourself with people who love *Star Wars* then you're going to know a lot about *Star Wars*, am I right, if you surround yourself with happy people, Allegra, then you can be happy. So worry not about Marion, Jamie and Cyclops, and this little turd who was rude to you in Dublin, it's all in your control.

Which is probably the most positive thing I heard on this trip home, even if Pops was just being polite about a theory he doesn't support. I take out my notebook again and begin to write.

Dear Amal Alamuddin Clooney

My name is Allegra Bird and I'm writing to you in the hopes that you will become one of my five. Let me tell you what that means. I recently learned the phrase from a guy who ripped up a parking ticket in my face. I'm a parking warden, you see, and he meant this phrase, you are the average of the five people you spend the most time with, as an insult. I suppose, as I'm writing this to you now I've realised that he also intended this as an insult to the people in my life too because he didn't like what he saw in me. We have since patched things up. Yes it was cruel but don't worry I'm not looking for legal advice. It did force me to take a closer look at the people in my life though. Who are my five.

I would have thought it was easy. But I'm returning from a recent trip home, in fact I'm writing this to you on a train, and I realise that my five people were from my previous life. I moved away, I'm kind of on a mission, and I currently find myself without a five. It's embarrassing, sad, I suppose, but I'm trying to see this positively now. I can curate my life. I can look to the people who inspire me, the people who would ground me, or lift me, or guide me, be honest with me, and by choosing the people around me and who influence me, I can choose who I want to be.

You are an amazing woman, Amal. You are an international law maker who is an advocate for criminal justice. I've read all the articles you've written that I could find online, I admire you representing Nobel Peace Prize winner Nadia Murad, journalist Mohamed Fahmy, former Maldives president Mohamed Nasheed, the Reuters journalists in Myanmar, and the fact that you represented Julian Assange in his fight against extradition makes you a hero in Pops' eyes. Plus you're a mother, a fashion icon, we have similar hair, though that's where our similarities end. I know that nobody has it all, but you seem to be doing pretty well at least making it look like that. Sometimes life is a bit of a kangaroo court, isn't it, I think I need someone who can recognise a kangaroo court when they see one. Someone who can restore justice and hope in my life.

Thanks for reading this,

Allegra Bird

PS I am sending a replica of this letter to Lake Como, the UN, Columbia University, Doughty Street Chambers and your house in Sonning Eye in the hope that you will receive at least one. I hope you won't consider me a stalker. Lol.

PPS this is more about just being inspired by people, the idea is that we'd have to spend time together so that you can directly influence me so I'm available for regular Skype or Zoom calls.

I have one hour left on the train.

Dear Katie Taylor,

Hi, my name is Allegra Bird and I'm from Valentia Island in County Kerry, Ireland. I've watched all of your fights, or most of them, and me and Pops even saw you win in the Summer Olympics in London in 2012, when you defeated Sofya Ochigava to win gold for Ireland and become the first-ever female lightweight Olympic champion. Wow what a moment, me and Pops went mental.

I'm writing to you in the hope that you could become a mentor of sorts. Not in boxing but as a person. I know you're incredibly busy training and competing, but it would be an honour if you could become one of my five people who influences me and shapes who I am.

I'm looking for people in different areas of life to help me become the person I should be and you most certainly tick the sports box! If we could meet a few times that would be great, or else a letter with words of advice and guidance will do too (preferably a few letters or Skype or Zoom because the idea is that we need to spend time together). It doesn't have to be sports-related, words of advice for general living would be much appreciated. My mailing address and email address are at the bottom of the page.

Yours in admiration,

Allegra Bird

I finish my final letter just as the train pulls into Connolly station.

Dear Minister Ruth Brasil

My name is Allegra Bird, I'm twenty-four years old. I'm from Valentia Island. I'm sending this letter to your constituency office, your office in Government Buildings and to your holiday home in Kenmare Bay. I'm also sending this to my aunt, Pauline Moran, who lives in Waterville and owns the Mussel House at Ballymacuddy pier. She tells me that you call in from time to time during the summer when you're sailing with your husband and that the steamed mussels in white wine and garlic are your favourite.

I'm not from a political family, there's a by-election on in a few weeks but as I've already been home for Easter, I can't afford to take more holidays. And no offence but travelling home to vote in a by-election doesn't sound like much of a break. But I'm an admirer of yours. I was delighted when the Taoiseach appointed you the Minister of Justice and Equality. I wanted to join the Gardaí when I left school and would have been proud to have you as my leader, overseeing law and order in Ireland. I like listening to you speaking and find you strong and firm but fair. I also think you're a compassionate person and must be because of your family law practice that you ran for so many years. I think you'd make a very fair judge.

I recently heard the phrase, you are the average of the five people you spend the most time with. If the phrase is true, and on long contemplation on the people in and on the course of my life, I think it is, then I want my five to be a mash-up of the greatest and most inspiring five that I can think of. I'm not looking for an intimate friendship, that would be weird, but whatever you'd be comfortable with on your terms. I suggest letters, emails, Zoom or Skype, but it's up to you.

It was recently brought to my attention that I have control of the five people in my life, it's not just who you're stuck with. So I can kind of curate the person I want to be. Sure we'll see how it goes.

I'd love to know who your five are. They must be very special for you to be the way you are.

I hope to hear from you.
Best wishes

Allegra Bird

I fall into bed as soon as I arrive back to the house at ten thirty. The McGoverns are still away on their sun break in Marbella, the house is dark and locked up. It's eerie to be faced with this great big empty mansion. There are a few night lights left on to make people think they're home.

I think I see Barley out on the grass sniffing around but then remember he's been sent to doggy day care and as the creature nears a garden light, its bushy tail reveals itself. *An madra rua*. The fox. I turn my lights off to get a clearer look. Sensing the change in light, it pauses and looks up my way. I hold my breath. It holds my stare. I don't want to blink. I don't want to look away. I'm not scared this time.

I gently move away to the fridge and take out a packet of ham. I go outside to the secret garden, hoping it hasn't left. It's still sniffing around the lawn. It's not a cub, it's a big one, an expert scavenger, fed itself nice and healthy.

I pull apart the slices of ham and place them down on the grass. The fox watches me from afar, through the entrance of the neatly manicured hedge.

That's for you, I whisper.

I slowly back away, far enough so that it's not threatened, but close enough to be able to see in the dark. It watches me, as if assessing me. Sizing me up. Can I be trusted. It decides I can and hurries forward, straight to the ham. Snaps it up and dashes away.

Pleased with myself, I turn around to go into the garage and the house alarm goes off, so sudden and so piercing it gives me such a fright I drop all of the ham and hurry inside.

By the time I get into my room my phone is ringing.
Becky calling.
Hi Allegra.
Hi Becky.
You're out of breath, where are you, she asks.
In Dublin.
Funny, she says, drily. Where exactly.
I wasn't being funny, I was home in Valentia for Easter, I reply, confused. I thought you meant . . . anyway now I'm back. I just got back a few hours ago.

Oh. Right, she says, so as you know the house alarm has gone off. I can hear it in the background. Gosh it's loud. It's probably nothing, but the security company just called me about it . . . they've contacted the guards and they'll be over shortly.

Okay.

Allegra, she says slowly then pauses. You didn't go inside the house did you.

Why would I, I say, rushing around the room to put a tracksuit on. Guards, she said, guards. Detective Freckles.

You sure you didn't go near the house or hit the sensors . . .

I stop and frown, realising this is sounding like an accusation. No, I say bluntly.

I grab the super flashlight that's beside the fire extinguisher. Advertised as the world's brightest flashlight, it must come close with a blinding 4,100 lumens. I remember pointing it at bats with Marion, Jamie and Cyclops. You're so weird, Marion had said with a laugh, watching me pack my bags to leave. What are you going to do with that in Dublin. It's a city, there'll be lights everywhere. Apparently you can barely see the stars there. Well, Marion, who's the weirdo now.

Okay, well I didn't want you to get a fright, Becky says, all nice again, as if she hadn't just accused me of breaking into her house. But I don't care, I'm excited the guards are coming.

As I pull the garage door closed behind me the flashlight illuminates the entire garden. I don't know if Donnacha's studio has an alarm. At five hundred euro for a small bowl that doesn't hold anything, there's a lot of value in that room. With the house alarm wailing in my ear I check the studio door. It's

144

locked. No smashed windows. I shine the light inside and see all his work in various levels of production and completion. All is still.

Hey there, I hear a man call.

I turn around and see two guards entering the garden from the side gate. My stomach flips with excitement. The male guard has got a tiny little torch, nothing like mine. I shine it in their direction, not in their face, I'm not stupid, and walk towards them. As I get closer I recognise them from the local station. The female garda is the cool one I see around the village. She wears lots of make-up and her blonde hair is tied up. She's not much older than me. Could have been me, I think whenever I see her. I always say hi and wave at her as I pass the office. I smile at them now but they don't reciprocate and I'm a little disappointed, in fact a lot disappointed that they don't recognise me as the parking warden. My job is to essentially assist them, after all.

I'm Allegra Bird, I say, my hand extended. I'm the McGoverns' tenant. I live above the gym. I point the torch at my room to show them. Becky told me you were on the way. I was worried about Donnacha's studio, he has some valuable stuff in there, so I checked it out. No signs of forced entry. I haven't checked the house yet. I turn my torch to the work studio and they take a few steps in that direction. The male garda walks up to the window. Looks inside. Checks the handle on the door. Same thing I did. I watch their every move. It could have been me.

Did you see anyone, he asks.

Nobody, I shout. The alarm is still wailing, it's piercing my ears.

The female garda studies me, then they go to the

145

house, checking windows and doors. They said it was the back garden sensor, she says to him.

Ah that would be here, I say, showing them the area around the patio immediately from the back wall of the house. It's protected by sensors so it triggers anyone approaching the house.

You wouldn't have set it off, would you, he asks.

No I came in the same way as you did. The sensors don't protect that gate, so I can come and go without disturbing them. I shine my torch at the pedestrian gate they entered and highlight the route I take through the garden to the building in the back. I got home at exactly 10.30, so it couldn't have been me anyway.

I'm sure they're impressed by my detail. They're taking me in anyway. Give me a job, I want to say to them, but I know they can't just do that.

I was over there in the secret garden when it went off, I say.

Where.

I show them with my torch.

Why were you out here.

There was a fox. Oh, it was probably the fox that set off the alarm, I say, suddenly realising.

What did you say your name is, he asks.

Allegra Bird. I'm a parking warden in the village.

Oh yes, the woman garda says and I'm relieved she recognises me.

I wave in at you from time to time, when you're in the office, I say.

You do, she says.

I applied for the guards, after school.

Well you've done a good job here, Allegra, she says. We'll just take another look around.

It was probably the fox, I say following them. It could have been going for the bins. It usually comes in this way, somewhere behind here — I use the flashlight — and makes its way around here. Bins are over there. Recycling bins haven't been taken since they went on holiday. It must have smelled the food.

The alarm finally goes off, but I can still hear it ringing in my ears.

Do you have a spare key, he asks me.

No. Next door do. Or Becky's assistant comes to take in packages and deliveries when they're away.

Hope you can get back to sleep, Allegra, she says.

Thanks, Garda. I'll see you around the village, on the beat, next time maybe you'll recognise me in my uniform. I'll see you to the car, I walk with them, my flashlight lighting the way to their car. By the way, if you ever need parking ticket information, it would help place someone at a particular location, or something like that, then I'm your girl. We take photos of the cars now, you never know what shows up in the photos.

We usually get that information from the county council, he says, and I deflate a little.

Of course.

Thanks, Allegra. Good night, she says. More friendly. Good cop bad cop.

Do you have a card or anything, I ask.

He doesn't budge. She roots around in her pocket and hands me her card.

Laura Murphy.

I watch their car until the tail lights disappear and then I grin, I can't stop grinning, and I feel like I'm floating as I head back to bed.

I like her. Garda Laura Murphy. An ideal one of five.

16

I'm up. Uniform on, high-vis jacket, lightweight boots. Birds are singing. It looks like it's going to be a glorious day. No raincoat needed. Lunch is packed. Edam cheese on granary bread, no butter, a Granny Smith apple, candied walnuts, and a flask of tea. I leave the McGoverns' grounds, looking out for any signs of foul play in the morning light but all is still intact after last night's intruder. I walk through Malahide Castle grounds, pass the man in the suit with the headphones and jaunty walk, pass the leaning jogging woman. The dog walker with the Great Dane. An old man with a wheelie walking frame and the younger version of him. Good morning, good morning, good morning.

I'm back.

The trip home has helped me. It stripped people away from me, yes, but it gave me something back. A mission. Another one. Though they are linked. I have a spring in my step. I have the letters in my possession that I wrote on the train, signed, sealed, waiting for stamps and delivery. Though I've more than three letters, with duplicates for each person to go to as many addresses of theirs that I can locate, I have a total of sixteen envelopes for four people in my backpack. I don't need to write to Pops, he's one of my five whether he likes it or not, and I plan to contact the fifth person on Instagram. Garda Laura Murphy is a new recruit to the list but I'd like to befriend her in the flesh. That's eight people I'm reaching out to but

I'm realistic; the odds of Katie Taylor, Amal Alamuddin Clooney and Ruth Brasil all writing back to me are very slim. Maybe it will be just two of them.

Back at the Village Bakery for the first time in a while. Whistles is outside eating a doughnut, a hot coffee on the ground beside him. He gives me a nod as I enter. There's a woman sitting at the counter at the window, head in her phone, lost in whatever social media wormhole she's been sucked into. She stuffs the last of her croissant into her mouth, followed by a slug of coffee. I recognise her from around. She drives a silver Mini Cooper. Black top. Two door. Always parks on St Margaret's Avenue. I've never had to ticket her and for that she has my respect, so she gets a good morning from me as she thanks Spanner and leaves.

Freckles, it's you pal, long time no see, Spanner says. I was beginning to think you'd defected to the other side. Deconstructed apple pie today the grand chalkboard has revealed this morning. Deconstructed my arsehole, Freckles, isn't the whole point of baking to construct, he asks, isn't it already deconstructed on the shelves when you buy the ingredients. What'll you be havin, the same as usual.

He's busy with his back to me, banging and pouring, all elbows and shoulders.

How's Ariana, I ask.

She's great. She's a fuckin princess, he says, back still turned, pouring the batter into the waffle machine. She had her first Irish dance feis on Saturday.

He turns around, wipes his brow with his dishcloth on his shoulder, and reaches into the pocket in the front of his apron for his phone. He shows me a photo.

There she is. Had her spray tan done for the day

149

an' all, she was bleedin delighted. She'd all the gear on, youngest in the group, hadn't a feckin clue what she was doin, dances like her ma, stomps like a horse, ah no, only jokin, her ma was all-Ireland champion, not that she'd be able to kick her legs now with all the extra weight, but I'm sayin nothin about nothin. They say people get fat when they're happy so she must be delirious.

So everything's okay then, I say.

She said if I showed up she'd call the guards, but I wasn't missing that for nothin. I stayed for her dance and left straight away, she didn't win a prize or nothin. Ma and Da were both there, no drama, I left her paedo boyfriend to himself, watchin the kids performing with sweaty palms. Didn't even look at the ugly sisters. Happy with that, and then this morning I get this fuckin letter, he reaches into his pouch and retrieves a wrinkled letter and hands it to me. Take a look at that, Freckles, and you tell me what the fuck is goin on.

I look at my empty coffee cup sitting at the coffee machine, and my waffle in the waffle machine, concerned, but Spanner's just looking at me, so I lower my gaze to the letter and reluctantly read.

Whistles shuffles in. No amount of coffee can remove his stench. It makes me thinks of Pops and his clothes and I'm glad I've washed everything from his wardrobe so there's nobody thinking the same thing about him that I'm thinking about Whistles right now. He whistles to get Spanner's attention, and I look up from the letter. Whistles is holding the half-eaten doughnut up in the air.

What's up with you, Spanner asks.

He jiggles the doughnut while whistling.

Jam, Spanner says, you don't like jam.

He whistles a high tone. Correct answer.

Well, your highness, Spanner bows dramatically, if you please do let me know which of my pastries are to your liking, I'd be most delighted to oblige you, seeing as I've nothin better to be doin around here.

Whistles is squeezing the doughnut too tight, the jam oozes and drips from the doughnut on to the page I'm holding.

For fuck sake, Spanner says, literally throwing his towel down.

Whistles jerks around nervously, whistling sporadically like he's a radio that's lost its signal.

I grab a napkin to clean it but to be honest I'm more concerned about my waffle still being in the machine, burning. The crowd from the Dart will be coming soon and I don't want to be squeezed in here with them and their morning breaths and moods.

I know this is a bad time, I say to Spanner, who's coming round the counter to either grab Whistles or the strawberry-jam-smeared letter, but I'm hungry so I say to him, my waffle.

It stops him in his tracks and gives Whistles a chance to escape. He looks angry, that I can tell, but I don't know if it's at me, at Whistles, or because of the jam on the legal letter, at Chloe, or at the waffle. I don't know, I'm not good at this stuff. He finds patience and goes back around the counter and opens the waffle machine. They're burned. He starts again, which is frustrating because time is ticking away.

They can't do what they're saying, I say finally, they can't stop you visiting your daughter.

I know, Spanner says, haven't I been sayin that for the past few months. First it was Chloe keeping her away from me and now she wants to make it legal. I didn't cause the fight at the christening, the paedo boyfriend hit me, not the other way around. I only hit him because he hit me first. Bringing up the assault and battery charges from years ago, before I even met Chloe, is a low fuckin blow. I was nineteen, that was a long time ago, I served my time. I've never harmed Chloe, or Ariana, and I never would. His voice cracks and he looks away to compose himself.

The light on the waffle machine turns green. Spanner is still composing himself, muscles working in his jaw but I can't let the waffle burn again. It will delay me even further and I have a routine, a schedule to keep. I don't do well when it's broken. And I have to call Pops.

My waffle, Spanner.

Yeah. Sorry, he says, shoulders drooped, and turns to the machine. Just one of those days, you know.

I place the legal letter on the counter. Spanner hands me my coffee and my waffle wrapped in newspaper, or greaseproof paper made to look like newspaper. He's forgotten the icing sugar. The bruise around his eye is gone but maybe because I know it's there I can still see it. I suppose that's what happens when you know people for so long. You know about all the bruises and marks that were once there and you can still see them even when they're gone.

Here give this to him outside when you're passing, will ye, Spanner says wearily, handing me a plain doughnut.

★ ★ ★

152

The village is sleepy due to the school holidays. Monday will be back to normal, crankier heads than usual. It helps that the spring weather is actually spring-like, which for us is like summer. Traffic is non-existent right now but will amp up as the day moves on, as people make their way to the coastal town. Most people are using their legs on a day like this in dresses and skirts and shorts. Arms and legs coming out of hibernation. Chins are up. Little for me to do in the way of checking parking tickets but I do my bit. The silver BMW still isn't outside the hair and nail salon, she must be away. On holidays too. The kids off school. The girls are laughing louder than usual inside, or maybe I'm imagining it. I feel protective on her behalf, feel like I've to keep an eye on things while she's gone. Her space has been empty most mornings, like if she can't park there, nobody else is good enough to park there. I look at the empty space for a while, I don't like it not being there, then move on.

I visit the post office on my break. It's lunchtime and it's busy, as if all those streets were quiet because everyone is in here, looking for stamps. I join the queue. Queuing gives me too much time to think, rethink what I've written, what I'm about to send. All of a sudden I'm at the top of the queue and I'm not ready. I get nervous, I leave the line, play out this little silent act like a bad mime artist, as though I've forgotten something and exit the shop. I take a few steps away and then join the back of the queue again, which is now longer and snaking outside.

I flick through my envelopes. Amal in Columbia, Amal in London, Amal in her London office, Amal in the UN. Katie at her fan club, Katie at the Olympic Council of Ireland, Katie at Bray Boxing Club.

153

Hi there.

I jump, startled and drop my envelopes on the floor. As I'm picking them up, in a jittery frenzy, I see the wanker Prada trainers.

Rooster, Tristan, I say standing up, feeling flushed. I feel a little shaky, I wasn't expecting to see him.

Freckles, Allegra.

He's holding enormous padded parcels under his arms. Doing your post, I say.

He smiles. Yeah. You too, he asks.

Yeah. I squeeze my envelopes tighter. I hope you're posting your parking permit form.

Jazz did it last week.

You should have it soon, I tell him. I gave you a ticket today.

I know, he winces, sorry.

You don't have to apologise to me.

I feel like I do.

Oh.

Did you have a good Easter.

Yeah I went home.

Where's home.

Valentia Island.

Oh cool. I've never been there. I thought I detected a country accent.

Feckin Dubs.

You've family there, he asks.

My Pops.

That's right, he smiles. Pops. Number one of your five.

I look at his face properly since we started talking, grateful that he's remembered Pops. That means a lot to me. I saw the others as well, I say, but realised they're not part of my five any more. So now I'm just

154

down to one.

Oh. Man. Wow. Sorry to hear that, he says. What happened.

My best friend is sleeping with my ex-boyfriend and she's pregnant. And her ex-boyfriend came on to me. And my aunt Pauline is staying away from me, I say, suddenly realising the other hole in my life. I know the reason but it's not going to change so . . . she's off the list too.

Jesus.

It's okay, I'm going to get four more people.

He laughs and I look at him, confused. He stops laughing.

Sorry I thought you were joking . . . Look that's great that you're finding more. How do you plan on doing that.

I finally stop squeezing the envelopes so tightly to my chest. I've written to them, I say.

We step forward in the queue. Ten people in front of us, in a winding queue. One of those rat mazes.

He looks at the envelopes in my arms and asks, how many people have you written to.

Oh just four people but for three of them I didn't know their exact home addresses so I'm sending copies to a few different places.

I try to read his solemn face. Why, I ask, am I doing it wrong.

Allegra, there's not . . . there's no right way to do it, he says gently but irritated. I never lose my temper, honestly, I'm kind, and patient, usually, and I don't know why I lost it with you. You clearly didn't deserve it. You're a good person with a kind heart and you should continue on as you were going. I feel responsible that you're doing this, he says, looking injured.

The staff room door opens and a worker steps out, chewing, wiping crumbs from her mouth as she sits down and organises her work station. Finally the two cubicles are open. She takes away the *dúnta* sign.

Two people step up. We step forward. Only eight ahead
of us.

I look down at the envelopes. I'd handwritten all the letters. I figured there was no point in writing beautifully to Amal in Como and typing to her in Columbia University. How am I to know which one she'll end up seeing. It has taken me a long time to write these letters and now he's telling me to just drop it all.

So I'm wasting my time, I say. As I pull them away from my chest to study them I realise I've given him an opportunity to read who they're addressed to.

Amal Alamuddin Clooney, he reads.

Embarrassed, I press them back against my chest.

Is she married to George Clooney, he asks.

He's married to her.

Do you know her, he asks.

No.

Silence. We step forward. Six people left ahead of us.

But I'd like to, I say.

He nods. But no Oprahs, remember, he says, you have to . . . know them.

I want to know her. That's what I'm asking her, I say. Is it stupid, I ask.

He has to think about it.

If you have to think about that, then it is.

No, no, it's not that at all, it's —

What.

It's —

156

Stupid, I say.

It really shouldn't matter what I think but I don't know what's in your letter.

I told her about the five people theory, I say. I told her I'd like her to be one of my five. I look away, feeling embarrassed.

Four people in front of me now. A woman clears the desk. Only three now.

Who else have you written to, he asks.

I feel panicky now. So close to the desk. I feel like telling him everything just so I can decide whether to do it or not. I flick through my pile. Katie Taylor, Ruth Brasil. He raises his eyebrows and I stop.

Katie Taylor the boxer, he asks.

Yeah.

Ruth Brasil, the politician.

Yeah. Minister for Justice and Equality. She's my favourite one. The only one I really know, to be honest.

And what about the other letter.

Which other letter.

You said you'd written four, he says.

He reaches out and pinches the envelope at the back, closest to my chest and pulls.

My heart beats like crazy and I hold on tight to it. I drop all the others, and as they scatter to the floor I tug the remaining envelope from his grip and rip it up frantically. Wildly. Like a crazy person. Everyone in the line is looking at me. So are the postal workers, now both available and staring at us.

Next, she says.

Tristan bends down to pick up the envelopes I dropped, while I cling to the ripped one in my hands. I stuff the torn pieces in my pocket, feeling mortified

157

by my outburst.

Tristan hands me the letters. I think, he says gently, that's the one you should definitely have mailed.

I walk to the desk and with shaking hands ask for stamps, he goes to the desk beside me. His business is more complicated than mine. His packages are travelling internationally, they need to be weighed and registered, sent in all kinds of complicated ways, forms to be filled out. Trembling from my outburst I pay for my stamps and when she offers to take them for me to put in the postal bag in the back, I say no and leave. I hear Tristan call me but I hurry before he has a chance to catch up with me.

I remember what the ripped letter said, word for word. I remember it because I had written it out over and over dozens of times in my notebook until I considered it word-perfect, though it could never be. After Garda Laura Murphy and her partner left, I stayed awake until 4 a.m. reading it, re-reading it, and then when I couldn't find any more words to add, change or subtract, I rewrote it over and over, neater and neater in cursive, each time. As if the perfect curl of my f or the dramatic swirl of my s would make a difference to how the reader would perceive me.

Though I've been writing it in my head for years.

It was a letter to Carmencita Casanova. My mother.

17

I moved here to meet my mother. I left everything and everyone I loved — all my five — to move to Dublin to meet one person. I suppose I didn't think it would take me so long to actually introduce myself to her but, looking back, I certainly knew it would be a long game or else why would I train for the parking warden job, and seek out employment in the village she lives in. I wanted to immerse myself in her life, get comfortable. I was never going to walk up, knock on her door or tap her on the shoulder and say, Howya, Carmencita, it's me, the daughter you abandoned. I don't think I ever thought it would be this long on the side of never meeting her, definitely wanted the time to be on the side of us spending time together and getting to know each other. The trip home to Valentia tells me that, judging by the words of the one I kept and the four I've lost or thrown away, they all thought there'd be quicker results. Did you see her, did you talk to her, have you done what you went there to do. No one mentions her name. No one uses the exact words.

Have you introduced yourself to your mother yet, Allegra. I'd tried to find Carmencita once before when I finished school. While everyone else went to Croatia to a music festival during the summer before we received our exam results, I booked my flights to Barcelona. Marion was coming with me. Pops knew nothing about Carmencita or had heard nothing from her since the day she handed me over to

159

him. All he knew, and all I knew, was that her name was Carmencita Casanova from Catalonia. But I do know what happened twenty-four years ago. She'd panicked when she'd found out she was pregnant, at twenty-one years old. I don't blame her for that. A baby fathered by a music professor at university no less, in a drunken stupor, in a moment of vulnerability, possibly desperation. I don't blame her for that either. I don't exactly have the best track record. She'd dropped out of university for the last semester and then went back after having me and continued on like nothing had happened. Pops had helped her. She'd wanted to get away, out of Dublin, in case she met anyone who noticed her growing bump, and so for the last three months of her pregnancy she moved to my aunt Pauline's B&B in Kinsale. Carmencita had stayed there for only two months, because I was born one month premature.

Complicated, Pauline would describe Mam as when I asked. Her English wasn't great, she'd add when pushed for more information as I got older. Disturbed, she'd add sometimes if she was feeling honest. I don't believe it was my age that made me want to know more, some days I just felt more curious than others, depending on what I'd heard or learned that day in life. It either made me care more about who she was, who she is, where she is, or didn't intrigue me at all. Sometimes I thought Pauline's stories of their time together could be something I could hold on to, something revealing about her character. Something to find myself in. I don't know. It's never that simple. Mostly I just wanted to know. Women always want to know, says every man I've ever known.

Complicated. Her English wasn't great. Disturbed.

She disappeared for two weeks while staying with Pauline. I know this from Pauline. From Pops. From my cousin John. From Dara, who disappeared with her. Nobody's hiding anything but I don't know where they went. For her to know and for me to find out, Dara said. Pauline's concerns had been running a B&B during the busiest months of the summer while her best room, the master suite, was being used by a heavily pregnant Spanish student, and I suppose the effect her stay was having on her two sons. Mam — Carmencita I'll call her because that's really who she is — had no interest in Pops the moment she found out she was pregnant, probably the moment after they'd slept together. She had wanted nothing to do with him. But she did need his help. She took his offer of help. She couldn't tell her family about her pregnancy, she couldn't return home. She needed Pops and he wanted me. This is what they told me.

Confused, Pauline had said on another day.

Complicated. Her English wasn't great. Disturbed. Confused.

She was holed up in the master suite for six weeks, only opening the door for breakfast, lunch and dinner. What did she do in there all day, I'd asked. She watched television but back then they only had four TV channels. Three of them were in English, one of them was in Irish. She watched videos but they were in short supply, my cousin Dara would get them from the local video store — it sounded like the Stone Age — and she didn't read the books that Pauline left for her on the food tray. I asked my cousin John about Carmencita too.

Bitch, he said.

Complicated. Her English wasn't great. Disturbed.

161

Confused. Bitch.

I tried, Pauline had said once, exhausted from the re-telling of it, as if there was a concealed accusation beneath my questions, that if Pauline had done something differently then Carmencita would have stayed, she wouldn't have given me up. No one thinks she and Pops would have gotten together and I'm glad she and Pops didn't stay together. I'm glad she gave me up. I'm maybe not so glad that she left me completely. But she did always sound like a bitch.

I see Pauline's side. Fifty years old, two sons, a business, a husband, minding a stranger night and day, waiting on her hand and foot, a young woman carrying her brother's child. Her brother's student, who regularly lashed out and wanted nothing to do with Pops or the baby. I can feel her stress, the pressure. She said she was terrified. She'd accused Pauline one time of holding her captive in the house. Pauline had told her she was welcome to leave if she wanted, that she was helping her because she said she had no place else to go. She left for two weeks and then came back.

She was dramatic, Pauline said.

Complicated. Her English wasn't great. Disturbed. Confused. Bitch. Dramatic.

Carmencita stayed until she had me. Pauline said Carmencita never talked about her hospital appointments. No one ever knew if the baby was healthy or not, if I kicked or not; Carmencita wouldn't tell anyone anything. Apart from Dara, my cousin, the weirdo with bad wiring. He didn't think she was a bitch. He must have felt he'd met his spirit animal. Someone who was wired the same way as him and despised my family just as much as he did. He was the one who drove her to hospital appointments and to wherever

162

she was hiding for two weeks. I'd like to think she and him didn't have a thing going. She would have been over six months pregnant, but Dara was always a bit weird. Still is.

Of course I've thought about it from Pops' perspective too. Especially when Katie said that pervert thing, I had to process it. Lonely but convivial music lecturer. Single man living in Dublin. A beautiful woman who just so happens to be a student meets his eye, wants him. He's not used to being wanted. Not like that. Not from someone like her. He's older and he's lonely; quite frankly, is the kind of man who looked old even as a teenager. Only it's not to be. She discovers she's pregnant, wants nothing to do with him. She wants to get rid of the baby but he wants it. Maybe she's scared to get rid of it, maybe she thinks it's wrong, who knows, but she doesn't. He'll do anything for her, to help her, and he wants to keep the baby. Because he knows he'll never be lonely again. He leaves his job, whispers and rumours have broken out. He's not the first lecturer to sleep with a student, not his own student, but still people talk. Just as well he's gone far away. He raises the baby alone but knows happily he'll never be lonely again.

He never loves again. Not as far as I can see.

How can I be angry with him for loving me and wanting me.

When I was five years old and started boarding school, he was able to take on a big job again. He got the job in Limerick University. I came home on the weekends. The teaching job was ideal because he was free in the summers when I was off school so he taught classes from the house or at summer schools. If he had to travel for those then I stayed with Pauline,

163

which I loved because a B&B in the summertime was always so exciting. Different people from different countries travelling through, bikers on cycling tours, or hikers and golfers. Artists, crafts people looking for inspiration in our beautiful landscape. American golfers, Danish artists, French cyclists. Coaches bursting with Japanese tourists blocking narrow cliffside roads, trying to pass coaches filled with Germans. Our little patch welcomed people from all over the world.

I'd help Pauline bake apple tarts and pavlovas for dessert, brown bread, Guinness stew and buttery cabbage for the tourists. We'd eat the fresh fish that Mossie caught. The cockles, mussels and clams. Even better, I used to take off on my own into the back garden, acres of Wild Atlantic Way land that rose and fell, rocky and dangerous enough for my imagination, detective on investigations, while I waited for Pops to return.

I don't ever remember feeling any more lost or empty than any other child. I had my moments, I was only human, but not because of Carmencita, not because I didn't have a mother. Not even when I had to explain it at the first week of school or the first time I'd meet someone, which was rare because who ever really cares. My mam's not around, I'd say most of the time. I never knew her, if I wanted to offer more. My Pops raised me. I loved saying that. I loved the sound of it. If I'm honest, it made me feel special. Different. Anyone can have two boring parents, that's easy. And I certainly wasn't the only one at secondary school with a different homelife. There were separations, divorces, deaths, two mams, two dads, all kinds of goings-on. We used to joke about whose parents would be next to split up, some girls actually wanted

164

it to happen, and those with single or separated parents would discuss how gross it would actually be to have parents living in a house together.

Anyway I didn't get to Barcelona in the end, to find Carmencita. We went to Croatia to the music festival. Marion really wanted to and I hadn't told her why I wanted to go to Barcelona, so I went along with the change of plans. Maybe felt a bit relieved.

And then the moment passed and I wasn't really arsed about finding Carmencita Casanova. It had been kind of a romantic idea that appealed to me after school, when I felt free, and before I was to begin my training as a garda that never happened. So I forgot about her and went back to thinking of her as I knew she was. Disturbed. Erratic. Complicated. Troubled. Confused. Bitch. Dramatic. Until one November afternoon when it was too early to be dark, but was, and I was working in the gift shop in the Valentia Skellig Experience, on a day that the centre was empty. Nobody could take trips out anyway, it was so stormy, and driving along the coast to see the two islands was out of the question because the air was so thick with low heavy clouds, mist and rain that you couldn't see past the end of your nose. Short days, long nights, just waiting for it all to pass when I came across an announcement in a left-behind local newspaper:

Earlier this month, the Malahide Chamber of Commerce elected their new president, Carmencita Casanova. The chain was passed on from Mark Kavanagh, who has presided for the past three years. Carmencita Casanova, a resident of Malahide in north County Dublin for the past ten years, married to Fergal D'Arcy, with two children. I

165

will bring great energy, imagination and commitment to the chamber and I'm honoured to have been elected president of the Malahide Chamber of Commerce, she said, there are many areas I wish to focus on, but I wish to especially continue the work I did in the main committee on specialist areas such as parking in the village which has affected the local businesses.

It was her. Who else would have a name like that. In Ireland anyway.

And I looked at her. And I looked at her. Pretty face. Dark eyes. Glossy black hair. Immaculate make-up, heavy on the eyeliner and smoky eye shadow. A big beautiful gap-toothed smile, looking straight into the camera lens.

Complicated. Disturbed. Confused. Erratic. Non-English speaker. Bitch. Dramatic. She may have been these things to everyone else, but she wasn't just that any more. When I saw her, something new happened. She was my mother. I decided for the first time in my life that I needed her. Not just because it was her but, I think now, in hindsight, that the idea of her offered me a place to go. And I already wanted to leave.

18

Tuesday evening live art class. My heart's not in it. Probably sounds stupid to suggest that you can put your heart into sitting naked for a bunch of strangers who paid twelve euro to capture you, but you can. I think you can put your heart into almost anything. And you can take it out too.

The student guy that I slept with before Easter, James, is here again. Or is it Henry. He looks like a Henry. He's all eager beaver, but there's only one in the room this evening. I'm not in the mood for sex, which is odd for me. I feel tired. Pops called me at 3 a.m. to say the mice were dodging the new traps in the piano. He'd fecked out Gerry's after he'd betrayed him by telling me about Majella. First thing this morning I'd checked with Posie, our neighbour, Pops hadn't left the house since I left. I don't know where he got the new mousetraps and he must have run out of food by now. Posie says she'll drop some food around and I'll transfer money into her account. Pops has money of course, or at least I think he does, unless he has more secrets, but if it was his decision, he'd refuse the help.

Posie is the woman who minded me when I was a baby. She took me at four weeks old while Pops worked. She ran an unofficial childcare service from her home that got rumbled when the new laws came in and now has a doggy day-care service instead. She smells of dog biscuits and wet grass. And now I'm asking her to take care of Pops. Funny how the world works. Not haha funny.

Anyway I'm in Monty's Gallery, sitting on the chair, naked, or nude, or whatever, with no clothes on, my tits out, feeling colder than usual. Legs closed. Doors shut. Do not disturb sign. I didn't say anything about the heat but Genevieve disappeared from the room and returned with a small heater. It's facing me now and as I feel the chill leave my bones somebody actually tuts. Maybe it's because they've made a mistake or maybe it's because they've spent most of the session working on almost blue skin, or erect nipples, or goosebumps which have now disappeared. Henry or James is scribbling frantically with charcoal, his tongue hanging out of his mouth like a dog in need of water. I don't want to think of what he's drawing but I'm guessing it's less of what he's seeing here and more of what he's fantasising about. Or remembering. I remember a skinny dick. Long pencil dick. He could sketch his picture of me with that. In a way, he does.

The artists pick up on my doom and gloom. Their finished products all have something in common. A pervading sense of sadness. In my face, in my hunched shoulders, my knees pressed together, shut tight, as if to say no one's coming in, no one's allowed in. I don't want to be looked at. Seeing my feelings reflected back to me just makes me feel worse.

Genevieve senses something is up, kindly asks me if I'd fancy going for a drink. I do. At first it's just me, her, and Jasper but after a while a few people trickle in and the rosé takes effect, loosening my mind and my tongue. I tell them about Rooster, about the five people theory and for the next few hours I listen to them both going through their five people, which takes a long time as they decide anecdote after anecdote who has been more influential than others. As the hours go on and our conversation intensifies and after too much rosé, everything is better than it's ever been. It's past midnight by the time we leave. We, being me and a fella whose name and face I can barely remember. I don't know how we got from the gallery to his place but I remember leaving a cottage in Stoneybatter at 4 a.m., while he's asleep, so I don't have to wake up in his bed, and walking the strange streets for a taxi. The dawn journey costs what I earned for posing nude, which I'm not happy about. I stumble from the taxi to the gym in the back of the garden, I think I even bump into the wheelie bins at one point. I remember an alarm sounding, and Donnacha's arms around me, pulling me up from the ground, while I try to explain to him that I should be left there for the next collection day. But when I wake a few hours later in my bed I wonder what was true and wasn't. My head is pounding, unbelievable throbbing from all sides, and as soon as I sit up and open my eyes to the April sunlight, I have to run to the toilet to throw up.

I throw up so violently I'm left lying on the floor, my cheek to the tiles in an effort to cool down and steady myself. I feel sick from the alcohol but also with myself, a kind of guilty fear that I've done something terribly wrong, that my life has changed forever and something bad is about to happen. The fear. I keep getting flashes of last night. Snippets of conversations, of touches, of glances, or moments entwined. Recollections of things I shouldn't have said, not aloud, not ever. I heave, over and over again in the shower, barely able to stand up, wanting to get it all out, the alcohol and my thoughts and memories.

I force a coffee into me, I won't make the walk to

the village without it. I down a pint of water, don't bother making my lunch, leave without it, unable to bear the sight and smell of food.

I'm passing the McGoverns' kitchen, the ground moving unevenly beneath me as if I'm on a boat, when the clever glass door slides open. I keep walking. As soon as I near the bins I remember falling into the bins, wonder if that's got something to do with the bruise on my hip.

Allegra, Becky calls. She's wearing a navy blue pant suit, a navy blue silk shirt buttoned down enough to reveal a little of her black lace bra. She's fresh faced and glowing after her holiday. She looks amazing. I've never felt like such shit. I'm wearing the darkest shades I could find.

Good night Allegra, she asks.

Maybe I didn't fall into their bins, set their house alarm off at 4 a.m. and have to be pulled to my feet by her husband. It may or may not have happened and I don't ask and don't apologise. I mutter a response, not really a yes or no.

She wonders if I can babysit tonight, something about friends, Hong Kong, dinner, and I can't concentrate. I never care about the detail, I just want to know what time I'm needed. Why do so many people bother with the detail. I interrupt her halfway through. I have to. I feel like retching again, my throat is completely dry and, despite the coffee, toothpaste and water, I can still taste the putrid vomit in my mouth. She's a little put out by my interruption but I don't know why today of all days is the day she decides to talk, maybe because she feels like bonding over the stupid thing I caught her doing and the revelation that I'm a human too.

Seven p.m. please, she says, and she takes steps closer to me, looking back to the kitchen to make sure the coast is clear. She lowers her voice: Allegra, about what happened a few weeks ago . . . but I can't allow her to finish, I can't. I really think I'm going to vomit. I feel hot and sweaty, as though my entire body has broken out in a hot flush. I shouldn't have worn my hat until my shift began but I needed to hide behind my sunglasses too. I must look like Robocop. Her voice is low, not the assertive one, it's gentler, soft, another version of her I'm not familiar with, which on any other day would be intriguing. But unless she wants vomit on her navy blue Prada suit she needs to withdraw immediately.

It's fine, I tell her, trying to breathe but feeling sweat prickle on my forehead, beneath the heat of my hat and hair. It's none of my business what you did or what you do, I say, I won't say anything to anyone. You have my word.

She studies me. Probably difficult to read me under the Robocop disguise. Then she nods, relieved.

But just maybe not in my bed again, I add. That was manky.

She holds her hands up in surrender, suddenly mortified at the details and not wanting me to continue. Of course not, she says, never again.

I wonder if she did it before, but maybe it's best I don't know.

A toilet flushes, loudly, and we get a fright. I look up, to the room above the sliding glass wall. The window is wide open, the bathroom window of the master en-suite. I briefly look inside the kitchen to see if Donnacha is there, maybe it was one of the boys in the toilet, but he's not in the kitchen and the three

171

boys are. Becky is frozen. I feel sick for her. And me.

You didn't say anything specific, I say quietly. Though to myself I think, I was the one that mentioned my bed.

I can see her running the conversation through her head. I can tell she doesn't want to go back inside, face the music.

See you at seven, I say, backing away, leaving her there.

As soon as I can, I down water from a glass bottle. No plastic. I pass the enthusiastic man in a suit with the headphones, a backpack on, bouncing as he takes long strides to the music. I'd like to know what he's listening to. He never even looks at me. I wonder if he ever notices that he passes me every single morning or if he notices when I'm not there, or if he wonders why we pass at different points some morning. Maybe not. Maybe not everybody's made like me. I feel a little better, the shaded tunnel through the trees is cooling, I can breathe. I remove my hat. I pass the leaning jogging woman. She's so tilted I don't know how she's staying up. Sweat drips from her brow, glistens on her chest, she's not moving very fast, I could walk beside her faster. The top of her head is soaked, her hair slicked to her scalp and her boobs bounce and swing as she jogs. Not the right boob though, it's held in place by her arm that's rigidly up by her side, the tilted side, the other one moves like she's doing a choo-choo train. It looks so painful it makes me want to cup my own breasts in place.

She looks at me but sees through me. Probably doesn't even see my small smile that's meant to be encouraging. And she's gone around the bend and I'm faced with a long path ahead of me. A beautiful tree-lined path that arches over my head. But I can't do it today. It looks endless, as though it leads to nowhere. And I don't necessarily want it to end. I feel safe here, cocooned in the fresh cool air. As soon as I leave the grounds I'll be faced with people, and smells, and traffic, and noise. And consequences and repercussions. Not today.

I take a few weary steps to the bench that says Lucy Curtain sat here, and I sit down with the ghost of her, weariness enveloping my body, aches and pains in parts of me that I don't want to think about the root of. The dog walker and the Great Dane. The Great Dane off the leash, sniffs at my boots. I haven't the energy to move him on. I may as well be a park statue. I expect a bird to poop on me. The old man and his son slowly walk by. Good morning, good morning, good morning, I practically whisper.

Then I know I'm good for a few minutes before anyone else appears. I close my eyes and go for one of those meditative mindfulness moments to convince myself that the world is okay, that I didn't do last night what I think I did. It doesn't work. Instead I'm alone to stew in my hangover. A sprinkle of cringe, a sprig of self-pity, a handful of regret. Low simmer for twenty-four hours.

I can't say that I do the best job that morning. I try, but my efforts are weak. I issue more tickets than usual. I feel so exhausted, mentally drained, that I don't have the brain capacity to work out whether to give a car twenty minutes' grace or not between tickets. I just issue the tickets and leave. At one point I question whether I'm working on a Sunday, as so many cars haven't paid. Rooster's yellow Ferrari included. After my little breakdown at the post office yesterday,

173

I move along quickly, and I'm too tired to feel ratty that he still hasn't sorted his permit. If anything I wonder why Fingal office are taking so long granting his business permit. Maybe I should call them. Fidelma in the office is helpful.

The usual stuff all morning and then I am so relieved to take a break. I sit on the bench, with my bottle filled with water again. I just want to lie down and sleep. I'm pondering lying down on the bench, and whether doing so would get me fired, when Tristan joins me.

No lunch, he asks.

Too hungover.

Ah must have been a good night.

I groan and he laughs.

You didn't ticket me.

Too hungover.

Wow, you must be really bad.

I have to give you fifteen minutes' grace if your ticket has expired.

Parking wardens and grace don't usually go together.

Those are the rules, I say. I down the water. I feel him watching me.

Where were you last night, he asks.

I don't want to talk about last night.

He laughs even though I'm being serious.

Okay. I've been thinking since we last saw each other. Which was yesterday, in case you've forgotten, before your alcohol poisoning.

I roll my eyes.

I think your letters are a good idea. You should post them. I'm sorry that I was unsure about it. I feel an extra responsibility over the decisions you make as a result of what I said. I don't want to make your life worse.

It couldn't get any worse, I say. I surprise myself with saying that.

Shit.

No it's okay. It's my fault.

We sit with that for a while.

So you're going to post the letters. To Amal Clooney and Katie Taylor and Ruth Brasil, he asks.

I sigh. I can't think today. I don't know. Maybe not.

Give them to me.

What, no.

I won't read them. I'll just post them for you.

I don't know. Tristan, no, I slap his hand away. I don't know. I can't think.

That's a good thing. You shouldn't think about it. Thinking about it stopped you yesterday and you should just go for it. Sit there. Be hungover. I'll post them. What's the worst that can happen.

I embarrass myself.

No. No one will ever know.

You know.

I won't tell a soul. Allegra, he fixes me with a serious stare, what's the worst that can happen.

They don't reply, I say.

Exactly. He shrugs. Who cares.

I care. I care if they don't respond.

Do you have the letters on you.

They're still in my bag from yesterday.

Let me see.

I open the zip in my jacket and fifteen of them slide out. I never rewrote the one to Carmencita. I didn't have time after work yesterday even if I'd wanted to, and I don't know what I want right now. At some stages this morning, in my worst moments of fear, I was considering going back home, giving up this

175

job and this half-life in Dublin, but after the trip I've had, I don't know what I'd be going home to. I've more going for me here, which isn't saying a lot, and I should at least finish what I started.

Suddenly Tristan grabs the letters and runs. I think he's joking and that he'll stop running any minute, but he doesn't. He continues across the road, almost gets hit by a car, disappears around the corner. I grab my stuff and chase him. I see him racing up Townyard Lane. Despite my state I take off after him. I'm breathless by the time I reach the top of the lane and see him outside Insomnia café, by the big green postbox, a grin on his face, and the envelopes hovering halfway to the postbox. He wobbles them threateningly close to the slit.

I'm so out of breath I feel like I'm going to pass out. I lean over, my hands on my knees. Dizzy. I'm never drinking again, I say.

Famous last words, he says, with a smile. Come on.

I straighten up.

The letters are no longer teasingly dangling in the slit, he's holding them out to me. You've got to do this yourself. Post them. Finish what you started.

It's like he read my mind earlier. How could he have known. He doesn't, it was just luck of course, coincidence, but it's enough for me. I take the envelopes and post them, one by one, a smile growing on my face as each one disappears. Three people, sending my wishes out to the universe. Just posting letters really, but all the same.

Now what, I ask, feeling elated, my heart pounding with excitement and not just from the run.

Now, you wait, he says. For a response.

Oh. I feel myself deflate.

176

No. Now you don't wait, he says, changing his mind. That was only three people, wasn't it. What about the one you ripped up.

I'm still working on it. It's kind of a long game.

Are you going to tell me who it is.

Maybe. Sometime.

He looks at me intensely, then at his watch. Are you still on your break, he asks.

I check the time. Fifteen minutes left.

Do you want to come on a tour of the office, he asks to my surprise.

19

This is Andy, Tristan says as we poke our heads into the first office on the right. I'm inside at last. I take a good look around, finally able to penetrate the Cockadoodledoo building of mystery. High ceilings, a white marble fireplace. I wonder if they can light it or if it will burn out a family of wood pigeons. Expensive-looking candles line the mantelpiece, pure white wax in glass. Panelled walls. Two workstations with white desks and enormous white Macs. Dark wooden floors, polished. A white fluffy rug. I look at everything in the room before I turn to Andy.

Andy looks at me warily.

Ah, I say, Andy's your parking angel.

My what, Tristan asks, grinning.

Some companies employ them. A team, or in your case a person, to move cars every few hours, or top up the meters.

Tristan laughs. What a sweet parking angel I have.

Andy doesn't like this job description. Sits back in his leather chair, swinging left to right, legs splayed to communicate that his penis and balls are too enormous to be able to push his thighs any closer together.

I'm EVP of production and development at Cockadoodledoo Inc, he says lazily.

OMG, I say flatly. I'm not impressed. Which bothers him. His title is designed to impress.

Where's Ben, Tristan asks.

He stepped out for a minute, Andy says, scrolling through something on his computer. I step back to

178

look at his screen. Sports cars.

He has the phone call with Nintendo this afternoon though, Tristan says.

I think they postponed it until tomorrow, Andy says, still not looking up.

No, I spoke with them this morning, Tristan says. They were ready. It's taken me literally months to set that conversation up.

Andy shrugs, which annoys me, I can't imagine what it does to Tristan.

Sounds like Ben cancelled the meeting, I say, and Andy glares at me as if I've ratted out his friend, because his obnoxious responses were doing such a good act at hiding the truth. What's in there, I ask, looking at the panelled double doors. White, of course. With this headache, the brightness should hurt but it's calming. Maybe it's off-white. Grey. I don't know.

I'll take you in there, Tristan replies to me. Maybe tell Ben to come up to me when he's back and has a chance, yeah, Tristan says, his voice is soft, too friendly, too quiet, giving Ben a million reasons to not bother.

Sure, Andy says, his full attention on his computer screen. Tristan glares at his back before leading me out of the room and into the room next door. The phone at Jazz's station in the hall is ringing. She's not there. Tristan ignores it and twists the doorknob. It's locked. He tries to shoulder it and knocks but nothing happens. We can hear people inside. The phone at reception is still ringing. He answers the phone.

Cockadoodledoo Inc.

As he says this there's a roar from the locked room. He pushes his finger into his ear to hear what's being said down the line. She's not here right now, eh yeah, sure let me write it down. He searches the desk for a pen and paper. Finds a large manila envelope that I recognise. There's another roar from the locked room. What, he asks, face all screwed up in frustration, blocking his free ear again. A nail appointment, yeah fine. He scribbles it down, then hangs up, his face a picture of irritation. Still holding the envelope, he storms over to the locked door, tries to open it again and then bangs on it with his fist when it's not answered immediately.

Finally it opens. A pug comes rushing out and down the hall to the back of the building. I follow Tristan inside, removing my hat and my jacket and high-vis vest. The room is enormous, goes back deep, an extension, a kitchen leads off it, into the garden. An immaculately kept courtyard. This is another picture straight from a landscaped garden, colourful bean bags placed all around the paving. Mirrors and picture frames hanging on the concrete walls, an Instagram dream. But it's the room we stand in that's most fascinating. The walls are lined with old-school arcade machines. I count eight people crowded round one machine in particular.

Pac-Man.

Go on, Niallo.

As if he's competing for gold in the Olympics.

Jazz is there. Long glow-in-the-dark yellow nails, bicycle shorts and an oversized hooded top. Black boots. Like a Boohoo ad.

What's going on, Tristan asks, but I'm the only one who hears him because they let out a roar again and Niallo steps back from the arcade, his head in his hands. It's Pac-Man. You'd think it was something like Street Fighter but no, all this testosterone and drama for Pac-Man.

They finally break up and look up at Tristan and I expect them to give a shit that their boss has walked in on them like this, but they don't. I can't tell if he's annoyed he wasn't a part of the game or because they're not working. They don't seem to care either way and excitedly fill him in on who scored what and who is next to play.

The phone rings in the hallway at Jazz's desk. She doesn't move. She eyes me warily.

Jazz, the phone, he says gently. His tone is notable.

Come on, he says to me, I'll show you the rest.

If you're going that way, you can answer it, Jazz says breezily.

He answers the phone. I sigh. Wuss. I walk away from him, down the corridor. Steps lead downstairs. I take them. I'll give myself the tour. The basement level is broken up into cubicles. I look in the rooms and see computers with seats, headsets. The walls are soundproofed and are decorated in photographs, cuddly toys, postcards, funny beer mats, personal items. Like each isolation unit has been personalised.

Game pods, he says suddenly behind me. This is where we test the games and film for YouTube.

I then notice the cameras inside, attached to the computers. More pets wander around the halls. The cat from before and another dog. Each room is empty. No work being done in this building at all. We head upstairs, back to ground level and up again. The pug tries to catch up with us and races through my legs. There are only two offices upstairs.

This is Uncle Tony's office. I want you to meet him, he says, knocking and entering. There's no one inside. A large office that takes up the front of the building, with a stunning view. Over the tennis club.

181

The sea. The one that reminds me of home. I can see my bench at the corner. I can see a lot of my beat. You could watch me move around the town like a mouse in a maze from here.

He should be back soon, he says, leading us to his own office. It's not as impressive. It's at the back, over-looking rooftops and chimneys, the uglier parts of the village, the working parts. The backs of kitchens and salons and shops. Staff parking, alleyways, skips. It's not an awful view at all. I can see the hair salon. The marina, the estuary. A van with hazards on double yellow lines.

Look at you, Tristan says laughing, you're like a predator sniffing out blood.

I sit on the leather couch and look around at all his things. It's not as neat and tidy as the rest of the building. His is a working desk, a working office. I don't know him well but it feels like him all right. Avenger figures. Merchandise. Gaming phrases framed on the walls such as *I'm a gamer, I don't die, I respawn.* Piles of paperwork on his desk. A lot of computers; a large Mac, two laptops, a large flat-screen on the wall, computer console, PlayStation, Nintendo, a Wii, Xbox, a driving seat with a wheel before an enormous flat screen, and some other consoles I don't recognise. He has old ones piled on open cluttered shelves, a Nintendo and Nintendo Game Boy from the Nineties, everything updated and replaced over time but kept. Honoured, even. The walls have framed posters of Mario Brothers, Sonic the Hedgehog, Call of Duty, Grand Theft Auto, Pac-Man, Tetris. All his pin-ups. His shelves are lined with how-to business books; *The Essays of Warren Buffet, 7 Habits of Highly Effective People, Shoe Dog, The Greatest Salesman in the World,*

182

The Lean Startup, all of which go to explaining his Jim Rohn regurgitation. Behind his desk is a large canvas of an old computer with rudimentary graphics.

Space War, he says. The first computer game ever invented. The platform is a PDP-1. It was made in 1962 and influenced the first commercial arcade video games.

He's animated, speaks with excitement. Loves his videos and facts.

I like this room best, I say.

Thanks.

You're obviously doing really well to have a place like this. To employ all of these people.

I did do well. But we've only just begun. We're developing our own games but we're at the early stages.

That's exciting, I say.

Yeah . . . I needed to grow the business. I've always had ideas about games, I saved them up over time. Think I got as high as I could go as a YouTuber. It's a competitive arena. Feels like now's the perfect time to move into my own business. Uncle Tony was the business brains, saw me playing on YouTube all the time and saw the possibilities before anyone else did. He got me the endorsements, sponsorship, merchandise, all that stuff. Got me from just being a kid who liked playing games to . . . well . . . He throws his arms up to display his surroundings.

To an older kid who likes playing games, I say.

He laughs. Yeah, maybe. An older kid who likes developing games. Hopefully successful games. Tony thinks I should have kept going as I was, you know, Rooster on YouTube, just playing other people's games, but I had to give it a go. I took the risk. It needs to work now.

Suddenly the business classes and inspirational quotes make sense to me.

How's it going, I ask.

Honestly, slowly. I was hoping to have launched the first game by now. It's not moving as fast as I'd like.

I wonder why, I say.

He misses my sarcasm. That's the reality of business I guess, he says.

Hard to move fast when your staff are busy playing a Pac-Man tournament I suppose.

Oh that. Well, he shrugs, then lights up. Want to see some of my sample games, he asks, excited. He goes through his stuff like a little boy showing me his toys in his bedroom, talking fast and quickly about ideas and how they're not right but they're almost there and please give your honest opinion but the blood and guts in this one needs to be better and I was thinking of literally being able to blow heads off but being more Tarantino about it and make it animated instead of real because the age is, well I don't know, we're debating that. This character literally got his sound from a food waste disposal in a sink, this guy is based on my physics teacher who was a monster.

And on he goes. Flicking through USBs and CDs and opening and closing contraptions, flicking through settings with one remote control and then another.

I should be getting back to work now but I really don't want to. Even the van with the hazards on isn't tempting me. I put my head back on the soft leather couch and close my eyes as he sits down beside me and plays, saying things like, it won't be as bad as this, and this guy is going to be more muscular, have a thicker neck, I think he should be bald, maybe a tattoo on his head. A web or a spider or something — I

184

don't know yet. And this will have different music and this guy is going to be a girl and that car is going to be a helicopter with an option to turn it into a boat, and here you'll have your inventory and there you'll get the bomb but it won't have this it'll be more like that.

I could sit here all day. It reminds me of the Rooster videos I watched on the train from Kerry; he's right here, live and in person, speaking in the same excited breathless way. So many words, not enough time to say them in. More grown-up but not really. A deeper voice. Still with the same child-like enthusiasm. Suddenly he goes quiet and I open my eyes. He's looking at me.

Boring you, he asks softly.

Not at all. Hungover.

He smiles. I'd really like to know what you got up to last night.

I think of the fella I went home with. I can't picture his face. But I can picture other parts of him. I feel sick.

No, I say, you really wouldn't.

He was that bad, he guesses. Will you see him again.

I look at him, study him. What would he think of me if I told him I'd slept with a stranger, a fella I don't know and whose name I can't remember. That it was far from the first time I'd done that. What would he think if I told him I pose nude for money. Would he think I am disgusting, would I shatter his innocent little gaming world. Peter Pan playing with his lost boys. But there's something a bit lost about him. I feel right at home with him.

What, he says.

Our faces are so close I can feel his breath on my skin. It's warm. I smell coffee.

185

I was just thinking of you as this Peter Pan figure who's trying to grow up, but it's like a double-edged sword. You have to keep some part of your childhood, your imagination, in order to do all of this gaming stuff, but then you have to grow up or you'll end up giving away the best view to everyone else around you.

Whoa, he says, his voice a whisper. You got me back.

I wasn't trying to.

He's silent. I don't know what he's thinking really. Another insult for me. I'm expecting anything. Relaxed about it though. I know it won't come from a malicious place this time.

Did you get drunk last night because you were upset about yesterday, he asks, about what happened at the post office.

Probably.

My fault again, he says, annoyed at himself.

I don't correct him, I don't have the energy to keep soothing his ego and unravelling knotted sensitivities.

Who was the letter for that you ripped up, he asks.

I sigh. My mam.

He looks at me for more. Cornflower blue eyes. Pity he hides them beneath the manky cap.

I've never known her, I explain. She left as soon as I was born. Pops raised me. I've never missed her, not really thought about her. Well I did, but not in a way that made me want her. In the way where I'd taste Turkish delight and like it when everyone else hated it and think, I wonder if Mam likes it. Or watching a TV show I'd wonder if she'd like it too, was she watching it too at exactly the same time, are we seeing and hearing the same thing. Random stuff like that. But I never wanted her. I never needed her. Until suddenly I did. Want her.

Because of what I said about the five people, he asks.

No. Before that. She's the reason I moved here. I came to meet her.

His eyes widen. She lives in Malahide.

Carmencita Casanova, I say. My heart beats faster at saying her name aloud. Admitting it. The family secret, out in the big bad world.

He frowns, I can see the name has triggered something.

Casanova, he says, the hair salon.

Yeah, that's her. She owns it. But don't ever say anything to her about me, she has no idea who I am. Who I really am. I've spoken to her three times, I explain. Once she said good morning, the second time she saw me checking her business permit and was worried something was wrong. She came out of the salon. I couldn't breathe, I didn't know what to say, made a fool of myself. I could barely string my sentence together.

I cringe at the memory of my mumbling.

And the third time, he asks.

The third time, she said, and I imitate her Spanish accent, A day for the ducks. I hear her tone clearly in my head. I hear it on wet days, over and over.

He smiles. Sweet, he says. How long have you been here.

Six months.

And she still doesn't know who you are.

Don't you start too. Everyone at home was asking me about her. My Pops, my friend, my ex.

Did he want you to come here, he asks.

My ex, no I broke up with him to move here. And now he's fucking my best friend.

He laughs, then apologises. I meant your Pops.

Oh. Just before I left I asked him how he felt. If I was doing the right thing, and he said, Probably not.

So he's your honest person.

He's definitely that.

I'm glad you ripped up the letter to her, he says. I don't know what you wrote but that won't have been the best way to get her — you'll never know if she opened it or if it was delivered, too many variables. So your hangover is not in vain. But I see what you were doing, you can't just rock up to the salon and say, Hey, I'm your daughter. Okay, he drums his fingers on his Prada trainers, what's the best way for us to do this.

I smile at the use of us.

He examines me, our faces are so close.

Do you look like her, he asks, and it's as if he's scanning me for comparisons to her as his eyes run over me. I feel goosebumps rise on my skin under his gaze. Do you not think she'd guess who you are, he asks. I've seen her a few times. I mean, you look Spanish. And your age.

I'm silent.

Say it, he says.

How do you know I've something to say, I ask in surprise.

When do you never have something to say, he says.

Okay. Some people see themselves in other people, how they're similar, and some people only ever see their differences. I feel like she's the type not to see herself in me. But because of that I thought she'd know me straight away. Because when I look at myself, I don't see her, I see my Pops' freckles.

Rooster babe, the door bursts open and Jazz rushes

in. Hey, she looks at him and me on the couch, heads close, lips even closer, not actually doing anything but it doesn't look good. We're having an intimate chat about how I approach my long-lost mother, there's bound to be a mood. I couldn't give a fuck, especially as she has just called him babe and it's a confirmation they're together, which is so predictable and annoying. She's shit at her job but she's hot. Why else would she be here. He sits forward, as if he's been caught doing something. He's made it look worse than it is.

I was just showing Allegra the new wreckage game, he says nervously, nodding at the paused screen, eagerly, gently. It's pathetic.

She looks at me. I smile. I like it, I say. It'll be better when the organs fall out of the bodies and self-combust though.

He actually sniffs a laugh because he didn't mention anything about exploding organs.

So . . . Katie and Gordo are getting married, she says, eyes wide. Getting fucking married. She sits down on the footstool in front of him, long shiny legs straddling his. And guess where the wedding is.

I don't know.

Rooster, guess.

She's from Kells, isn't she, so —

Ibiza baby, she says, doing an excited little jiggle, her mouth open in a silent cheer. It's gross and I have to leave now.

Thanks for the tour, Tristan, I say, standing up.

Tristan, Jazz says in a sneering way. No one calls him that. Only his mother.

Well she'd know, wouldn't she, I say easily, and Rooster is a big boy now, so he gets a big-boy name. I look at him. Remember to tell Jazz about her nail appointment being changed. I pick up the brown envelope that he's unknowingly carried from room to room since he took the message downstairs. And uh-oh, don't forget to mail this. I drop it on the table.

Tristan peeks in the top and slides the paperwork out. It's the parking permit form. Jazz, he says with a sigh.

I'll see myself out, I say.

Cool. Don't forget your high-vis jacket, Jazz says.

What a fucking day.

★ ★ ★

I've never been so pleased to see Paddy as I am at the end of the work day when he pulls over at the bus stop opposite the church on Main Street.

Hop in. What happened here, he says, looking out all of his windows, concerned.

The gathering crowd stare at me as I get into the car.

They look angry, Allegra.

They are angry, Paddy.

What did you do.

I sigh. A fella pulled into the bus stop. I issued him a ticket. He'd been there four minutes with his hazards on.

That was decent of you.

I thought so, I say. But I don't think Paddy really does think it was decent. He's the kind of guy that trawls cafés and shops, looking for parking offenders to let them know they're out of time rather than give them a ticket. Paddy's a popular character around the village. They hate it when they're stuck with me, and I don't care.

190

There's no grace period with that malarky, he says. You did the right thing. What was his excuse.

He'd pulled over to help an old woman who'd fallen, I say.

He snorts. Pull the other one.

That was actually true.

He looks at me in surprise. And you gave him the ticket, he asks.

Paddy you were my supervisor, you trained me yourself and you were the one who said, Without mercy; we're paid to be impartial upholders of rules. We want to make sure traffic is flowing and drivers are doing the right thing, we want to make sure everything is perfect, not be distracted by sympathy.

Yeah, I know, I know, he says quietly.

People would miss us and there'd be chaos on the roads . . . I repeat everything he taught me. The guy went apeshit, I told him to appeal it, that's what the appeal system is for. I was only doing my job.

He's silent and I feel his judgement.

I issued loads of tickets today. Did you, I ask. All along the estuary. You'd swear everyone thought it was a Sunday. Everyone wants something for free.

Paddy's silent, thoughtful. Did you check to see if the pay and display machine was working, he asks.

Shit. I want to kick myself. Rookie mistake.

How many tickets, he asks.

Ten, maybe more.

They'll appeal, he says. That's what the appeal system is for.

He's not even trying to be funny.

He drops me off at the house and before I get out he says, you got the rules right, Allegra, you did, no doubt about that, well done. But sometimes, just

191

sometimes, you have to make allowances for people being human.

You see that's the problem, Paddy. That's the bit I don't get. The human bit.

I can't give you a rule book for that part, he smiles.

As he turns the car around, I ponder which take-away I'll order for dinner while babysitting the boys and try to ignore how lonely I feel right now. It happens sometimes.

Fucking hangover.

Paddy lowers the window as he pulls away. I'm having a barbecue on Sunday, for my birthday, do you want to come.

He's asked me to a few things before. I never went and he stopped asking. But maybe he's picked up on my mood. I nod and smile, grateful. Thanks, Paddy.

Have you heard the one about the traffic warden, he asks. As he was being nailed into his coffin, he regained consciousness and hammered on the lid to be let out. I'm sorry, said the undertaker, but the paperwork's all done now.

We both laugh.

I'll drop you a text about Sunday. He drives off, his arm out the window in a grand farewell.

20

Later that evening, after hours of playing, and showing the kids Rooster videos which they're not as interested in as I'd hoped because he doesn't play the up-to-date season of Fortnite, I put them to bed and download Instagram. Time to set up an account. I have Facebook and Twitter accounts that I never post anything on, they're just for looking at what other people are doing. Every now and then when I'm in the mood I post a comment. You get the most fun out of riling up the perpetually offended.

Most people at school have private Insta accounts, but plenty don't. They're happy to display their lives; travel, nights out, favourite motivational quotes. The person I'm looking for is Daisy Starbuck, with an account by the name of the Happy Nomad. Her profile photo is of her smiling happily with cliffs in the background. Non-Irish ones. Somewhere exotic. Somewhere far away. There's a breeze in the air and a few strands of her blond hair have blown across her face. She's looking away from the camera, an enormous open-mouthed smile that reveals her perfect teeth and glowing skin. Oozing happiness, confidence, freedom. Her bio reads: *Here. There. Everywhere. Happy.*

Daisy was in my year at school. She was enormous. Not in size but in personality and character. To me she glowed, she stood out in every room. All students liked her, even the bitches. The teachers liked her, even the bitches. In transition year she starred in the lead role in *Grease* when we paired up with the local boys' boarding school for the annual production. I was a stagehand. She ended up dating Finn, who played Danny. They were the sweetest couple, the kind of couple you were so sure would end up getting married. More mature and settled than everyone else, they went on proper dinner dates and acted like grown-ups together. They broke up in sixth year just before the leaving cert exams because her parents were worried about them being too serious and wanted her to focus on her studies for her final exams. The entire year felt like we'd broken up with him too. I think he was so distraught he had to repeat his exams. Don't know if I quite wanted to be her but I wanted to watch her as you would a favourite film, and listen to her on repeat as you would a favourite song. She had a magnetic effect, she drew people in, but unlike other popular girls she didn't use that power and loyalty for her own ends. She was nice and she was kind. I was never her friend, never in her inner circle but now that I know what I know because of Tristan, I wonder what being in that circle would have done for me. Maybe in that supportive tight little group of five people, who all ended up doing exactly what they wanted to do in university and who knows what since, maybe it could have rubbed off on me and I would have become a garda.

I haven't seen her since our leaving cert result party, but I've often thought about her and wondered about her.

I can't just sit around waiting for Amal, Katie and Ruth to write back to me. I need my five people sooner rather than later. I need to be who I want to be sooner rather than later. I don't have time for natural development, I've got to move this evolution on. It's time to reach out.

Though Daisy was always kind I don't expect her to remember me or befriend me instantly. I need to lead her to me, reel her in. I comb through the internet for travel photos, amateur but impressive ones, and I copy and paste my favourites into my account and save them to drafts.

I spend time thinking of captions that someone like Daisy would like — usually humble, inspiring phrases. Always positive but not so much that it's saccharine. She does humour too, but she's clearly a person in search of herself and is doing a good job of looking.

I dispense with the cheesy inspirational quotes and try to find the happy balance. I need to retain a part of me too or I won't be able to keep up the charade. I find a photo of a sunset over Valentia. Caption: *Home*. Happy contented face emoji.

I think of my morning walk to the village, the pathway through the trees, and post a photo of the sunlight beaming through a tunnel of trees. Caption: *Breathe*. I use a yoga girl emoji.

I find a coffee and Belgian waffle photo, a hand holding it that could pass for my own. It's set up on a pretty mosaic table with flowers and a little blurry view of water and green in the background. Seated outside. Caption: *Treat time*. A cake emoji and face with tongue emoji.

But I need to show that I'm fun.

I find a photograph of a couple getting married on a beach. It's from a hotel website advertising weddings. I have no idea who the people are, they're probably models, I post it. Caption: *Making memories with friends. Amazing day*. Hands pressed together in prayer emoji.

For observational animal humour, I find a photo of a baby beaver looking like it has collapsed on the floor with the caption *Dam it* and post my comment, *Happy Monday folks*. I hate puns. They're my least favourite kind of funny, but she seems to like them. It'll do.

I look at my collection in my saved drafts. I'm missing something fun. Something that tells you that I'm the girl you want to go on a night out with. Something that doesn't say I sleep with strangers who paint me naked. I find a lightly naughty photo of a group of friends jumping into a swimming pool at night; all the guys are pulling moonies, bare bottoms out in the air. Caption: *These guys!* Emoji, that one with the zany eyes and tongue sticking out.

Instagram name: Freckles. Bio: *You are the average of the five people you spend the most time with.*

Looking at the photos, I seem the kind of girl that a girl like Daisy would want to spend time with. I post them all. I follow Daisy, and go through her posts, liking some photos, commenting on others, using praise the lord heavenly hand emojis for photos that I think she's particularly proud of, all those scenic views and the likes.

Then, just as I did when I posted the letters, I wait.

When Donnacha and Becky return I'm asleep on the couch. I jump up when I hear the key in the front door and try to gather myself. I look a mess, I've had drunken dreams reliving the night before with the mystery fella and I feel parched, sweaty and disoriented.

Everything okay, Becky asks.

Yeah, I'm fine thanks, I mumble sleepily, just wrecked.

I meant the kids.

Oh yeah. Yes, all fine. I try to fold the cashmere blanket and attempt to display it in the way it used to be, stylishly slung over the corner of the couch, but I don't have the knack for that stylish touch. As soon as I've placed it, Becky picks it up and restyles it. I don't think she even notices what she's doing.

They went to bed at nine, I say. I read them a book. We couldn't find Banana the monkey, so I stayed with Cillín until he fell asleep.

She smells of alcohol and a light odour of cigarette smoke. They both seem jarred. Donnacha retrieves a pint of water and then pings from the bannister to the wall as he goes upstairs, like he's on a boat. Maybe I'm imagining it, but it feels like there's an atmosphere between them. A tension. Maybe he heard our conversation this morning when he was in the bathroom. Maybe he's not an idiot and can tell when his wife is sleeping with another man in her own home. Nothing like too much drink to sort out a domestic.

She keeps her voice low. Has he said anything to you about —

No, I reply, getting my bag. And I wish she'd stop bringing it up and making me feel like I'm her co-conspirator. A goodnight and I'm gone. As I walk on the sandstone stepping-stone slabs to the gym, I feel like I'm being followed, I turn around and see the fox dart into the shadows.

Hi Trimble, I whisper, and reach for a packet of peanuts in my bag. I sprinkle them in the secret garden. It's just for us two now. For the privacy of this family. I stand back and it slowly ventures into the secret garden. When it sees me, it pauses. I don't move. I'm not a threat. It sniffs the peanuts. It makes a choice. It

197

slinks forward, keeping an eye on me the whole time and it eats while I watch. My phone rings suddenly and the fox darts away.

I grunt with annoyance and answer the phone.

You don't sound very happy, Pops says.

The ringtone chased away the fox.

What fox.

I've been feeding a fox in the garden.

You shouldn't encourage it, Allegra.

Just like you shouldn't encourage the lamb.

A lamb is not a fox. One of the greatest lessons I thought I could teach you, Allegra, is when to recognise the difference.

I know the difference between a lamb and a fox, thank you.

But do you, he says and leaves a pause. Anyway, I'm calling you to tell you I spoke with Pauline and she wanted me to tell you that the politician, eh . . .

Ruth Brasil, I say quickly, excited.

Yes, Ruth Brasil, was in the Mussel House over Easter and Pauline passed on your letter. What's that about, Allegra.

I dance around the room listening to Pops waffle on about me befriending foxes and writing to politicians and he really wishes Pauline would have told me herself and maybe I'm right, maybe she is avoiding me, and on and on.

When I wake in the morning, I check Instagram before my eyes have unstuck themselves and I see a red number one beside the arrow signalling private message.

The Happy Nomad has said: *Freckles! so good to hear from you.*

Yes! I punch the air and leap out of bed.

* * *

It's a beautiful morning. It's bright, sunny, hot — a heatwave, they say. The first week of May. Cherry blossoms bloom. I even say hello to the man in the suit with the backpack and jaunty walk. He looks confused, as if he thinks I've mistaken him for someone else. But that's okay. I smile at the jogger. She smiles back. I pat the Great Dane. I ask the owner how old he is. Three years. What's his name. Tara, he says. We laugh. Good morning, good morning, beautiful morning, to the old man and his son.

I bounce along to my next destination, the Village Bakery. Whistles is outside eating a cream éclair, a steaming black coffee beside him on the ground.

Spanner is beside him, smoking. He flicks his smoke, Whistles goes for the end.

Spanner holds the door open for me with a Howya, Freckles, and we go inside.

He pours the batter into the waffle machine, even though I haven't ordered. He knows me. It's this simple act that makes me feel closer to him. Close enough to suddenly start talking about my recent visit to Pops and unload my worries about him. About how quickly he changed as soon as I left. How quickly he could lose everything if he doesn't have people around him.

Ye see it's the fuckin stress, Freckles. It's the stress that'll do it to ye. Cancers, strokes, Whistles.

While Spanner works he unloads more of his worries about his restraining order. He hasn't been able to see Ariana since the Irish dancing feis because of the order against him coming near Chloe. He can't even contact her directly, so has tried to get friends and his ma to contact her. Have his ma pick up Ariana,

199

but Chloe's having none of it. You know what, all you women — sorry, Allegra — but you with your rights and unequal this and unequal that, it's fucking fathers who need to have the next revolution. I've never had a restraining order against me in my life and I've put Deano's head through a window, the thieving fucker, even though it turned out it wasn't him.

You're right, I say, to his surprise. My Pops raised me on his own.

Power to the Pops, he says, raising his fist, tattooed biceps winking at me.

But you need a solicitor, I tell him again.

All of a sudden, I feel a thump in my back as a fella comes rushing by me. The coffee splashes up from the drinking hole in the cup onto my skin. It burns. I shake my hand in the air, suck my scalded skin.

Oi you, he shouts, firing himself into the shop, finger pointing at Spanner, all aggressive. What have you been saying about me.

Well if it isn't the paedo muppet, Spanner says, a glint in his eye but a tone in his voice I've never heard from him before. It's dangerous.

I'll fuckin kill you, the fella yells.

Spanner removes the dishcloth from his shoulder, opens his arms out in a welcoming pose. Bends at the knee, muscles in his thighs tensing. Go on and try it.

How do I get in there, the fella spits, pacing up and down the counter.

Spanner picks up a whisk, waves it around like he's Bruce Lee and it's a nunchuck, then he throws it at his enemy. It makes a sad sound against his chest. Splashes him with egg batter.

Fortunately — or unfortunately for the fella, who I now realise is Chloe's boyfriend — he can't get to

Spanner. The counter spans the entire width of the shop; the only way to the other side is at the end of the counter by unlocking the door in the lower half and lifting the counter, but he's so consumed by his red mist he can't figure that out. So he lashes out, arm swinging over the counter, body somehow miraculously going halfway over it too. The beautiful carrot cakes lining the top shelf get smushed. It's such a shame, they were so pretty. The banana bread and the blueberry muffins are lost too in his second attempt to slide over, arm swinging and punching the air.

He's having the greatest kerfuffle with confectionery that I've ever seen, and he seems to be losing.

Should I call the guards, I ask.

They're only down the road, I could be there in minutes. I'd love the excitement of including the Gardaí, another chance to spend time with Laura, and I could impress them with what I've witnessed, but I don't think Spanner would want them on his premises. Not with the looming custody battle. He doesn't hear me anyway.

Spanner laughs loudly, taunting him. A bad idea. Because suddenly the lad has pulled himself over the counter, his T-shirt covered in sugar, cream and jam. The sweetest-looking bad guy you ever did see. Spanner looks dangerous. He has too many items at his disposal. A bread knife, jagged and sharp, used for the thick doorstep loaves he baked that morning. The boiling hot water in the coffee machine beside him. Frankly a sourdough thrown at speed to the head would knock a man out. I see him registering everything, his eyes quickly moving left and right. Don't mess with the village baker. His legs are wide and bent, a strong stance, arms out and ready. The size of him, all muscle ripping from his white T-shirt and his jeans. His hands opening and closing into fists as he moves from side to side like a tennis player waiting a serve.

Maybe I should have run to the station.

Don't, Spanner, I say, and he looks up at me, as if suddenly remembering I'm here and where he really is. Think of Ariana, I say.

Hearing her name does something different to both of them. It fires up Chloe's boyfriend, who goes for Spanner, charges at him, but he slips on what I assume is a very messy floor and goes down. The sound of her name softens Spanner somewhat. The difference between choosing the bread knife and the banoffee pie, with its beautiful topping of perfect cream peaks and chocolate shavings, and he shoves it in his face.

You muppet. Get out of here, he says, the danger gone from his voice.

His opponent blinded by the cream, Spanner drags him out the back door.

I watch the door, waiting to see what happens, listening for the worst.

Spanner returns and looks down at the floor. He swears quietly, then back at me.

Sorry about that, he sniffs, straightens his apron, his hat. Could have been worse, he says. I was this close.

I'd seen the way he'd looked at that bread knife. He's lost his bravado of earlier and seems shaken up by what could have happened, what he could have done.

Thanks, Freckles, he says. I mean it.

★ ★ ★

202

I take the coffee, still hot and untouched, and the waffle, and carry it to James's Terrace. Despite the drama in the bakery I'm on a high about my Instagram friend. I want to share the news with Tristan that the second of my five came through.

As I pass the garda station the door opens and out step two familiar faces. Garda Murphy, I say loudly, and she looks up.

Hi, Allegra, Laura says, and I'm so chuffed she's remembered my name. My heart soars, I could honestly dance. Maybe I'll be three for five by the end of the day. Back on the beat, I say.

Just finishing she says, got to get home to the little ones. Her partner ignores me and goes round the other side of the garda car. She stops at the driver's door, in the driving seat. I like that. Well done, Laura.

You know where I am if you need me, I add, as she gets inside, signalling my ticket machine and referring to the last conversation we had where I offered to help them.

Thanks, Allegra, she says with a smile and I feel pumped.

Yellow Ferrari is there, Tristan's in. So, unlike the fella I first thought he was, he didn't earn his Ferrari by being a flake. Still, good work ethic doesn't earn him the right to drive a banana-yellow car. That will never be cool. I hop up the steps to number eight and ring the doorbell. No one answers. I ring again.

Jazz, I hear Tristan's voice yell. The door. Where are you. He pulls it open, I think I'm happier to see him than he is to see me and that maybe this visit is one too many, but I know he'll care.

Hi, I say, upbeat.

I'm doing my make-up, Jazz yells from somewhere

inside the building. You can open the door yourself, can't you.

He closes his eyes and that face, the hulk face that lost it with me and ripped up his parking ticket, is suddenly visible beneath the usually kind face.

I brought you a coffee from the bakery I told you about. Much better than that muck you drink.

Who's that, Jazz yells and Tristan makes a decision. He steps outside and slams the door. He takes the coffee cup. Let's walk, he says.

He walks fast. I've long legs, and usually walk faster than most, but I run along beside him to keep up at one point. We walk to the seafront. He looks like he wants to wade right in and never come back.

Which way, he asks.

What do you mean. Where do you want to go.

With you. Want company for a while, he says. I could do with getting away from that lot.

Sure. Let's go this way, I say. We take a right, not because it's my route but because he looks like he could do with some coastal air and a long walk away from people, any people.

So. One of my five contacted me, I say, excitedly.

Your mum.

No.

Amal.

No.

Katie Taylor.

No.

The Minister for Justice.

No.

He rolls his eyes then. Your Pops called you.

No, I laugh. Well, he did, but that's not who. It's a girl from school, Daisy. She was the coolest girl in my

204

year — but cool in a good way because she was kind and nice and I think I wanted to be her. Anyway, I hunted her down, aka found her on Instagram.

Stalker, he says through a fake cough.

I followed her and when I woke up this morning she'd followed me back and sent me a private message.

That's great, Allegra, I'm happy for you. So are you going to meet . . .

I don't know.

Then what's the point of all this.

Maybe she can influence my life via Instagram.

Instagram influencers are not included. You've got to have real-life interaction with your five. You are the average of the people you spend the most time with, remember. Spend time with, he repeats. His eyes darken for a moment, as if he's just thought of something. Anyway, what's your Instagram account, he asks, taking out his phone.

I don't want to share it because it's not really me on the account. But he's not going to give up, and he's in on everything in this scheme so far, so I tell him.

He scrolls through his phone. I focus on the windscreens that we're passing, stopping occasionally to get a better look at a ticket.

Did you take these photos, he asks.

No. I got them online.

He stops walking and bends over laughing. He's laughing at me, which should sting, but the sight and sound of him in fits is irresistible, it's contagious, and I join him. He can barely speak, he's laughing so much. Allegra, I think you're missing the point of this.

I shrug.

What's her name.

Daisy.

On Instagram.

Oh. The Happy Nomad.

He frowns as he types, lips slightly pushed out, which makes me smile. He's fast at typing, fingers moving furiously, two-handed texter, flying across the buttons. Ah. There she is. He scrolls through his phone, zooms in, out, examines her from what seems like every angle in his mind.

She's nice, Tristan, I say. I looked up to her. I have zero friends right now.

He drops whatever smart remark he was about to make about the Happy Nomad. He taps away on his phone and then puts it back into his pocket. I'm following you now. You have two followers. This is really good coffee by the way.

Told you. Spanner in the Village Bakery.

What kind of name is Spanner.

What kind of name is Rooster.

What kind of name is Freckles.

What kind of name is Jazz.

He sucks in air. Jasmine.

So what's with the stinky mood this morning.

I called an early meeting. No one showed up. After yesterday, showing you around, I was embarrassed by their unprofessionalism. But it's hard to get your mates to work for you.

They're your friends.

Most of them from school. We grew up gaming together. My dream is their dream and as soon as I could set up this business, I asked them to work with me.

For you.

Yeah well.

206

For you.

Okay.

And your uncle with the fancy office with the best view in the building, who does he work for.

Well he's in kind of an advisory, consultant, management, agent type role. He did the deals for me from the beginning, organised the sponsorship. He's the one who saw the potential in a fourteen-year-old gamer on YouTube.

What does he do now in his big office.

He, well . . . he, well, there's no actual product yet for him to sell. All the games are in development — loads of them actually, are in development, some of the ones I showed you yesterday. I brought Andy and Ben in for that. They're qualified game software developers, they're focused on the more technical side of building the game, whereas I'm on the creative side. I need them all. The more time I'm away from gaming though, the less of a fan base I'll have, so my uncle is keeping that Rooster awareness campaign going. Conventions, sponsorships, the occasional game endorsement, teaming up with other YouTubers, that kind of thing.

And you pay him. He works for you. Just as your friends do. You're the boss.

I'm not. It's a different kind of business. I'm young, they're young, he's my uncle, my mum's his sister. I can't be . . . you know, barking at them. I prefer to create a place where people want to be. That's why we have the pets, the games room — they're allowed to have fun, so they want to come to work.

Only they don't.

I don't want them to be afraid of me. I don't want my mum to be stuck between me and my uncle.

They don't have to fear you to respect you. Jazz doesn't know her arse from her elbow, Andy's one of the rudest people I've ever met, and they're masquerading as people who know what they're doing.

You always say it how you see it.

Sugar-coating is for Belgian waffles, I say. Now I understand why the phrase was on your mind, why you passed it on to me. You are the average of the five people you spend the most time with. You're the one who has built a team around you. You're trying to surround yourself with a certain type of people to become a certain type of a person. But did you get the people right, I muse. Hmmm. Have you, too, become lazy, obnoxious and working in the business you used to love for all the wrong reasons.

Ouch, he smiles.

We walk in silence for a while.

You hated me before I said anything to you, he says.

That's true.

Why.

Your car.

Don't you think that's very closed-minded of you.

Yes, it is. Because you're actually quite okay.

He shakes his head and laughs.

It makes me confused about the yellow car. It doesn't seem to match who you are.

What's wrong with a yellow Ferrari.

What's right about it.

I bought the Ferrari because it was my dream to have a sports car. Like most boys. And when I bought it, I felt like it was the best moment in my life. That I'd made it. But you're right about it not fitting me and my life. I still live at home with my parents . . . Truth is, I can't drive it home because of the speed bumps in the housing estate, so I have to park it at a garage every day. I call my dad and he meets me there and drives me home on his way back from work. So much for independence and making it in the world.

I laugh.

And the reason it's yellow is because it was the only one they had in stock. I actually wanted a silver one. Gunmetal with a red interior, but I had to wait months for that . . . I was so excited, I couldn't wait. Shouldn't you be giving tickets or something, we're just walking here.

You know there are a lot of days when I don't issue many tickets. I'm not an animal.

What about them.

We look across to a van parked on a wide pavement. Two men are fitting windows to a house. When working with glass, I explain, rules state you must park very close to the spot, so they're allowed on the pavement.

Oh.

You're disappointed, I laugh.

I want to get someone. I want some action.

It's not about getting people, Tristan, it's about observing the law, respecting the rules.

You really believe that.

Of course, why do you look so surprised. You think I was doing this to catch people out. Rules are a gift. Wouldn't you love a rule book to help you out of your little hole at work right now. I mean, why else would you be looking for motivational quotes. You want to be guided. Isn't that just another way of following rules.

He gets the action he wants when we circle back to the village and see a white van parked on double yellow lines outside a house. Hazard lights on. The hallway door is open and the builder is inside sawing wood.

Go on, get him, Allegra, Tristan says, as if I'm a guard dog. Cats, he hisses in my ear.

I stop and watch the guy.

Come on, Tristan urges me.

Wait, I say, keeping an eye on the time. When two minutes is up, I approach him. Excuse me, I say, you can't park here on double yellow lines.

I was just loading, he says, barely meeting my eye.

No you weren't.

He looks at me like he wants to use the saw on me.

I was loading, he says slowly, as though I'm stupid. Therefore I can legitimately park. I'm old enough to know the rules of the road, young one.

I feel Tristan tensing beside me and I put my hand out to stop him from advancing. Let me, I say quietly.

I've observed you for two minutes and there are no signs of loading here.

I'm impassive as he roars at me, drops his stuff, grabs his keys, swears at me as he gets in the car and speeds off.

Jesus, Tristan says, watching him, anger pumping through him. Do you get many like him.

Sometimes, I smile. Sometimes people are nice and will apologise when I give them a ticket. Most are defensive and some are aggressive. It makes you realise what people are going through. It's a trigger that can let loose built-up stress, I say the words that Paddy said to me when he was training me. Now I understand them better. Oddly Tristan has helped me to understand that. Maybe you can learn about humans.

I don't think I'd have the temperament to be talked

to like that, he says, which I think is nonsense because I've witnessed his staff speaking to him in what I consider unacceptable ways but I don't say this.

Who was the worst person you ever had, he asks.

You, I say quietly. You got to me the most. And I walk on.

21

I browse through Daisy's Instagram photos to get a sense of what she wears on a night out. We're going out tonight, Saturday night. But first I have the live art session at Monty's. I no longer have the physically sick feeling when I think back to Tuesday night. The *I will never drink again* mantra has left me, which is timely because I'm going to need some Dutch courage to meet up with Daisy after all this time. Her life is phenomenal. She works with an international aid charity, she travels the world. She's selfless and sophisticated. She has a level of class that I just don't have and I'm hoping some of that can rub off on me. Right after I pose nude for a group of strangers, some of whom I've slept with.

We're meeting in a place called Las Tapas de Lola, on Wexford Street at 8 p.m. I've had tapas plenty of times before, in fact Pops used to bring me to tapas restaurants and order the Catalonian specials, even encouraged me to take Spanish lessons in school in an effort to feed my cultural heritage. When it came to eating out I chose the Pakistani restaurant, and at school I chose to learn French instead. I don't know, maybe I was trying to reject Carmencita like she rejected me. Maybe I was afraid that I wouldn't be able to learn the language and I'd fail again without her knowing.

Maybe I just wanted to learn French and eat different food.

But first I must face the gallery. The details of our

night out are still pretty hazy and I cringe as snippets of conversations with Genevieve and Jasper come back to me. Things I said and shouldn't have said, things I don't think I even meant but liked the feeling of saying aloud. I arrive very close to starting time, deliberately so, less time to chat. I hope when I enter Jasper is busy with a customer but I'm afraid not. He looks up: hi Allegra, hi Jasper. Cringey-cringe-cringe. I walk up the steps, out of his view. Genevieve is on her phone, thankfully, talking to an artist, rolling her eyes at me as he or she blathers on. For someone who loves art, she has complications with the artists. Needy fuckers, she always calls them.

I disappear behind the changing screen. The room is being aired, the chairs and easels are set up. I feel an uneasiness about doing this today; it's difficult to sit and wait when you're excited for something. Time goes especially slow. I never had a problem sitting in all the weeks and months before, because there was nothing to be excited about.

I came across the job advertisement before I left Valentia when I was looking for accommodation. For the first two weeks in Dublin I was house sharing with two professionals from the tech sector, so the advertisement said. They were looking for a male or female, 125 euro per week for a box bedroom with a single bed . . . It didn't go down well when she found me in my single bed in my box bedroom with him. They never said they were together. Not once. Never shared a touch or kiss in my company. They had separate rooms. How was I supposed to know. I was happy enough to leave. I lived there for a month, during training, and when I was placed in Fingal for work it made sense to move out there. I got the job at the gallery to cover the cost of the house share, paid them in cash. Thought I was being clever but Dublin's expensive, money goes fast. A coffee, a sandwich, a small run to the shop and bam it's gone.

I remove my clothes behind the screen and listen to Genevieve discuss a picture frame for longer than a frame ever needs to be discussed.

I moisturise my skin and wrap the kimono around me just in time to hear the artists arrive. Genevieve tells Vincent she must go but she'll call him later to pick up where they left off.

Needy fucking artists, she mumbles as she hangs up.

Hi Allegra, sorry about that. Bloody Vincent.

I heard.

She dips her head behind the screen, and gives me a once-over and asks if I'm ready.

I nod.

The session passes by surprisingly fast as I think about the conversation Daisy and I can have, which parts of me and my life I'll tell her and which parts I'll edit, and before I know it I've been captured . . . pensive, is the word I'd give their overall depictions of me. One is quite forlorn, I look lost in a whirlpool of pencil, and a man who has given me a sympathetic stare throughout has drawn my scars as deep incisions, battle wounds, raw.

★ ★ ★

I arrive at the restaurant early so that I can settle myself and my nerves, but Daisy is there already. Oh my God, Freckles, look at you! She stands up and opens her arms wide and gives me the tightest hug.

214

She smells flowery and sweet. Her arms jangle with layers of delicate bangles, one with a star, one with a moon, one with the sun, one with a flower. She steps back and takes me in. You look amazing, your hair . . . She reaches out to touch it gently. Wow. It's been way too long, can you believe it's been almost seven years since we left. So good to see you, I can't wait to hear what you've been up to, let's sit, do you want a drink, I ordered tap water, the food here is delish, have you been here before.

No, never, are my first words as I sit down and she waves for the waiter. A pretty smile, a delicate movement of her hand. Can we get another glass for the table, it's missing, thank you, here's the wine menu, she offers it to me.

I wonder if I should drink even though she doesn't. I order a glass of Cava and Daisy tells the waiter to bring a bottle.

We get down to the fine art of studying the menu before we begin the conversation. I order Manchego cheese with honey and traditional Barcelona spicy meatball with alioli sauce. She orders chorizo in white wine, prawns with garlic, chilli and olive oil, mussels with house marinara sauce and I lose track there as she signals for more throughout the meal.

We do the usual expected chat, talking about the big characters from school, who we've kept in contact with and who we've seen or heard about, what everyone's up to. There's no break in the conversation, I don't know what I had to worry about.

So enough about everybody else, Freckles, she says, what have you been up to. When did you move to Dublin.

I moved to Dublin five months ago, I say. I just got

the urge for a change. I'm working for Fingal County Council as a parking warden and really love the job.

This part of my life I'm proud of. I love my job.

Wow. A parking warden. She says, then her eyes run over me quickly and I'd love to know what she's thinking. Didn't you always want to be . . .

Detective Freckles, yes. We laugh. And you always wanted peace and equality in the world, I say.

Ha yes, she nods, and in real life that means building. I work with Brick-by-Brick, an international human rights organisation that focuses on building and rebuilding homes, schools, care centres, sanitation facilities and community buildings in developing countries. So I've gone from wanting peace and equality to making bricks, plastering and painting. She tenses her tiny little biceps in her arms. I can't imagine her doing any of that.

That's amazing, I say in awe. I spend my days distributing parking tickets.

All self-effacing, it's no big deal, she wants to move on.

What an amazing job you have, I say, hating how much of a sycophant I sound but genuinely meaning it. Visiting somewhere different all the time. Seeing the world, helping people.

They are all things that I'd hate but that's the point of the five people theory, isn't it, they're supposed to rub off on you in some way. I have Pops for honesty and for grounding me, he's not a yes-man, and Daisy can be my source of inspiration, my person who can give me aspirational thoughts about being better than I am. It's happening already. I mean, I don't want to move to a developing country to build a school, but I'd like to think that I could find it in me to want

216

to help communities fighting poverty and disaster. I could be that person.

Georgie, she says happily, all of a sudden.

A guy who has just walked in pulls a chair from the table next to ours, gives Daisy a kiss on the cheek, and sits beside us.

I'm with these guys, he says to the waiter in a posh Dublin accent. She asks if he'd like to see a menu and he says uh no thanks. I'm fine with the wine. He takes a wine glass from the empty table beside us and places it down beside him. Hi, he gives me a big smile, whiter than white teeth. Tanned skin. Smooth skin. Heavily moisturised. Shiny. I'm George. Friend of Daisy's. He holds out his hand.

Georgie this is Freckles, Freckles this is Georgie.

Nice to meet you, I say.

Nice to meet you, he imitates my accent. A bad posh Dublin version of a Kerry accent. He makes me sound like Darby O'Gill. He laughs and drains his glass.

I hate him instantly. He oozes asshole.

Take a photo of us for Insta, she says, thrusting her phone at him and coming round my side of the table. She pushes her head close to mine, I feel her forehead against mine. Higher up, she tells him, and he stands and points it down at us at what feels like an unnatural angle so that I feel like I'm straining my eyes and looking up through my eyelids. I feel awkward, not sure if she's smiling big or not at all, I want to look at her to check but don't. I'm not sure what I settle on, but if I was to be painted, uncertainty would be the air.

She examines the photo, I wait for her to laugh at my face, or say something but she doesn't, she twiddles around with it. Posted! Right, she drops it into her bag. Shall we move on. We ask for the bill. When it arrives, she grabs it in that way that people who insist on paying do. Halves yeah, she says, taking it and calculating it on her phone. I had two dishes and a bottle of Cava, of which I had two glasses, her friend Georgie Porgie downed the rest. She had two espresso Martinis and so many dishes we had to place them on the next table. I reluctantly hand over my card feeling the heat of injustice. They both go to the toilet before we leave and I wait outside. I check Instagram. She's tagged me in her photo.

Caption: *Old friends. Good times.* A peace sign and kissy lips. I look stilted and awkward beside her. Straight back and rigid, when she's all loose and cool. I post it to my own Instagram. Rooster is one of the first to comment with a thumbs-up emoji. Suddenly I have eight new followers, girls from school I half-remember and some I'd forgotten about.

Freckles!! oh my God!! blast from the past! one says. I don't know who it is, her ID is nutty_for_nutrition and her profile pic is an avocado. When I click into her account it's magazine-type photos of food and I still can't figure out who she is. Not until I scroll down and see the gym workout photos, the abs, the muscles, the weights. It's Margaret, who used to stuff her face at night with mini Crunchies. Well well well.

Finally George and Daisy emerge, linking arms.

I just got a message from Margaret Mahon, I tell her. She's changed. And we talk about Margaret until Georgie yawns in our faces and tells us that talking about old times is as interesting as listening to peoples' dreams. We arrive at our next destination. I offer to buy the drinks and I'm glad when she says she only wants water. I don't ask George because I think

218

George and I know where we stand but he announces he wants a gin and tonic anyway, Jawbox gin specifically. As I go to order, I see Daisy casually swipe someone's drink from the bar. It has a beermat over the top, which suggests they're outside smoking. She does it so effortlessly. I watch her drinking fast, downing it and placing the empty glass on a table far from where she stole it. I find Daisy and George outside talking to a group of people whose names I instantly forget. George was specific about the slice of cucumber in his gin and he takes a sachet of red peppercorns from the inside of his jacket pocket and drops them into his drink. The only thing that makes me feel better is knowing that I ordered the cheapest gin there was, not the Jawbox he requested.

He doesn't bother making conversation with me. He talks loudly and obnoxiously, the life and soul of the party to the group, while I have a quieter conversation with a girl who's expecting her first baby and can't wait to go home. The fellas in here seem to be playing who has the most tanned skinniest shaved ankles in the room as I notice all the guys are wearing short trousers and no socks. I try to think of anyone on Valentia dressed like this in our local and I have to fight the smile from my face, Jamie with his bandy chicken legs, hairy delicate little ankles, and Cyclops with his skeleton calves that wouldn't look good in a pair of skinny jeans. How we'd laugh about this — but we won't, because we're not friends any more. I've lost that five, I'm searching for a new five. Am I going to find it here. I down my drink and I'm glad when Daisy takes my arm and pulls me away. We're off to a new place and this is how it goes for the next few hours.

If I was to sketch Daisy, I'd draw her perfectly still and then scribble over her. If she got one thing right on her Instagram feed it's her bio: here, there, everywhere. It's when she bundles me into the toilet cubicle with her and takes something from her cross-body bag that I realise I'm an idiot. Of course. Cocaine. I'm not anti-drugs, I've had my moments with Cyclops, but never cocaine. There's something a bit tosspot about it for me. A bit too Dublin arsehole. Ironically, aside from the dinner bill, it's the first thing in the whole night she's been happy to share with me. Well two things; a cubicle and cocaine. I watch the back of her perfect head as she sniffs the powder up her nose. I kind of deflate. I thought Daisy was different, I thought Daisy was someone I could aspire to be. This messy act of hers is too easy. Is too mundane. Is too nothing. I could find this girl just about anywhere.

I think of drawing her again. If I was to draw her, I would draw her perfectly, then I would take an eraser and run it over her. Rub her out in places, but not completely. She's here but not here. Stable in places, lost in others. She offers the powder to me but I shake my head. She doesn't push. No big deal but maybe she feels judged as I watch her sniff my line off the top of a manky toilet. When I step out of that cubicle the real me steps out. And perhaps the real her does too. No pretence now, we're on an even footing. She can do her and I'll do me.

The rest of the night is an incomplete jigsaw. Holes in a picture that stop me from seeing the entire image in its totality. A series of places that not so much as blur smoothly into each other but jut sharply in and out of each other. At one stage we call by a dingy building that ends up being Daisy's place. She shares a bunkbed with a stranger, a Chinese girl who's shouting at us for turning on the light while she's trying to sleep. George is laughing, and so is Daisy. She's searching under her mattress for something, I don't know what, I assume drugs or money and I leave the room when the roommate throws a hot-water bottle. It just misses my head and then explodes against the wall, and I feel scalding water drip onto my arm. There's a shower at the foot of their bed, a microwave on a desk. Daisy gets a drawer in the hallway outside. She tells me this as she rifles through all those beautiful Instagram clothes that are under lock and key in this dusty drawer in the hallway, not looking so picturesque right now.

I say to George somewhere that working for charity obviously comes at a price, and I admire Daisy for giving up her life to help others. I'm not sure I believe what I'm saying but I'm still hopeful that the vision I had of Daisy can be salvaged anyway. George laughs at me. Daisy, work, he asks, she hasn't got a job. Her parents pay for her to go and volunteer to make it look like she's actually doing something with her life. They treat it like rehab. She doesn't have a choice.

At some point, outside, linking arms, walking to the next destination, I ask Daisy about Finn. Her boyfriend from school. Perfect Daisy and perfect Finn, Sandy Olsson and Danny Zuko, the dream couple of our year. Does she ever see him, what's he doing with his life. The last delusion of her, I suppose. And then the final petal falls and the beauty truly becomes the beast.

Oh my God, she says. Finn O'Neill. He was done for possession of cannabis, that's why we broke up. All hush-hush of course. He was up in court on intent to supply. He was facing five years in prison. Last time I saw him was a few months ago and he was standing on a bar pissing on someone's head.

I remember laughing at what she was saying, laughing because it was all so ridiculous, not funny. I dreamed of being in a relationship like Daisy and Finn's, just as most girls in my year did, we collectively grieved for them when they broke up. And now here we are, turning over the rock to find the woodlice beneath.

We end up in a dark sweaty basement club called Moonshine that plays dance music with a beat so monotonous I have to leave. I don't know where Daisy and George have gone to and to be honest I don't search too hard. I've had enough. So I leave alone and start walking to D'Olier Street for the Nitelink home.

As I'm walking I can hear laughing. At first I think it's nothing to do with me and then I realise it's directed at me. I don't turn around, I don't want to be drawn into a 3 a.m. street fight. And then I can't take it any more, what is so very funny about the way I'm walking. If these Dublin gobshites want a fight I'll give them a fight, this evening has not been what I wanted it to be, I'm ready to knock somebody out. I spin around and catch sight of Daisy and George hiding behind a rickshaw, then see them from the corner of my eye as they race across the street to a bin. They're playing spies, and it's all so childish that I can't help but laugh. They want to continue the party, back at my place.

It's my stupid ego that makes me say yes. I've put Daisy up on a pedestal. Her job, her clothes, her Instagram account, while I'm nothing. But now I want her to see my life in comparison to her rat piss ugly room.

We lose George outside a bar when he stops to talk to some people and I guide Daisy away. As we walk further from him, I'm hopeful she's going to be better without him, that it'll be easier to have her to myself. Maybe she'll go back to nice Daisy once she's sobered up and has gone thirty minutes without putting something up her greased lightning, boho chic Daisy. Happy nomad.

22

The pay-off is, when she sees the house, she's impressed. I have to tell her to keep her voice down. I have to tell her to shut up rather forcefully. It's 4 a.m., the family are all in bed. They have kids. It will be bright soon. Shut up please. In the gym she puts full lights on and climbs on machines, drops weights with a clang. Like a monkey let loose. I follow her around, tidying up, putting things back, telling her to keep it down, trying to drag her from the gym. I see the light go on in Becky's bathroom and I quickly turn off the gym lights and hustle Daisy upstairs. Regardless of the fact I'm not smiling or replying, Daisy talks incessantly until 5 a.m., about nothing really, if I think about it. Then she takes her clothes off and falls asleep in her underwear in my bed. I take the couch. Even though I'm exhausted and hungover, I wake early. I make a pot of coffee and keep an eye on Daisy. I needn't have tiptoed around, a herd of elephants wouldn't have woken her. I have to violently shake her awake at noon. I need to leave for Paddy's barbecue.

Daisy is quiet. I give her a coffee. She looks out the window and slowly wakes up, I wonder if she's recalling events from last night. Bit by bit, like it happens for me. Never in the right order and never completely recovered. I await the realisation. The apology. The some sort of something. But she doesn't apologise. Doesn't appear to be embarrassed. Nothing. Apart from a little smudged mascara in the cracks beneath her sleepy eyes, she's make-up free and perfect. Apple faced, high cheekbones, plump juicy lips. Seemingly no conscience. She sips her coffee.

I offer to book her a taxi. I tell her where the bus stop is. Where the train station is. I google the timetables on my phone. I'm doing everything to get rid of her. She doesn't really respond to anything, well she does, but she doesn't commit. The same Jedi mind trick from last night where she has the ability to change the subject without appearing rude. It's like nothing sits with her, nothing stays, everything is fleeting. Maybe she's stalling. Maybe she doesn't want to get back to her shithole room to her flatmate who'll be raging with her today, but I don't care about the hole she's dug for herself. I need her to leave, I have a place to be. I promised Paddy and even though I have never wanted to go to anything he's invited me to, I feel a sense of duty today.

Where are you going, she asks.

It's my colleague's birthday. Paddy. He's having a barbecue.

Her eyes light up. I love barbecues.

And that's how it happens.

⋆   ⋆   ⋆

I'm grateful Becky and the kids have gone out, I don't need to hang my head in shame again as I exit.

Wow, Daisy says as we near the house, she leaves the path that I'm supposed to stay on for the privacy of the family, and moves closer to the house.

Don't, you'll set the alarm off, I say quickly.

She hears me but she keeps walking.

Daisy, I grab her arm and pull her back. They have

225

an alarm set, sensors all around the house, I say. If you pass them, you'll set off the alarm.

She laughs. I bet they've made it up.

It's true, I say. It's linked to a security company who alert the guards. Come on.

The guards, she laughs. You're making that up.

I'm not.

She looks at the house as if it's tempting her. She looks at it like a little child who's just been told they can't do something and they're going to do it anyway. I watch her, that intense face, the selfish gaze of wanting what she wants because she wants it, because I said she couldn't. All wrapped up in this ethereal-looking thing, in last night's clothes that look fresh as, well, a Daisy.

Girls like her get away with murder.

She steps in front of the sensor. And the alarm instantly wails.

It's the wide-eyed innocent whoops that makes me want to throw a whisk at her tits.

* * *

I don't hang around for the guards to arrive. I text Paddy to see if it's okay for me to bring a friend and he replies the more the merrier with two lines of food emojis. We stop at a shop on the way to get a present, it's a fancy shop where they do expensive gourmet foods. Daisy trails along, tiredly, as I browse the shelves.

He loves marinades, I say to her, he'd marinade something for a year if he could. That and simmering. I think he simmered a lasagne for twenty-four hours. He loves food, he doesn't stop talking about food and how he cooks it.

Do I sense a little . . . She raises her eyebrows suggestively.

God no, it's Paddy, I laugh. Wait till you see him. I work with him. We're not even friends.

I spend a bit more than I was planning to on the marinades. On behalf of me and Daisy, seeing as she doesn't buy anything for him. I've never been to Paddy's home. I've tried to imagine it a few times, what it would look like but other than his love of food, I don't know very much about his life. As a blow-in to Dublin, Paddy proudly tells me all about where he's from. The Liberties is a city neighbourhood. It's the heart of the city, he'd say. On my first few weekends here I took his advice and explored the areas he told me to and he was right, the heart of the Liberties is the heart of Dublin's history; art, political, religious, military history. And as Paddy says, full of the most down to earth, salt of the earth, honest to goodness, funniest people you'll ever meet. He'd never leave it because he'd miss it something terrible.

We arrive at a ground-floor flat of a four-storey block of 1940s council flats. The flat next door has been boarded up, with smoke stains around the walls.

The last barbecue didn't go so well, Paddy jokes when we arrive and takes the marinades with absolute glee.

The weather is balmy, it's sunny and it's perfect barbecue weather. We're not the only ones with the idea, I can smell barbecues from every direction of the city. The flat has a small paved square yard, that proves to be a baking tin for the heat. A gate leads to an alleyway that runs behind the back yards. Kids play football, the gate rattles and bangs as the football occasionally

227

hits against it. The gate's rusted hinges are off and it needs a sand and repaint. Daisy takes a bottle of beer and leans against the splintered wood. She makes it look like a cool rustic location shoot, reclaimed wood is all the rage, and asks me for a photo. I'm fixing my hair, bringing it over one shoulder just as she's done when she hands her phone to me and I realise she wants me to take the photo of her.

Paddy notices and takes the phone from me, pushes me in beside her and I awkwardly pose against the door, beside her, wondering how she manages to hide the fact that the rusted hinges hot from the sun are searing into her skin as it is with mine. She examines the photo, with a grimace.

Paddy has set up a small BBQ covered by a golf umbrella, which is dangerously balanced between two TK Red lemonade bottles.

It's just us and Paddy.

Is anyone else coming, Daisy asks me.

My best pal Decko is in the loo, Paddy answers. Mammy is coming. Out for the day. And I invited Fidelma, he says, moving the sausages on the grill. She works with us. She'll drop by later.

I've never seen Paddy out of his work uniform. He's wearing a Dublin football jersey, a size too small and that's being kind, with a sweat patch across his back and under his moobs. His glasses steam up over the barbecue and sweat drips down his face. His sandals are Birkenstock. I'm afraid to look at his toes. There's no shade in this space, only the sizzling meat has the benefit of the umbrella's shade.

Decko steps outside, head down, eyes on the ground, hands in his pockets then out again, then in again, then scratches his face, then his head. Fidgety, nervous. Paddy introduces us and he nods, howya, barely able to look us in the eye. Not rude, but achingly shy. I try making small talk with him, and he's nice, he warms up a little, but Daisy is just achingly rude.

Ah here's Mammy now, Paddy says, as an old woman in a wheelchair is pushed to the door that meets the patio area and is left there, as a woman, presumably her carer, faintly visible in the darkened house, lifts a hand and leaves.

Thanks, Cora, Paddy calls. See you later.

So now it's me, Daisy, Paddy, Decko and Mammy. I look over at Daisy. Maybe yesterday I would have felt embarrassed by this party in front of her. But I don't today. She's texting, not paying the slightest attention to anyone around her.

Hiya Mammy, Paddy says, kissing her. Mammy says nothing but her jaw works left to right as if she's a cow chewing on cud. Wiry hairs on her wrinkled chin and lips all pulled in as if a drawstring around her lips. Looks like she has no teeth. We're having a barbecue, Mammy, you like sausages don't you, he asks.

She looks up at him then, a flicker of recognition in an otherwise confused state. She either recognises him or sausages. I think of Pops and his mice and hope it doesn't come to this. It would hurt me, scare me if Pops didn't recognise me. He's all I have. What happens when the person who knows and loves you the most, the number one of your five, no longer knows who you are. Would it mean I'm erased.

The doorbell rings. I know who this is, Paddy announces again, genuinely excited at the guest arrival part of his day.

When I hear the voice at the other side of the door

my stomach flips. Georgie.

I look at Daisy, open-mouthed. How did he know we were here, I ask.

I texted him the address, he's going to drive me home, she says, and I feel relieved that she's going to leave and not at all insulted.

In Georgie strides, in his tight shorts and T-shirt, body popping with muscles, thick neck from his rugby days, if he ever played. Collar up on his pink polo shirt. Slip-on shoes. Boat shoes. In case he's going to be hopping on a yacht here in the Liberties. Plastic bags clinking in his hands.

Good afternoon all, he says confidently. What a smashing day. It smells good, Paddy, he says as if he's known Paddy forever. I brought the Heino.

He doesn't work here. His confidence, his accent, his voice, his posture, his energy. It doesn't fit into this small yard, or this neighbourhood. The perfect gentleman, he thinks, as if butter wouldn't melt, but to me he's all rotten inside. All private school politeness, all dirty spoiled privileged cock on the inside and he shouldn't be here with real honest to goodness people.

The doorbell rings again and I offer to get it, to escape the maddening sense of anger that's rising in me for this guy I barely know. If Decko doesn't give him a hiding, I will.

I open the door and Fidelma's there with her daughter in her Holy Communion dress, hands pressed together in white-gloved hands in prayer, a position she's been no doubt forced to take for every door they knock on. Decko, Georgie and Daisy, Paddy, me, Fidelma and her daughter Matilda all stand around sweltering outside, not a spot of shade in sight, not a bit of breeze. Mammy's in the kitchen wearing a heavy cardigan and drinking water through a straw.

Time for food I reckon, Paddy says. He hands the food around on kids' paper party plates. I try to make polite chit-chat with Fidelma who works in reception in Fingal County Council. I ask one question about the Communion and she goes through the entire Communion ceremony for me, from prayers to songs. Matilda spills tomato ketchup on her white dress and cries. Decko doesn't want anything with lettuce, peppers or onions. He doesn't eat vegetables. He tries the burger and won't eat it because there's something on the meat. Paddy tells him it's been marinated that's all, but he won't finish it. He lights up a cigarette instead. The lack of breeze keeps the cigarette haze trapped in the hot square and at some stage we all cough. Paddy makes a joke about opening the gate and letting the heat out but that's as far as he goes to complaining.

The food is delicious. The best barbecue I've ever had. Even the gherkins are a taste sensation. I eat every morsel and lick my fingers and hold my plate out for more to a deliriously happy Paddy. George eats the steak, no carbs, and declares it to be smashing. But his overuse of the word dilutes its genuineness. Daisy demolishes her chicken and I see her wrap a sausage in a napkin and put it in her bag when she thinks no one is looking. I try at one stage to get a group conversation going about Daisy's charity work. Her next trip is Nepal to help build and repair classrooms damaged by earthquakes. I'm sure Matilda would like to have heard about her building schools but the Happy Nomad is no more interested in talking about her volunteering adventures then Decko is in trying a barbecued banana for dessert.

231

Fidelma's chest is burning in the sun. It's sizzling and starting to bubble with a heat rash. She swiftly leaves with Matilda. I give Matilda a fiver, it's all I have spare. Decko gives her something too. Paddy of course has a card ready for her, but Daisy and George don't even notice the guests leave. The party is over but they don't pick up on the social cue to go. Or even when I say let's go.

Instead, George blares music from his iPhone and they begin dancing to 'Rhythm is a Dancer' in their own worlds thinking they're fun and fabulous, more fun than anyone ever placed on the universe. They look pathetic. Georgie's boat shoe accidentally kicks the barbecue legs. The barbecue falls over, makes an almighty noise as it clatters to the ground. Mammy gets a dreadful fright, she starts crying. Paddy goes for Mammy, Decko goes for the barbecue, George and Daisy are almost peeing themselves laughing.

George's boat shoe slips off and he trips over his own feet, falls back, his weight too much for the gate that is already hanging on one hinge, and the door falls inwards, towards Decko who is bent over picking up the barbecue.

I call out but it's too late. It bashes against his back, he lets out a yell and along with the sound of the gate against the metal barbecue, it sends Mammy into further distress. George and Daisy's wicked, twisted sense of humour perceives this Laurel-and-Hardy-like scene of devastation to be hilarious.

I look around the mess, the sound of Mammy crying, the sound of George and Daisy laughing uncontrollably, Decko groaning as he attempts to straighten his back, it's all horrific. Paddy's face.

Stop, guys, I say, but they don't hear me. They're

still snorting at what has happened. They're trying not to, of course, they know it's wrong, but that only makes them laugh more.

Stop it, I yell at the top of my voice.

Everybody stops doing everything. Daisy and George stop laughing. Mammy stops crying. Decko pauses fixing the barbecue, Paddy stops comforting his mammy. Everyone stares at me.

I think you should both leave now, I say to them, quieter now. More in control.

They look at each other and giggle again but I can see Daisy is changed. Something nasty in her stare.

Freckles, I don't even know why you brought me here, you said Paddy wasn't even your friend, she says, eyes wide again.

Paddy's face. It breaks my heart.

I leave through the hole in the wall where the rotten door was.

On the bus, I try to think of a message of apology to send to Paddy but I'm too embarrassed. There are no words that can fix what happened. He invited me into his world, I brought them into his world. I'm responsible. In my drafts in Instagram I have the photo of me and Daisy against the rustic gate along with the caption: old friends. New beginnings.

I delete it.

You are the average of the five people you spend the most time with.

I do not want to be like her.

I unfollow Daisy.

And I'm back to having one out of five.

23

I drag myself out of bed after pressing the snooze button three times. Pops called me during the night. It was still dark so sometime before 4 a.m. I'm grateful that this time it's not about the mice in the piano, though he's not sure if they're still there because he hasn't played recently, which worries me. I feel that his music would ground him again but he says he's had no time. He's been busy. He rages about another post office being closed.

They're ripping the heart out of Ireland, he says. Don't they realise, they're not just closing down a post office, they're closing down communities. I've joined a group. We're going on a march. In Dublin. I'll let you know when. We'll begin at Trinity College and make our way to Government Buildings, where I'll demand to speak with the minister. The island's being decimated, how is this place to attract a hub of new business if we don't even have a post office. They'd want to fix the Wi-Fi for a start.

And on and on it went, all pretty lucid until: I'll start a pigeon carrying service, that's what I'll do. First the closure of the transatlantic cable communications, that chased my family away from this island, and now the post office. What next. No car ferry. Will the islanders have to swim next. No no. I have to do something about this. No wonder the rats and mice are all moving in, they think the place is deserted, it's like the scavenger birds on a hunt. They're circling, Allegra, they can smell the rotting of community and of human decency . . . And so on.

After I've pressed the snooze button, I just lie there. I can't move. I don't want to move. My head is heavy and my body is weary. I'm physically and mentally drained. I want to stay in bed all day. I want to hide from the world. I want it to leave me alone. I'm trying, I really am, to get my shit together and be someone. Someone that I like. But I can't even do that. I've messed up at home, nothing there to return to. I've messed up with Daisy. With Paddy. I'm afraid to step outside in case I'm confronted by Becky about the alarm being set off yesterday. I have to babysit tonight and how can I face them. I'm afraid for Pops. I'm relieved the mouse hunt has ended, happy he has found a new goal. Joining a group means human inter-action, even if it's a small fringe group. But I don't know. I'm exhausted from it all. My careful life that I always worked hard to have under control is turning to shit.

It's Monday morning. Maybe everybody has the same fear. Maybe everybody wakes up and moves around with the same dread that this isn't what they had in mind. This life isn't going to plan and what was the fucking plan anyway. And then a cup of cof-fee and it's fine, a news story and it's fine, a favourite song and it's gone. An online purchase and it's no longer there. A chat with a friend and it's buried. A scroll through social media and remind me what was the problem again.

I check the postbox even though I know the postman hasn't been yet. You never know, Amal Ala-muddin Clooney, Katie Taylor or the Minister for Justice and Equality could have quietly hand-delivered their replies during the night. There's nothing in the

235

postbox and I feel the rejection three times. Boom, boom, boom. In the gut.

My sluggishness leads me to missing the man in the business suit, the jogger, Tara and her human, and the old man and his son. Missing them doesn't knock me off as it usually would, it seems fitting to my current mood. As I walk over the humpback bridge into the village I realise that I feel different. Lighter, but not spiritually. I've forgotten my backpack with my lunch and my wallet. I picture it sitting on the counter where I left it. I don't have time to walk back before my shift begins. Maybe I can go back at lunch but for now, no coffee. No waffle. No sugar-coating. No Band-Aid. My mood worsens.

Every driver will feel my wrath today, there will be no mercy. I do feel vengeful, I do feel hate. After all this work on myself, I'm back to only having one of five. It's pathetic that I ever thought I could control my life. Pathetic that I could ever be the person I want to be. Pops was right, I shouldn't have let that stupid phrase get in on me.

I don't hit James's Terrace until lunchtime and by then I'm so hungry my head is pounding. The yellow Ferrari has a pay-and-display parking ticket that ended an hour ago. His parking angels have let him down again. Instead of being angry at Tristan as I would have been — progress — I'm annoyed with his staff. His good-for-nothing lazy staff all riding on his coat-tails. I feel Andy and Ben's eyes on me as I storm up the steps. The door opens before I have to chance to press the bell.

Allegra, Jazz says with a disarming smile. Come in, she says cheerily.

I step inside. Her welcome replaces my anger with

suspicion. Perhaps he had a word with his staff. I'm proud. I was looking for Tristan, I say.

Rooster is in a meeting, she says, emphasis on the Rooster. How can I help you, she asks.

If there are problems, for whatever reasons, with posting the business parking permit forms, I say, trying not to sound catty, then there's an app that Tristan can use. He can pay for parking from the app on his phone. He'd probably prefer an app.

I'm trying to sell it to her. I'm trying to make her do something for Tristan. Something that will actually benefit him.

It's called Parking Tag, I continue, with a registered debit or credit card it will text him to remind him when his parking is going to expire.

Mmm. She's thoughtful. Come on upstairs. He's in a meeting with Tony so we can't disturb him, but we can set it up on his phone right now.

Pops used to say never confuse politeness with stupidity, just because you smile through an asshole comment doesn't mean you don't understand the insult. I'm not always the best with people, but I know that whatever lack of synchronicity I have with them doesn't mean I'm stupid. There's a catch here somewhere but I can't think of what it is and so I follow her upstairs, the pug at my heels. Tony's office door is closed, I can hear a quiet murmuring. I follow Jazz into Tristan's office.

His phone is in here she says, lifting it from the desk, and I can tell she's one of those girlfriends that rifles through everything, reads every text message and checks his social media accounts with the belief he belongs to her. She enters the pin code with her long apricot-coloured nails. She must know he follows

237

me on Instagram, she probably has noted every comment he's made so far. She's probably searched my posts psychotically and checked out my followers and who I'm following. She probably knows more about me than I do.

Here you go. She hands his phone to me, to my surprise.

Maybe I'm wrong about her. Maybe the hollow rumbling in my stomach is making me wrong about everything.

His credit card is here too, she says, opening a drawer. You should maybe use his business one, yeah. She looks at me and I'm not sure if it's a question. For a business expense, she adds.

Oh yeah, okay, I say, but I don't know about these things and I'm still suspicious of her intentions. I look at his phone in my hand thinking this is it, this is her trick, there's something on the phone she wants me to see, a screen saver photograph perhaps of the two of them together, or a text message she expects me to nosily discover, thinking that I'm like her but I'm not. She won't reel me in. I go straight to the app store feeling cocky and self-assured that I have dodged a bullet, I have not played into her hands.

What were you guys doing in here last week, she asks.

I try not to smile. A-ha. That's what she's up to, fishing for info. And so I supply it. He was showing me sample video games, I say.

Here's his card, she hands it to me.

I sit on the couch and concentrate on setting up the account. Name, registered business address, credit card details.

It's fun seeing how it all begins, isn't it, she says.

238

Yeah it really is. So interesting to see the inspiration for these things.

She's already turning the plasma on. Did you see this one, she asks.

I purse my lips to stop myself from smiling at how obvious she's being. She's testing me, did I really see the videos or were we screwing on the couch.

Music starts up, some fancy swishing sounds, but I keep my eyes down as I insert the long credit card number and then double-check that it's correct. I mean, I could be a fraud. I could steal his details right here right now and all she's worried about is whether I kissed her boyfriend or not.

This game is only early stages but Rooster is excited about this one, she says. It's been developed faster than any other game they have. I play this one a lot.

Now that gets my attention. I didn't think she was a gamer and I look up to see the words fire across the screen: Warden Wipeout. They diminish in a bloody slither down the screen.

So the idea of the game is to hunt down the parking warden when you get a parking ticket, she says perkily.

She's sitting on the arm of the chair, long shiny legs out before her. Ankle bracelets around her thin ankles. Handling the PlayStation controls like a pro.

I look at the screen, my mouth suddenly completely dry. Cotton mouth. I watch the half-developed town centre that looks like it's modelled on Malahide. A Main Street, a diamond shaped intersection and laneways growing from it. There's a lone person walking the paths, dressed in navy blue and a high-vis vest. There's a map on the top right hand of the screen with a red dot showing where the parking warden is.

And a timer. A countdown that tells you when the parking ticket has expired.

Suddenly a siren sounds, as she's issued a parking ticket. Jazz's avatar takes off in the direction of the target on the map, to the parking warden whose features come into view. The warden is female, she's dressed exactly as I am now. She has a nasty face, twisted in a scowl like a witch, a long nose and chin, all elongated bony features. It would scare children.

And freckles.

Look at this, Jazz laughs, and suddenly her avatar lashes out and punches the parking warden.

The warden's hat flies off and blood gushes from her face, flying into the air in a big red spray. The avatar high-kicks, gets her right in the stomach, and she doubles over, blood dripping from her mouth. The warden's equipment falls to the ground, the avatar picks it up, throws it at the warden's head. More blood and sprays, so that the warden's face is like a bruised plum. Then the avatar stomps on the equipment, stomp, crunch, smash. The warden starts to run away, tickets and papers flying around her like confetti. The screen vibrates with Warden Wipeout thumping high-paced music and the avatar — let's be honest, it's Jazz — continues her attack. Thumps, kicks, headlocks. The warden doesn't fight back, but she makes sounds. Yelps, oomphs and uhhs. Pained sounds with a horrified expression beneath the bloodied and bruised face. Then Jazz picks up a pay-and-display parking meter, uproots it from the concrete, and whacks it across the warden's head. The head flies off, blood sprays from her open neck, the headless body wobbles drunkenly around in circles on the pavement for a moment before collapsing in a heap on the ground, the head rolls.

I'm not a sensitive creature, usually, I can tell the difference between a game and reality, but this is a new kind of nasty. It's Jazz's cruelty that hurts the most. I feel every one of her jabs and kicks. I knew she was casting a web, I saw it coming and crawled straight into it anyway. The psychological mindfuck of it all, the way she sits there now, knowing she is intentionally hurting me, and is enjoying it, makes it impossible to pretend that I'm not.

So there it is, she says, placing down the controls. Inspired by you. Rooster's particularly proud of this one. He thinks this is the one he can launch out into the world.

I don't know if she's expecting a comeback, an argument or a physical fight, but she's not getting it from me. I feel winded.

Okay, I say, finally finding my voice. I get it, Jazz.

I stand up, place the mobile phone and credit card down on the coffee table, account set up, parking app downloaded. My work here is done. And I leave. Just like that. I pass Tony's office, raised voices drifting through the wall, and I let myself out. I hold back the tears as I walk down the stairs, along the terrace and down the steps to the road where I'm hidden from view of number eight. The humiliation of it. The hurt. I could cry right there, but I don't. I don't stop moving and then the need to cry disappears and the anger comes. Not at Jazz so much. But at Tristan. He is exactly who I thought he was in the first place. The Prada-wearing wanker who drives the yellow Ferrari. The man whose insult about my character and private life was death by a thousand cuts. Who set me on a path of further destruction, trying and failing to

241

find friends. To find me. To make me the best me I could be so that I'd be good enough to meet my mam.

I march on, ignoring the cars I pass by, not really sure where I'm going but driven by anger to just move. I near Casanova salon and see a strange car parked outside where the silver Mercedes should be. This angers me further, the fucking nerve of a stranger taking Carmencita's parking space. How could she let this happen. Was she late this morning and missed her spot and if so, why was she late, did she have to park elsewhere and did she mind. Was it a bad start to her day. Did it bother her. Did it ruin her morning. Do I need to step in and defend her. Did she show up to work today, is everything okay at home, did she crash, did she move house, is she gone again before I even got to say hello.

This final thought angers me. I'm hungry, I'm weak, I'm hurt, she can't leave me again, not until I get the time I deserve with her. Heavy-breathing, overthinking, angry, frustrated, hurt, hungry, weak, humiliated, I could yell and scream and shout right here right now. I want to kick the car, do a Britney, whack it with an umbrella, pull the wing mirrors off. This fancy SUV. I look around for her BMW but there's no sign of it. I pace up and down the pathway. The Range Rover has taken over her spot. It will have to be punished in some way. I'll find a way. I examine the windscreen. There's no parking ticket. Ha! gotcha. Hold on, it has a business parking permit, though. I see it is registered to Carmencita Casanova. The jeep is hers. I look at the insurance disc and motor tax for more information.

I look inside the salon. She's in there. I'm relieved that she's safe, there's still time, I haven't lost her. But

I also haven't lost my anger. It was directed at the vehicle and now because it's her vehicle, the anger naturally transfers to her. She's shaken me. She could so easily have just upped and left again and I'd never know and never find her.

She sticks a poster to the window. *Women in business. A gathering of women in local business, a discussion and celebration. Hosted by the president of the Malahide Chamber of Commerce Carmencita Casanova. A drinks reception in St Sylvester's GAA hall, 8 p.m. on 24 June. Tickets €6.* She's very proud of it, I can tell. She's removing it from the window again, getting the levels just right, she doesn't want it to be slanted or crooked. Her big night. Too much to the left, too much to the right, bit more to the right, yes, she commits, presses the double-sided sticky taped corners to the window. So happy with herself and her life.

I look back at the jeep. Still feeling the anger surge. The Range Rover has children's car seats. Booster seats. They must be over five years old to be out of car seats and into booster seats, I calculate. I see toys on the floor of the back seats. A car, an action figure, an enormous complete and total sticker book for girls. Complete. Total. Everything she needs whoever she is. Could have been me. The anger rises. My heart pounds. I press my face to the back windows.

Carmencita kept this girl. Was it the way she cried when she was born, did she do something differently than what I did. Such a silly baby I was, I should have known better, I should have known what to do, that those few seconds of our first meeting would be our last. That I had only a moment to convince her. Was my cry too loud, too piercing, not desperate enough. I didn't succeed in changing her mind. I couldn't win her over. But no, she kept these two little ones. These little dirty rats who drop their toys and make a mess. My forehead is against the tinted darkened glass. I peer in for more signs of who they are. Who are they. Do they look like me too. Brown-skinned, Irish-Spanish kids. Without the freckles probably. They don't have the Bird gene. The part of me she couldn't love.

I see Tristan round the corner from James's Terrace, he's running, with a scared expression, and when he sees me he slows.

Allegra, he says, in a low voice as if he sees me holding a gun to my head. He looks worried. He knows what Jazz has done, what I've seen. She must have told him. Pleased with herself.

I ignore him, press my face back against the window, heart thudding even more.

Is everything all right out here, a voice from behind me says.

The anger swells, swells like a storm inside me. The booster seats, the abandoned toys. The wrong vehicle for the business parking permit. Complicated. Bad English. Disturbed. Confused. Bitch. Dramatic.

Fuck her. She wanted to deal with the parking crisis in the village. Well then let's begin.

No, I say, turning my attention to my ticket machine, my weapon, and getting to work. Unfortunately this car isn't the vehicle registered to the parking permit, I say.

Don't, I hear Tristan call out and I ignore him. He's hanging back, away from us both where she can't see him but he wants to stop me from making a scene.

Her eyes look left and right as she thinks. She understands what's happening but she's going to pretend. I may not read people well but I know people when they're caught out and about to lie, I see it every day and her, I know. I know more about her than she thinks.

No no, she says, wagging a finger in the air at me as though I've been a naughty girl.

Wrong move, Mother.

Just a moment, she says, going inside her salon.

Allegra, don't do this, Tristan says. I know you're angry with me but don't ruin this with her because of me.

Not everything is about you, I snap. Leave me alone, I say, before she reappears.

He holds his hands up in surrender at the sidelines.

She returns, car keys in her hand. Big bunch, key rings, photographs with smiling faces. She's going to show me her permit, that it's all paid up, that it's all in date. She's going to take me through this kangaroo court, Mickey Mouse show. I fucking know it all already, where's Amal when I need her.

Now, she says, all business, not even looking me in the eye as she brushes past. She opens the door, a Minion toy falls out. Children, she puffs, blowing air out of her mouth as though I'm to understand.

How many do you have, I ask.

Two, she says.

Actually you've three, the third one is standing right here right now, your first one. But of course I don't say that out loud. I scream it in my head.

Tristan puts his head in his hands at what he's witnessing, jiggles nervously trying to get my attention. I ignore him.

Yes, I know it probably looks like more. They are so messy but they are not allowed to leave my car in this state. This is my husband's car.

245

Fergal D'Arcy, I say.

She looks at me in surprise. How do you know.

It says it on my machine, which is a lie, I didn't read it on my machine. I already knew. It was in the newspaper when I found it in the giftshop, her announcement as president of the Malahide Chamber of Commerce, mother of two married to Fergal D'Arcy. He works in a bank, high up. They do rather well. I look into the back seats again, then the boot, and see two scooters and two helmets among other things. I wonder if Fergal knows about me, and if he doesn't, what knowing about me would do to their family.

She slides the disc from the windscreen pouch. She's so close to me, her perfume is strong. I know I'll spend a while in Boots walking the aisles and trying to locate which scent it is. I might even buy it. She's wearing a colourful wrap dress, low cut, her boobs splurging out, shapely hips, wedges. She's curvier than me. I got Pops' slender frame, or maybe she did look like me once, before the babies. Three babies. I wonder if she has to correct herself when she tells people how many children she has. Does she almost go to say three and then say two. Does she sometimes say three to some people, strangers, people she'll never see again, just to test how the truth feels on her tongue.

You see here, she says, her Spanish accent still thick despite her years in Ireland. It is in date, it is registered to here, my business.

Yes, yes, I know all this, but I'm polite.

Yes, but it's not registered to this particular vehicle, I reply, realising I'm now actually enjoying our first conversation.

This vehicle, she snaps quite suddenly, is my

husband's. I'm borrowing it for the day. My car is at the garage. NCT test is coming up.

She didn't need to say test. NCT stands for National Car Test, so technically she has said National Car Test test. She probably doesn't know what it stands for, not very good English, isn't that what Pauline said. She was right about that. Let's see how accurate the other summary of her was.

You see everything is in order, she says in a very matter-of-fact final way, a woman who's used to getting what she wants. Speaking to me as if I'm a child, though she doesn't know I'm her child. There are no problems here, she says, sliding the disc back into the plastic shell on the window. She has a problem with authority. She's a mother, the owner and boss of her business, she's president of the Malahide Chamber of Commerce. She does not like to be wrong.

Only there is a problem because she is wrong.

The rules clearly state that if you change your vehicle, you need to apply to change the vehicle details on your payment, I say.

But I have this car only for one day.

She uses her hands to express every point. She also raises her voice. Temper temper. Dramatic. Disturbed. She hasn't changed. She rants and raves, loudly.

You people, she says to me and unleashes her tirade on how parking is ruining the small businesses in the village.

This is ridiculous, this is a disgrace, she finishes, then mumbles something in Spanish. Oh if only I'd kept up those classes. I could reply to her, see how she'd take that. The salon door opens. Is everything okay, Carmen, her employee asks. Carmen. People call her Carmen for short. I'm learning a lot about her now in this small exchange. Diamonds are formed under extreme pressure and boy is she shining now.

And this is not funny she continues, how dare you laugh at me, I'm going to complain to your superior, give me your name. And that is when it is all not fun any more, if fun is the word, which it probably isn't, insightful maybe, educational, because I definitely cannot give her my name because then she will know who I am. There aren't many Birds, she'll know immediately and I can't have her finding out like this.

Suddenly it hits me. What the hell am I doing. I'm making a mess of it all. Tristan can even see that. He's trying to stop me though I don't know why, what I'm doing to myself here is worse than every blow he could throw at me in his psychotic video game. You don't get a second chance at a first impression, this is how I'm beginning the relationship with Carmencita. What am I doing. Self-sabotage, I do it so well. I need to reel this in now, the anger inside me has dissipated and now I feel fear.

Give me your name, she repeats.

I can't tell her my name. When she hears my surname she'll know.

I understand your frustration, Ms Casanova . . . And I can't believe I'm saying her name out loud, to her. Hearing my voice makes me feel shaky. I hear it in my voice, the fear and awe of who I'm speaking to.

Oh now you're being nice, she laughs at me. Now you're afraid, she taunts me.

I'm here almost every day, I say, I don't know if you've noticed me, but your details are always above board.

She backs down a little at that, but she's looking

cocky. Like she's won and I can't let that happen. Not again.

I have already issued you a fine, the details have already gone through on my machine. But you are perfectly free to appeal the fine. It is my duty to call it in, but you can take your issue up with the council.

Oh I will, she says, hands on hips feistiness back. I'm the president of the Chamber of Commerce, I happen to know the council very very well.

Once your appeal is received the fine will be placed on hold until the appeal is decided, I explain calmly and rationally, as she continues to huff and puff. They'll look at the by-laws, the photographs I've taken, your evidence in order to make their decision.

Look how good I am at my job, Mother dearest, I want to shout. Look at me, listen to me, I'm following all the rules. If you were at home and I returned to you in the evening and told you about a woman like you, you'd be proud, cheering me on with how I've dealt with this. Look at me, Mam, look!

All such nonsense, you could have just let it go! All this work now, appealing it because I borrowed my husband's car.

Yes well, I look away, catch Tristan's face, one of such pity I hate him even more. I start to back away.

I'm just doing my job, I say.

And you are going to lose it. I'll make sure of that, you are nothing but a strange creepy girl, she shouts after me and she goes back inside her shop, banging her door.

Tristan catches up to me. Allegra, he says, all sooth-ing, and I could punch him right in his smarmy little lying face.

I stop and look him in the eye. I never want to talk

to you again, I say. Do you hear me. Stay away from me. I growl at him, feeling like an animal, the anger coming from somewhere so deep it disturbs even me.

24

A strange creepy girl. That's what she thinks of me. That's what I am to her.

Maybe she's right. Maybe she's summed me up after all. Maybe she is a great mother, she knows exactly who I am on a first encounter. Maybe that's what comes from a complicated, disturbed, confused, dramatic woman, when mixed with an eccentric atheist music professor. This is what comes of the illicit encounter. A strange creepy girl.

Forget work, forget the beat. Forget everything I came here for. It's all gone to shit, to piss, to utter rot. It's a plastic whirlpool in the middle of the ocean, an entire melted ice cap, a washed-up plastic choking whale, it's that poor little fella on the sand, the refugee, washed ashore on a fancy beach of a luxury holiday destination. The worst of the worst.

The intrigue and curiosity I felt when pushing her is gone. Now I'm forlorn. Yes that it's it, I'm totally empty, warden wipeout. But filled with so much contempt for myself. Why couldn't I leave her alone. Why did I have to pursue the ticket. If I had let it go, she wouldn't hate me, wouldn't in fact think anything of me, would go back to fine day for ducks and maybe good morning as we pass each other. Was it because I wanted to make her feel something, was that it, I wanted her to notice me, did I want to punish her, did I want to punish myself for being such a dope and having such hope. For letting myself get carried away with what might be instead of having the courage to try to make it something. Did I use up all my units of bravery moving here and fall at the final hurdle.

The tears are pumping out of me. I'm a snivelling wreck. Up Old Street, onto Main Street, past the Village Bakery. Are ye all right, Freckles, I hear from Spanner who's outside smoking. I keep walking, past the church over-flowing with communion ceremonies, over the bridge, into the grounds of Malahide Castle.

I'm the wicked warden from Rooster's game after all, punched, kicked, beaten down. I've thrown it all away, everything, forget this job, forget apologising to Paddy, forget the art gallery and my cheating guilty landlord, forget them all. I'm done, I'm finished. Over and out from weird creepy girl.

I pass by Donnacha in his studio. If he's surprised to see me back so early with tears dripping down my face, hiccupping from the lack of breath, then I don't know and I don't care because I'm not looking. Swollen face, snotty nose, eyes streaming. I walk across the flagstones planted in the secret garden, unseen, hidden, like no one would know I'm there. The creepy girl in the back of their garden. The way they want it, I suppose. It wasn't Donnacha or Becky, but a girl named Ava, Becky's personal assistant, who showed me around the back garden, pointed out the exact route I'm supposed to take. Through the side gate, past the bins, cut into the garden through the gap in the hedges, into the secret garden, over the flagstones that lead to the gym in the back.

For the privacy of the family, she said.

I could sit out in the secret garden, but not the rest of the garden.

For the privacy of the family.

252

I wonder what she'd think now of my privacy if I sent her the video of Becky screwing hairy arse on my bed. I wanted so desperately to get out of the box bedroom house-sharing situation . . . the atmosphere was awful, they were arguing every night, I couldn't leave my room. He wouldn't look at me, she looked at me as if she wanted to kill me.

Out, she'd shout at me, get the fuck out.

But I'd nowhere to go. Finding this place was a heavenly bliss, I thought I'd won the lottery. Five-star luxury, I didn't care about the secret garden or the family's privacy, or the fact it was in the back of a garden. It was a gift. I'd have agreed to do seven nights' babysitting to get away from where I was. I had to meet Becky first, of course, she had to approve Ava's choice. I didn't see the inside of their house until my first babysitting job. For the privacy of the family.

I throw off my cap, fall onto the bed and cry some more, this time loudly, frustrated, angry. It's not pretty. At some stage I fall asleep.

I wake to knocking on the door. I'm momentarily disoriented as I wake, expecting to be in my room in Valentia, and then in Pauline's B&B and then finally realise where I am. It's still bright outside so it's not that late, it doesn't get dark until 9.30 or 10 now. I look at my phone. Eight missed calls from Becky. And the knocking starts up again.

Allegra, it's Donnacha.

I push my hair back from my face, its wild mane like the weird creepy girl I am, and pull the door open. He stares at me, my face, then a quick glance at my uniform then at the bed behind me. He looks smart, like he's going somewhere fancy, and then I realise.

Oh shit. Shit. Donnacha, shit. I'm sorry.

I was supposed to babysit. I let go of the door, spring into action, grabbing my shoes, feeling woozy and having to steady myself.

What time is it, I ask. I look around for my phone.

It's 8.45.

I was due to babysit at eight.

Oh my God. Shit. I'm so sorry. Okay just give me a minute.

I start to close the door and he holds his hand out.

It's okay, don't worry, he says, Becky went ahead of me, she couldn't wait longer. It's some do at a friend's house. Her friends, not mine. I'm honestly happy to be delayed.

I'm not happy to delay you.

It's okay. I saw you earlier. You seemed upset. I thought I'd give you some time.

Oh yeah. I'm looking down because I feel my eyes spring with tears again.

Is everything okay, he asks. Dumb question, he corrects himself. Is there anything I can do. We can do.

No, no, thanks though.

Okay. Is fifteen minutes from now good for you, he asks. I should miss the awkward chats over drinks and if I'm lucky, the starters.

Okay I'll be quick.

Take your time, his voice drifts back to me as he makes his way down the spiral staircase.

I dive in the shower then change into loungewear, and with wet hair and flip flops, I make my way through the garden. For the privacy of the family. The boys are dressed for bed and drinking milk at the TV.

Donnacha looks at me caringly and I suddenly warm to him, feel bad for him. I don't know what he's like as a husband but Donnacha is a good dad. He

254

doesn't deserve what Becky did to him. But I would never tell. It's not my business.

Right. He looks around and then at me, as if he picks up on what I'm thinking and wants to say something. Maybe there's something to artistic antennae after all. But whatever it is, he changes his mind and says, Help yourself as usual to the fridge. Boys, I'll see you in the morning. He kisses the kids, and he's gone.

I sit with the kids for a while, feeling cosy with them in their winding-down mood. Cillín likes a cuddle and his warm body and soft breathing warms my soul.

At eleven thirty, much earlier than I thought, Becky and Donnacha return. Becky gives me an accusing look then goes upstairs without a word, there's that air of tension again. The bit before an argument. Donnacha saunters in to me as I gather my things.

The boys went straight to bed, I say nervously. Cillín came downstairs twice, once for water and the second time to ask about what would happen if you flushed a Pokémon card down the toilet. Don't worry, I fished it out.

He doesn't smile.

Okay thanks, Allegra. His hands are shoved into his pockets, and he looks behind him as if checking to see if the coast is clear. I can't have this conversation with him.

I quickly gather my things and move. Goodnight Donnacha.

I go to the flat, drop off my things, get the soft fleecy blanket that Becky had wrapped her sweaty sex body in and go back outside with some left-over steak. I place it on the lawn, in the area I'm allowed to be in, hidden from view. I sit down on a bench and light a cigarette. A few minutes later, Donnacha's figure

255

appears at the secret garden entranceway. I light up another cigarette. He walks over to me. Maybe the fight is over. Maybe it hasn't begun yet.

I didn't know you smoked, he says.

I don't.

He sits down beside me but far enough away to be okay. Me too. Any spare, he asks.

I hand him the packet and the lighter.

He lights up, inhales, prepares to say something, to fill the silence, but then maybe picks up on the mood, my mood or else just couldn't be bothered himself and doesn't bother saying anything. Unusual for him. I appreciate this. He settles into the silence, something I wasn't sure he could do. I keep watching the lawn.

What's that, he asks.

Left-over steak. It's for the fox.

You saw it, he asks. Becky thinks I was seeing things.

I think it's a female. She comes most nights. I think she's coming out from behind the shed.

He looks in the direction of the shed even though it's too dark to see. How do you know it's a vixen, he asks.

Her teats. She's lactating. I googled it, but I could be wrong. I think she set your alarm off when you were away, I explain.

He inhales his cigarette. I'll be honest with you, he says, the gardaí said they saw you walking around when they arrived. Found you suspicious.

What, I shriek. I was checking your studio. For you. Becky called me to see if everything was okay.

She said you were out of breath.

I was outside with the fox. I had to run back in to get my phone.

256

I wondered if maybe you'd fallen over, against the bins and set it off . . .

That happened once.

You've had a couple of wild nights lately.

It won't happen again. Did the guards seriously say it was me.

They told us to check the cameras.

Why don't you.

He doesn't reply.

I think back over my conversation with Garda Laura in the garden and then again when I met her outside the station. I had been trying to be friendly, to actually befriend her, and she had been suspicious of me. Hurt again by people. Deceiving, misunderstanding fuckers. Everything upside down and inside out. I don't get humans.

They came over again yesterday. They suggested it might be you. They didn't know for sure.

I groan. Yesterday was Daisy, I say. A kind of friend who's no longer a friend. I'm sorry. I told her not to walk past the sensor, but she has mental problems. Jesus, I sigh. I wanted her to be my friend, I say aloud even though I didn't mean to. I wanted Garda Laura to be my friend.

He studies me. There's better ways of meeting people than triggering alarms, he says.

I didn't, I splutter, so frustrated.

He laughs a little. Just kidding, Allegra, I believe you.

So you checked the cameras.

I did.

And.

Someone had wiped them. Odd, because they usually last a few months before recording back over themselves.

Well it wasn't me, I say, and then it dawns on me. It must have been Becky. To stop anyone from seeing her hairy-arsed guest's comings and goings. But as a result I've lost my proof.

I watch the steak, he watches me.

What are you staring at.

Your profile.

Please don't, I say, shuffling away from him a little. Weirdo.

He smiles and looks away.

There's a sound from the bushes and we both look. Nothing.

Should have put the steak in one of your bowls, I say and, despite himself, he laughs.

I'm not used to him being so quiet, but he seems weary.

Why do you make bowls, I ask suddenly.

Well that . . . he thinks long and hard, is a very big question.

Is it, I laugh.

Did you know there are seven different types of soup bowls.

No.

There's the soup plate, the coupe soup bowl, the soup-cereal bowl, covered soup bowl, lug soup bowl —

That's very interesting but I don't recall asking, I interrupt him.

Bowls are fascinating things really, he continues with a smile, and I think he's enjoying my ambivalence. So much more interesting than you first think, so much depth to them.

Not to your bowls. You couldn't fit a Weetabix in one.

He laughs. There's more to them, on closer inspection, he says, looking at me. Like most things.

He's doing it again. I look away, focus on the steak.

Anyway I thought they were vessels.

Inspired by soup bowls, I'll admit at least that.

I try not to laugh, who gets inspired by soup bowls.

Remember the soup kitchens in Ireland during the genocide, he says.

I smile. During the famine.

You say famine, I say genocide. Potato, potato. Pardon the pun.

Yes, I say, they were set up to feed the poor.

Not the poor. The deliberately starved. By 1847 there were three million people being fed every day. But they shut them down, expecting the next crop of potatoes to be good, which it wasn't. They told people that instead of the soup kitchens they could go to the workhouses. So the soup kitchens effectively became the workhouses, which became prisons for people who were being systematically starved to death. The local workhouse in the town where I grew up is the local library now. In its day it had housed eighteen hundred people when it only could accommodate eight hundred. Bad conditions, diseases spread, the places were hellholes. It became a private home then, to a rich noble family. My grandparents worked for them. My grandmother in the kitchen, my grandfather in the gardens. Right where their ancestors lay starving. One million people starved to death, while we were still exporting food from the country. So, I make soup bowls, he says simply, lest we forget.

Vessels, I want to correct him, but I don't.

He barely allows me to digest that humdinger before saying suddenly, It's you.

What are you talking about.

I have a solo exhibition coming up in Monty's Gallery.

I feel myself twitch at the mention of it.

I'm thinking of calling it Hunger, he says. All the ways in which we feel hunger. Hungry for love, hungry for power, for youth, for money, for sex, for success, for connection.

Sounds good, I say nervously. Inhale. Hold it. Exhale. Maybe you should call it scavenger. After our friend the fox.

I don't think he hears me. He wants to say what he wants to say. It's inevitable.

I was in there during the week to look at the space. I saw a few paintings in there, sketches, portraits from a live session that had just finished. They were all different of course. Each artist had a different perspective but as a collective, there was something distinctive about them.

Come on fox, come and rescue me. Appear and make him change the subject.

You're an intriguing character, Allegra, he says, on closer inspection.

He says it gently, then leaves.

A strange creepy girl, I whisper.

25

I take the day off work. I can't face anyone today. I finally build up the courage to call Paddy and ask him if we can switch zones for the next few days, which he agrees to. I can't be near Casanova. I can't be near Cockadoodledoo Inc.

I'm sorry about your barbecue, I say to him.

You weren't to know.

I shouldn't have brought them. Well, I didn't know George would show up. But I shouldn't have brought Daisy. Did they leave when I left, I ask, afraid to hear more. I never heard from Daisy again after that.

They stayed for a bit longer.

How long.

Around eleven.

Jesus, Paddy, I'm so sorry. Why didn't you tell them to leave.

Well I couldn't really. They stayed outside. In the sun. Too much sun probably, mixed with the alcohol. Not a good combination. She was sick.

I bury my head in my hands, mortified. I had no idea, Paddy. I'm sorry. I haven't spoken to Daisy since. She and I, we're not friends.

Funny, you said the same thing about me.

My heart pounds. I feel my cheeks blazing. I said it, I admit to Paddy, hearing the guilt in my voice. But not in the way you think I meant it. She thought that we were together, together, and I was trying to tell her that we weren't. That we just worked together.

That we weren't friends, he says. Good to know.

His usually happy tone has lost its warmth. He's flat and cold. Which is what I deserve. I'm so embarrassed.

Paddy, I'm so sorry.

He's silent for a moment and I think he's hung up.

I think, he says finally, taking his time, that we won't be seeing each other much going forward anyway.

Why not.

The transfer will be coming up soon.

What transfer.

We'll be moved. It happens every now and then. Wardens are moved around periodically.

But why, what for. I've been with you since the start, you trained me in, you were, are my support on the road. Would they move us somewhere else together.

No. We'll be split. It's to prevent boredom and over-familiarisation. Maybe it's a good thing, Allegra. For you. I don't know what's going on around Malahide, and frankly I don't want to, but maybe a change of scenery is what you need.

I end the call, the tears welling in my eyes. I can't be moved. I can't leave Malahide. I haven't achieved what I've come here to do yet. I've lost more people than even I knew I had and now I've hurt poor Paddy, the sweetest and kindest of them all.

Feeling low, I try to cancel this evening's art session. I can't go back there thinking at any stage Donnacha could walk in. I'm sure there's someone else that Genevieve can ask. I'm sure there are people lining up to pose nude, waiting for their lucky break, but when I hear her disappointment I somehow manage to be drawn back in. They have a full class today and she'll pay me more. I hear Becky, Donnacha and the kids out in the garden having a barbecue and I give in and agree to go to the gallery. It will be better to be away from here.

It's a stunning evening, I imagine what it would be like at home, the sun over the Skelligs, the pop of yellow of the birds-foot-trefoil to the landscape, blackberry brambles lining the roads. I close my eyes and imagine breathing it all in. The screams and shouts from the kids outside bring me back. Cillín is in his full princess dress, the princess from *Brave* with an impressive Scottish accent, and heels. He's climbing up ladders and jumping down fireman's poles and neither the dress nor the shoes hinder him.

I keep my head down as I walk through the secret garden and exit their garden. Past his Range Rover and her Mercedes, neatly parked, gleaming in the sun. I walk to the bus stop and get on the number 42, upstairs and to the front row. I love to see over the walls and trees, into gardens and homes that are hidden from pedestrians. As the bus sways and rocks, I start to calm down and pick over the carcass that is my life.

I take out my gold notebook and pull the lid off my pen with my teeth and start writing a letter to Katie Taylor. A reminder that I'm here and that she hasn't responded. The nib hovers over the paper, occasionally bumps against the page from the moving bus and the blue ink is dissolved by the page. A series of mistaken dots, but no letters, no words, no sentences come.

My heart isn't in it. Katie didn't reply to me because Katie doesn't know me. I'm a stranger looking for connection, what's in it for her. The same for Amal and Ruth. It hasn't worked well for me when I tried to make new friends. Certainly not with Daisy, and

Garda Laura thinks I break into houses. I'm getting something wrong here. I'm going about it the wrong way.

You are the average of the five people you spend the most time with.

I may not have friends here, but who do I actually spend the most time with.

I remember what Tristan said at the beginning, if you look outside of your family there are other influential people in your life who are having an effect on you that you possibly haven't considered. Perhaps the people you spend the most time with are the people you don't see. Look at what you've got and not what you don't have.

I look down at my dotted blank page. Dots. Dot to dot.

I don't want to write a list any more. This has always felt like a puzzle to me, a game of join the dots and so I draw the constellation Cassiopeia, the five-star constellation. In the shape of a w. Beside them I write a name along with my reason for the choice:

- Pops

No denying that. I draw a line connecting him to:

- Spanner

I see him every day. I know more about his personal life than anyone else's here in Dublin and actually he knows just as much about mine. I connect the dot to:

- Paddy

My work colleague. But I should have seen him as a friend. I link him to:

• Tristan

Whether I like it or not. He started this chain of change in me. I stick the nib in the circle, and I slowly pull the pen to the next dot. The fifth. Then I stop. Nothing. And I want to cry.

I push the door open to Monty's Gallery. I don't even look up at Jasper. I trudge up the wonky stairs that creak and move beneath me, feeling heavy and uncertain of how to do this.

Hi Allegra, Genevieve sings.

Hi, I say quietly, going straight to the changing screen. I sit down and undo the laces of my boots.

Mind if I join you, she asks, head popping in through the side.

Yeah.

She disappears and there's nothing. I frown and look around. Her head pops up at the top.

You sure, she asks.

Yes, I smile.

She disappears again. Silent. Pops back up in another direction.

Because you seem kind of down.

I laugh.

She disappears again. Popping up from another corner. That's better, she says, of my smile. Thanks for being here. I'm sorry I bullied you into coming in.

You didn't bully me. You guilt-tripped me.

I pull off my boot and drop it to the floor with a thud.

Bad day at work, she asks. I hope that guy with the

flashy car isn't bothering you again.

No not him. It's not work. I took the day off, I say, and I hear the wobble in my voice.

Are you okay, honey.

Are you okay. Three little words. When is the last time somebody asked me that. I can't remember.

I feel it all well up inside me. All the sadness and fear and anxiety and stress of it all. And the hurt. So much hurt. And I start crying.

Oh dear, well I knew there was a reason I had to force you to come in today. Talk to me, she says, reaching out to hold me. I take a deep breath and feel like I haven't spoken in at least seven months.

I tell her everything. Absolutely everything. About Pops, about Carmencita, about Tristan and the five people. About Marion and Jamie and Cyclops. I even tell her about the men in the art classes, and finding Becky on my bed. I tell her that I'm a weird creepy girl who can't seem to get anything right. I cry and we laugh, and she talks and she shares and my God it feels so normal and natural with her and nobody's life is perfect and that's good for me to hear. We're all just trying and all of us get it wrong sometimes. It's not just me. I feel nothing but relief when we're finished that not all humans are horrific species who misunderstand and blame, and twist and lie, and hurt others just to make themselves feel better. Some people are kind.

Later I sit on the stool before the full class, knowing my eyes are puffy and red, that my nose is stuffed from crying, but I can't hide it. I look out the windows above their heads, feeling lighter than I've felt in a while.

On the bus on the way home, I open my notebook

and go to the final dot of my invisible five people.

- Genevieve

Because she knows exactly what lies beneath.

26

A letter. For me. Handwritten.

Department of Justice and Equality
51 St Stephen's Green
Dublin 2 D02 HK52

Dear Allegra,

Your aunt Pauline gave me your kind letter when I visited the Mussel House last weekend, a glorious sunny day in Kerry, there's nothing quite like it, I'm sure you'll agree.

Thank you for your letter. What an intriguing theory you have raised. To think of those around you as those who help curate the person you are is something I will give some thought to over the coming days. Over a lifetime, yes of course I could name you five who have deeply influenced me, but to look around us now is a challenge indeed, one that is a wonderful way to honour and appreciate those around us. I'm honoured and flattered to think that I have inspired you in some way and all I can hope is that you continue to work hard and be happy with family and friends and that in your quest you continue to flourish and find happiness and kindness in those you choose to surround yourself with.

I'm very fond of your aunt Pauline, please give her my regards should you find yourself in Kerry before I do. You should look into doing a postal vote for the

Friday morning. A day off. Uniform-free, wearing the
best sundress and trainers I could find and afford, the
Minister for Justice's letter in my bag placing a spring
in my step, I nervously adjust myself and enter Casanova salon.

Welcome, welcome, my mother says to me warmly
as she guides me into the salon. I've never been inside,
I've never had reason to, have always been too afraid,
too unprepared. Oh don't you look beautiful, she
says, admiring my dress. Sunshine yellow, one of my
favourite colours to wear but girls like you and me get
away with it, yes, she asks. But she's not asking, she's
telling me.

Yes, I nod and smile. Girls like me and you, Mam.

She doesn't recognise me. Certainly not as her
daughter but neither as the nasty parking warden from
last week. She doesn't know I'm the weird creepy girl.

It's beautiful today, I manage.

Oh yes yes, she says, distracted, looking through
the bookings. Allegra, yes, she says and I nod, heart
pounding faster at the sound of my name from her
lips. She didn't name me, Pops did, I don't know if
she ever discovered my name, I'm guessing not, due to
her reaction, or if she ever learned it then she quickly
forgot it and me. I didn't give them a surname when
I was booking, I didn't have to, the girl on the phone

269

didn't ask for more, with a name like Allegra they usually don't need to. I don't know what I would have said if she'd asked for more. So far I have not lied, I have refrained from telling the full truth. I don't want to begin to lie.

Wash and blow-dry, she says.

I nod but she can't hear my nod so I force out a healthy yes. Should I tell her now that I'm the parking warden. It is better to get it out of the way, to get in there first. Let it come from me before she guesses or figures it out. Before one of the girls in here who witnessed our exchange recognises me and dobs me in. There's one other staff member, a blonde beauty in black, shampooing, and she stares at a distant thought in the future as she massages the woman's head, the woman with her head over the sink has her eyes closed and looks like she's dead, if it wasn't for the rising and falling of her chest.

I specifically asked for Carmencita to do my hair. I took the only slot she had left in the day, apparently all the women want her and she's more expensive too. She's the most senior, the owner, the manager, the president of the Chamber of Commerce, for God's sake. I had to make sure I had enough money for the experience. And there's the new dress I'm wearing today. Most people begin their pampering at the hair salon for a pending event; for me, the salon is the event and I prepared for her. It's worth it. She likes the dress, it's the first thing she said.

Where did you get your dress, she asks, leading me to the basins and patting the chair in a motherly way.

Zara.

Oh I love Zara, she says and goes into a long and elaborate story of how she found a dress she wanted and she waited and waited for it in the sale, hiding it in different points of the shop so that her size wouldn't be found, and she got it for fifty per cent off she exclaims, with such joy even the comatose woman beside us at the sink and the blonde beauty trapped in her trance start laughing. Because when my mother tells a story, she tells the entire room a story.

I think of that as my opening line of her eulogy. It may have taken us so long to reunite but when we did our relationship was so intense on many levels, and so moving that Fergal and the kids ask me to speak for them all. She loved us, her daughter would say, but really you were the special one, and so I would take to the altar and begin. The long-lost daughter, found and cherished. When my mother told a story she told the whole room a story, and everyone would laugh with fondness, take tissues from purses and wipe their eyes because, yes, that's so true, her daughter Allegra has hit the nail on the head, they all knew that about Carmencita and loved her for it and it took her eldest daughter to point it out.

But she's alive and she's here. She runs the water gently over my hair and asks if the temperature is okay. It takes a while for my scalp to feel it through my thick hair and as if reading my mind she says, My goodness, all of this beautiful hair, we may need a bigger basin.

Like Charlotte's hair, the blonde beauty says, and her voice is nothing like I thought it'd be. It's deep and husky.

Yes yes, like Charlotte, that's my daughter, my mother says. My heart pounds and splits at the same time because you see I am her daughter and she doesn't know and how I wish she'd be speaking proudly of my hair as she does of Charlotte's. I think of us gathering among her friends, us sharing the story of how we met, the humour of the parking ticket drama, and everyone would laugh, like we're ladies in some Victorian parlour taking tea. And my mother would say, But it was when I saw her hair, touched her hair, felt her hair, that I knew she was mine. And the ladies would ahhh and press the corners of their monogrammed handkerchiefs to their moist eyes and fan their faces before reaching for a cucumber-and-crab finger sandwich from the bottom layer of the afternoon tea tray.

Her fingers are in my hair now, they gently guide the water away from my forehead and face in a scooping motion so relaxing that my core stops rattling and finally normalises. I close my eyes and sink into the chair.

Is there a particular shampoo you'd like to use, she asks and I shake my head no.

I'll let you decide, I say with a smile.

She holds out the bottle before me. For dry, thick hair, coarse. I'm sure you don't need to wash every day, too much work with the blow-drying, so this conditions and . . . off she goes. She knows my hair, my mother. She could have told me these things as I was growing up, tips and guidance on hair products, packing them into my case as I headed off to boarding school, or would I not have gone to boarding school if she was around. Everything would have been different. I feel a lump in my throat, a little emotional at what I've missed out on. What both of us have missed out on, what I'm experiencing now at her hands and she doesn't even know it. Pops gave me baths, always entertained me with bath toys. I loved bathtime and then as I got older he ran baths and left the room for me to get in, feeling it inappropriate for a dad with a daughter, while he sat outside or nearby, talking to me, asking me to sing just so he knew I hadn't drowned.

And then of course I started showering myself. At five years old at boarding school. Charlotte's age, or maybe she's older. But I'm guessing her mother still washes her hair for her, runs her hands through her hair lovingly as she's doing now, massaging my scalp. More lovingly, I suppose. Pops would use a cup to scoop the bathwater and pour it over my head. Shampoo my hair roughly with heavy hands and thick fingers, shampoo and water going in my eyes, everything stinging. I hated that bit, it stressed him. He'd do it as quickly as he could, get it over with, wipe my stinging eyes and tears, and then he let me play.

She washes the shampoo out and massages in the conditioner, a long explanation of what that will do to my hair. I feel like I'm falling as she massages my temples, my scalp, my headache not gone but throbbing beneath her fingers, and I wonder if she can feel my head vibrate in her hands. She tells me about treatments that will help my beautiful hair, and I take it all in, every single word, commit it to memory as she tells me so I can add in a conversation sometime, My mam told me to use . . . Just like other people say without thinking about it. A sentence I've never said before in my life.

Is she feeling a deep connection with me under her touch, or is she staring idly into space like her colleague, the blonde beauty, her tenth shampoo of the day, thinking about what to cook for dinner, or the birthday present she needs to buy and wrap for Charlotte's friend's upcoming birthday party. I do not want this moment to end, my mother's hands on me like this, it's bliss. But unfortunately the water is turned off.

Now she says, loudly and brightly, shattering the silence and peace. My eyes fly open, a hairdryer goes on for another customer and the spell has been broken, but it's not over yet. She wraps a fresh towel around my shoulders, a towel around my head and leads me to a chair facing a mirror. I feel nervous again to be face to face where she can scrutinise me more. Pops used to dry my hair messily, roughly with a towel. I'd sometimes feel as if my head would pop off. He could never figure out how to wrap it around as my mother has done now in a turban style. Like I'd ask him to do, like I'd seen in the movies. And then the blow-dry, what a palaver. He hated drying my hair, it was so thick and so long, it took too much time. And so because of that we didn't wash it regularly, not enough anyway. No, hair was not his thing, but he was so good at so many other things. She is so good with hair and was so bad on everything else. But the positives, let's focus on them.

You have magic hands, I say to her and she grins, aha, as though she's heard it a thousand times and knows it already. She combs my wet hair so that it's perfectly straight.

How much would you like off. I think to here, yes. Get rid of the split ends. It's two inches.

Yes, whatever, I don't care, whatever takes the longest amount of time. Keep touching me, fussing over me, make it last forever. I don't know why I didn't do this months ago. I could have been having this contact with her for the past six months. I nod in response to her.

When did you last have it cut.

Almost seven months ago. I think back. Marion did it in her kitchen, the week before I. Before the home salon, before the goosebump baby that's probably now the size of an apple. My mother can't believe it's been such a long time. How often should I get it done, I ask her, and listen to her again about the weather, and the seasons and what signs to look out for and again I take it all in. Maybe I'll begin a Mother book, documentation of all the things she's ever said directly to me, like a scrapbook, so by the end of my life it will be full and rich and proof of a relationship over time and motherly advice. Tips from my mother to pass on to my daughter. From the grandmother she'd never met, or did meet when I brought her to the salon with me, in a buggy, or had her first haircut, all by a mother and grandmother who never knew. And why did you never tell her, my daughter will ask, and I'll smile, a secret kind of smile and say, I never told her, but she knew, pet, she knew.

She's quiet now, concentrating as she gets the ends even. Pulling them down and checking the levels. I study her face, now that she's not watching me. Every gesture. Now and then her stomach or her boobs press against the back of my head and I think, I was in there. Her fingers brush against my skin and I think: Those hands held me, those fingers touched me, at least once. This part I don't know, maybe they lifted me out of the room straight away, but wouldn't the midwife have placed me on to her naked chest, skin to skin, not for her benefit but for mine. The midwives would have cared, wouldn't they. I look at her chest in her low-cut wrap dress, shiny moisturised, great skin, a necklace with a heart that is trapped in her cleavage.

I wonder if Fergal gave it to her.

I would ask Pauline these things about the hospital but she wouldn't know. My mother gave birth alone. Driven to Tralee maternity hospital by my mad cousin Dara who wouldn't tell me much more. Pops was there, of course, in a waiting room or downstairs at reception, or wherever he was allowed to be, but no one was with her, no one but the midwife. I don't know how moving or cold our first and final moments were together. Not final, I remind myself, for look at us now. Reunited.

She's happy with the length, she can talk again.

You have the day off today, she says.

Yes.

What do you do.

And it was going so well. Perhaps it is our final moment, Carmencita, I think to myself. I take a moment then turn to her, even though I can see her in the mirror. I need to connect to her in real life, not make the stupid mistake with her that I made before. We've actually met before I say in a gentle polite voice, in a not so pleasant way that I'd like to apologise for.

She takes a step back, slightly, moves away, body language reads defensive, I know because I learned conflict management. She readies herself.

You know, I thought that there was something familiar about you.

My heart skips a beat at that. Did she feel something, a connection.

So did we meet, she asks. Tell me the terrible thing that I did. She's trying it keep it light but I can see how much she has tensed up. A defensive woman who always likes to be right, does not like to be surprised.

You did no terrible thing, I smile. I'm the parking

276

warden who issued you a ticket last week.

You, she says loudly, and the others stare. But you don't look like . . . you. Lady, high-vis yellow is not your colour, she laughs.

I know, I smile. I'm sorry about how it all transpired, I wanted to come here and I wasn't sure if you'd recognised me.

No no, well I didn't. I would have said. Of course. As soon as you stepped in, I would have said something. Well, well, well. She's flustered. She's annoyed. She planned on holding a grudge forever and I've ruined it. Now I'm a customer and there's nothing she can do. She doesn't know what to say, she doesn't look at me as she picks up the hairdryer and blasts my hair. Angrily. Not too dissimilar to how Pops would do it. Hair flies across my face and whips my eye.

I've ruined it.

My hair is so thick it takes a while and after fifteen minutes of no more talk, which I'm not sure there could have been anyway due to the noise, she switches it off.

I've never seen my hair look so beautiful and I say so. She has softened over time and this certainly helps. I'm waving the white flag and I hope, I think, she sees it.

Good, good, this makes me happy.

She removes the towel from my shoulders and our time is running out. Knowing who I am now, she may never want to take my booking again. Or she'll take the booking and allow somebody else to do it. She doesn't seem like one to turn away business. I feel desperate that this is the end of our physical connection. I don't want to leave. I look at the nail bar.

I don't suppose you have time for nails, I ask.

277

Ooh I don't think so. I don't think she's lying because she's looking through her bookings. Hmm. Not today and tomorrow, Saturday we're fully booked. Closed on Sunday. Monday is quiet.

I've work. But maybe on my lunch break. I really shouldn't, but I'd break my routine for her. I'd wave goodbye to the bench and my sandwich and walnuts and tea, to sit across from her, with my hands in her hands.

We agree on noon, Monday.

We're at the money part. I look at the poster that she has on the window, the one facing out about the women in business event. You must be excited about the event I say. I think it's a wonderful idea. Running your own business, and president of the Chamber of Commerce, I don't know how you do it all.

And the children of course. Most important of all, she raises her finger in the air.

Of course. Raising children is most important, I agree.

Sixty euro, I give you ten per cent discount for new customer, for making the appreciated gesture and for new beginnings. Yes, she says.

Yes thank you. I pay in cash because I don't want her to see my full name on my bank card.

I still will appeal the fine, she says, and I laugh. You should, I say, but I don't want to talk about the fine with her. I'll suggest your event to my friends, I say.

Yes of course, tell as many women in business as you can. The more the merrier. We're still looking for a guest speaker. We went to print with the posters and so it says with special guest speaker, but I don't have the special guest speaker. She hits her head playfully. Three weeks to go.

What about Ruth Brasil.

The politician, she asks.

Yes, the Minister for Justice. I could ask her.

Her eyes almost pop out of her head. She reaches out and takes my hands, squeezes them in hers. You know Ruth Brasil, our next Taoiseach, she asks. Our first female Taoiseach, I'm sure of it, and she ought to be with all this nonsense going on. He's a bad man, he has to go.

Yes I know her. I feel the letter from Ruth throbbing in my handbag. In fact I already told her about the event and she was very interested. She thinks it's a great idea. I'm quite sure she'll come.

It just comes out, straight out. I don't even think about it. I just want to make my mother happy.

Would she be the guest speaker, she asks.

I'll ask her today.

Oh! she squeezes me excitedly. My goodness, if you got Ruth, you would be welcome here, free for life!

I'll find out as fast as I can, I laugh.

She hugs me, hugs me with excitement though I think she'd hug just about anyone she's that happy. But she hugs me. My mother hugs me. Our first hug. Hopefully not our last. I leave the salon feeling a million dollars. Bouncing, new dress, new hair, fresh blow-dry, a relationship with my mother.

27

I walk, but feel like I'm floating, across the road to the park by the marina. My hair bounces, my button-down yellow tea dress flaps open around my legs with each step and I feel the sun on my hair and my skin and I'm happy. It's one of those days it's great to be alive, when you don't hate everyone, when you don't feel shame, when you don't want to hide. For me anyway. I'm sure there's someone somewhere living their worst day.

Foreign exchange students sit in large groups throughout the green area, wrapped in coats and jumpers on our warm sunny day. I sit on the grass and open the minister's letter again. It's handwritten but it's on her constituency office headed paper. There's an email address at the bottom. Now that she has replied to me, the correspondence has begun. I feel like I knocked on her door and she let me in. But it's quicker to email than write, and time is of the utmost essence now. So that her secretary doesn't think I'm a lunatic, I take a photograph of the minister's letter as proof, and attach it to my email.

Dear Minister Brasil

I was so delighted to receive your letter, thank you so much for taking the time to respond. It meant so much to me, it started the most incredible chain of events. You see I had almost given up, but your words gave me such confidence that I went straight to my mother, who gave me up at birth. I walked into her world and I've just spent the most amazing hour of my life with her all thanks to you. Do you see how inspirational you are to me.

Her name is Carmencita Casanova, she's the president of the Malahide Chamber of Commerce, and she's running an event in three weeks' time celebrating women in business. She would love for you to attend. If you have time to call by this event for even ten minutes, it would mean the world to the president of the Malahide Chamber of Commerce, and the businesswomen of Malahide.

But mostly if nothing more ever comes of our correspondence, I want to thank you for the gift you have given me today. Your response gave me wings, just when I needed them, and that is the power of being somebody's one of five.

Attaching a poster of the event to prove its legitimacy. I would appreciate it if you or your office would liaise directly with me for this event as I'm assisting the president with the organisation.

You'll be glad to hear I have taken steps to do a postal vote for the by-election.

Best wishes

Allegra Bird

I request to be contacted directly by the minister's office because I don't want to get cut out of anything further happening. In the event the minister decides to attend this event I want to use it to further develop my relationship with Carmencita. Then, when the time is right, I'll tell her who I am. But the time has to be right. I absolutely have to prove myself first. Carmencita is tough, she's strong, she's firm. She does not like surprises. I don't know her well but I know that I need to prove to her that I am someone she wants.

I press send, lie back on the grass, lift the camera and take a selfie. New hair, yellow dress, green grass, buttercups, daisies. It's a moment. It's an Instagram post. I'm getting the hang of this.

Allegra, a voice calls, breaking into my thoughts.

Tristan is beside me, looming over me, blocking my sun like darkness incarnate in that stupid red Ferrari cap.

Go away please, I say, getting myself ready. I throw my phone into my bag, carefully fold the minister's letter and place it inside.

I barely recognised you, you look amazing, not that you don't always look ... He hunkers down to my level. I saw your post on Instagram, you know you should turn off the location if you want privacy, anyway I took a chance that you were still here, he says, and I realise he's breathless from running over here from his office.

I do want privacy. Please go away, I say, standing up.

Tristan stands up too.

I've been searching for you all week. Where have you been.

I walk to the road, the green man turns to red, stopping my escape. Frustrated, I hit the pedestrian crossway button.

Allegra, Tristan says, keeping up with me in a polite way that shows he doesn't want to invade my boundaries but also doesn't want to leave. Please listen.

Look, Tristan, go away please, I don't want to talk to you. And I'm working very hard to be very polite now when all I really want to do is tell your smug stupid Ferrari-cap-wearing mug to go and jump.

Oh. He touches his cap self-consciously.

I tap on the pedestrian button over and over, trying to hurry the little green man along. The traffic is streaming towards the coast road on this beautiful day.

I've been telling your colleague Paddy all week that it's really important I speak to you, have you been getting my messages.

No.

I haven't spoken to Paddy since our phone call. He texts me the zones we're working. I'm intrigued, but I don't want him to know that. I want to punish him. Hurt him as he's hurt me. The traffic light explodes with video-game-like sounds to alert us that it's safe to cross. Tristan almost collides with a double buggy and a kid on a scooter as he follows me.

Sorry. So sorry. Allegra, where have you been, did you go home.

They switched our beats, sometimes that happens. Why, did you think that you had hurt me so much I couldn't bear to come to work and see your face, I ask, knowing that's exactly what had happened.

No, of course not, he lies badly, his face flushed. Look, I fired Jazz. What she did to you was abominable. I fired her straight away. She's gone. We're not . . . We broke up.

283

I stop walking when we get to the other side of the road. Tell me, Tristan, that game where people pulverise me to death, did Jazz design it all by herself.

No no — his hands in the air — that was me.

I'm sure Beavis and Butthead were only too delighted to help you design it.

He doesn't deny it.

Suddenly at the window of the hair salon my mother appears, waving.

Uh oh we should move, he says, trying to take my arm and guide me away.

I shake him off.

She motions at me to wait. Allegra, she shouts from the open door. I take a few steps towards her.

Yes, Carmencita, I say, enjoying the feeling I get from this closeness and with Tristan witnessing it. I feel smug, as if I can do anything now.

Did your friend, Minister Brasil, say yes, she asks excitedly. I was thinking, I'll print up new posters with her name on them as guest speaker. It's an extra expense and time to replace them all around the village, but it's worth it.

I squirm a little inside, not quite wanting Tristan to know how exactly I have made her warm to me. I've just emailed her, I say, I'm sure I'll hear back from her soon, maybe you shouldn't do anything until we have confirmation.

Of course, I'm sure she's very busy. I'm sorry, I'm just so excited. You really think she'll do it.

I'm sure she'd love to, I say. It's not a firm yes. We'll just have to wait and see.

She gives me a big thumbs up and a fingers crossed and everything else she physically can do to display her excitement.

284

Well that's a turnaround, Tristan says. Does she know you're her —

No. Not yet, I say, walking up New Street. I don't want him to utter the word aloud.

What have you done, Tristan asks, and I don't like the warning in his voice, the distrust, the doubt. I glare at him and he stops. Okay sorry, none of my business. But . . . okay listen to me, about the other stuff. I developed that horrible Warden Wipeout video game back in the first two weeks we'd moved into the office when I didn't know you, when you kept giving me tickets every few hours.

I was doing my job.

I know that now, but I didn't know that then. I was angry, angry at you and angry at everyone in the business. It wasn't personal, because I didn't know anything about you. You were just some horrible warden who kept ticketing me. Now I do know and I'm sorry that it hurt you. I really am. You're the last person in the world I'd want to hurt. You're the only person who treats me like I'm normal, the only person who tells me the truth, the only person who doesn't care about my car.

Because your car is tacky and nasty.

See, that's exactly what I like about you. No one says that stuff to me. Most people I know are proud of my achievements, you, not so much. I need to hear it. You're my non-yes person. You hate the cap, I'll throw away the cap.

He takes it off and squeezes it through the narrow hole into the bin.

I look at the bin in surprise.

When I first met you I said some horrible things, he says, but I was angry because I wasn't happy with my own life, so I like, transferred my feelings on to you. Don't roll your eyes, please, thank you. And then you actually listened to me and started to do something about it, you started to change your life or at least try. Anyway, just through watching you and talking to you, you've inspired me to look at my life and I realised my five weren't who I thought they were either. I broke up with Jazz, I've made some big changes in the office just in the last week and there's more to come. People are going to finally start listening to me, because you're right, I was a complete pushover. And I've talked to Uncle Tony too. We're not working together any more.

Whoa. How did he take it.

He says I'm unappreciative and he's suing me for everything that I have. Anyway, I don't care what Tony says he's going to do. It doesn't matter, the fact is I've made the changes and I can have a fresh beginning. And I've you to thank for that. Seeing you with your mother last week —

Was enough to put anyone off ever beginning new relationships, I interrupt, starting to slow down now as my anger loses steam.

Yes — but you were trying. I needed to be as brave as you. I glimpse at him quickly to see if he's being serious. No sarcasm. He looks embarrassed. I'm embarrassed for him. For me. He must be.

Okay. That's it. That's everything I wanted to say. Where are you going anyway in such a rush.

Nowhere really, I admit. Just away from you. I stop outside the bakery, then push the door open.

He follows.

Hi, Spanner.

Howya, Freckles. Where have you been, I thought

I'd scared you off. He looks Tristan up and down without a word.

This is Tristan.

Hi, Tristan says politely.

Spanner just nods, sussing him out. Your fella, he asks.

No way, I say, insulted.

Well, I'm a boy and I'm your friend, Tristan says, offended by my tone.

You're not even my friend, I say. Spanner snorts.

Are yis going to order something.

I'll have a cappuccino with almond milk, Tristan says and adds please as Spanner glares at him.

Are ye allergic to dairy are ye, he asks in a teasing way, changing his voice to sound more feminine.

More of an intolerance actually, Tristan says, it bloats me. Allegra, you'll have . . .

The usual, Spanner and I say in unison.

So I took your advice and got meself a solicitor, he says.

Spanner that's great news. His ex won't let him see his little girl, I explain to Tristan.

Tristan sucks in air. Tough.

Spanner looks like he wants to headloaf him. Tristan shrinks back.

All of a sudden Spanner punches the air violently and Tristan jumps, startled. He raises his two fists in the air as though he's Katie Taylor and he's the undisputed ultimate champion. I'll have my day in court, he says, I'll tell them that I lived with Chloe for three years before she got up the duff, thank you very much, and I lived with Ariana until she was four years old. I've paid for everything, I have my own business, I brought her to Montessori every morning while Chloe

287

was still in bed, thank you very much, and then I'll wait until they apologise: we're very sorry, Mr Spanner, for the in-con-fucking-venience, you're excused, here's your daughter back.

Or you could just ask Allegra's friend the Minister for Justice to help you out, maybe she could have a chat with the judge, Tristan says, barely able to keep the grin off his face.

Spanner looks at me, surprised. Freckles, you never said.

No . . . I . . . I mean, she might be coming to Malahide in a few weeks. I'm just waiting to hear back from her. She might not be free, though. I feel my face burning.

Three weeks. I can't wait that long, he says, bounding out from behind the counter to the door. Legs spread, wide stance. Spanner lights a smoke and stares down the traffic.

Tristan laughs. I'm sorry, I couldn't help it. He's intense, isn't he.

He'll do anything for his daughter, I say, and I'm surprised when the words catch in my throat. I have one like him at home, and I'm here. I'm briefly shaken by that negative thought, after the excitement of the morning. I'll just have to make it all worthwhile. This time spent away from him will all have to be worthwhile.

My phone buzzes in my hand to signal an email and I check it quickly.

Everything okay, Tristan asks, sprinkling sugar into his coffee and watching my face.

Yeah.

Was it her, the minister, he asks in a teasing tone, is she coming then.

Yeah, she is actually, I straighten up. And she'll be the guest speaker. I grab my coffee cup, leaving Tristan to pay. When he's out of sight I read the email again. And again, hoping for a different response.

Thank you for your email. Your message is important to us and we will respond as soon as possible.

28

Hi Pops, I answer the phone, walking back through Malahide Castle gardens in the sunshine, coffee still in hand.

Did you hear.

Hear what.

About Cork.

No, what happened in Cork.

An Post are closing their mail centre in Little Island.

Oh. He hears my indifference.

Two hundred jobs will be lost, Allegra.

I know, that's terrible. I'm sorry to hear that. Do we know anyone who works there.

No. But that's not the point, is it. The government just announced their new environmental policy, did anyone take this into account when they decided to shut down the mail centre.

What's the post office got to do with an environment policy.

Well how many trucks are going to be on the road now bringing the letters to the nearest depot, wherever that will be. It's another nail in the coffin for rural Ireland. The hearts of communities are being ripped out. Not just the hearts, it's a decapitation of our society.

What are you going to do about it.

I've spoken to Bonnie —

Who's Bonnie.

Bonnie Murphy, she used to be the post mistress over there in Glencar before they shut her down.

We've been working on this for weeks now, I told you. We're going to organise an association for saving post offices, we're going to mobilise.

But how are you going to do that, with no car. To mobilise, you need to be mobile. Posie says you're still not back at choir practice.

Posie doesn't know all my comings and goings, I've made sure of that, her son is a civil servant in Dublin, they can't be trusted. And you don't need to worry. I've been on to the insurance frauds for the past two weeks and they're fixing the car electrics, they've given me a temporary car until it's done.

But Pops, I spoke to them numerous times, they wouldn't believe me about the rats. They pretty much said scrap it.

Aha, Allegra, that's the thing about these corporations, you can't let them win, you can't give up. You don't take no for an answer. The last thing they'll do is replace the car, of course, but they'll spend their time and money rewiring it.

So you're out and about again, with this woman, Bonnie.

I am. Somebody has to, or before we know it everything will be shut around us and we'll be nothing but rats, nesting in our own deserted towns.

I smile. Sounds great, Pops. I'm glad to hear you're back. For a worthy cause, of course.

Well. He relaxes. Any news.

I know what he means. Have you seen her yet, spoken to her yet, does she know yet.

Well, yes actually. We've been talking.

He's quiet for a moment. A dubious, yes.

And I'm just judging my moment, Pops. I'm going to help her out with something, with an event she's

291

organising. I've invited Minister Ruth Brasil.

So that's what your letter was about. They say she'll be next Taoiseach, the way this government is going. What's the event.

For women in local businesses.

And she'll go, will she.

Yeah. I think so.

And you think that will win her over, do you.

I hate his cynicism. I want to get off the phone. I didn't say anything about his stupid quest to save post offices.

Yeah. Yeah, I do, Pops, I snap.

All right, love, all right. Keep me in the loop, as they say. But don't write it in a bloody letter or I'll never find out down here.

I laugh. Okay, Pops. Love you.

Love you.

While I've been talking, a text comes through from Becky, asking to meet me at seven-ish when she's home. The spring in my step just doesn't stop. Pops is on the mend, I'm working on my mother, with the help of the Justice Minister, which is like killing two birds with one stone. Everything is finally looking up.

You look different, Becky says as I enter the kitchen from the back door.

Thanks, I smile. I got my hair done.

I can see that.

There's a bottle of wine open on the expensive worktop that glistens as if concealing diamonds, it's breathing in a fancy decanter. She sends the boys out of the room to play their computer games, kind of barks at them, agitated. Cillín asks for my phone because there's a game on it that he likes to play.

Out out, she hurries him.

292

He moves away from the kitchen to the couch, in his own world. I feel apprehensive about them all being sent away like that. By her mood.

I look outside to the garden room to see if Donnacha is there, working on his solo exhibition.

He's not here, she snaps.

She pours us both a glass of wine, which should technically be a nice gesture but it feels aggressive. She's tense, she pours clumsily, the red wine splashes over the rim. She bangs the bottle down on the countertop.

I clear my throat because she's all of a sudden making me feel nervous.

Before I forget, I say, you might be interested in going to this. I retrieve a leaflet about the women in business event and place it down on the counter.

She doesn't pick it up.

They've already invited me. Someone from the Chamber of Commerce.

The president. Carmencita Casanova, I say. She's the one who did my hair today. I'm actually helping her with the event. I'm working on getting the Minister for Justice to attend.

I'm aware of how impressive that sounds, which is exactly what I'm trying to do with Becky. We've had a bad few weeks, hopefully I can turn that around. But my words don't have the desired effect. She looks at me oddly, her face kind of twisted in a weird thought and I realise she's already had a lot to drink, it's giving her an edge. So early, home alone with the boys. This is unusual.

The horrible feeling intensifies. I drink the red wine, take too much of a gulp, it catches in my throat and I splutter a cough.

She watches me with her cat eyes. Sips slyly. Smiles at my discomfort.

Before we begin, is there anything that you'd like to tell me, she asks, eyes searing into mine. Her pupils are so large her eyes seem black.

Confused, I rack my brain for something that I should tell her.

Em. No, I don't think so, I say slowly. But I could be wrong, I'm sure she's about to refresh my memory.

You don't think so. Right. She straightens up as if trying to stay calm and breathes in and out before saying, without kindness, You've broken the terms of your lease. We had a three-strikes-and-you're-out agreement. You're out, Allegra.

I haven't broken any terms of the lease, I say, confused. I search my brain. I broke a plate a few weeks ago but I told you about it. I said I'd pay for it.

Do you think I'm stupid, Allegra.

No.

Then you wouldn't be evicted over a plate, would you. There have been many incidents over the past few weeks. I was hoping I wouldn't have to remind you of them, that they'd be as perfectly clear and as memorable to you as they have been to us.

She's ready to list them, I can tell. She's been dying to do this. Probably saying them over and over in the shower, as she cleans the kitchen, empties the dishwasher, over and over in her head on a loop, all the terrible things I've done.

Donnacha had to scrape you up from between the wheelie bins when you set the alarm off, so drunk that he had to practically carry you to bed. Then don't think I didn't notice you had a friend stay over.

She's not my friend.

Well, she laughs angrily, nostrils flared, that's even worse. You brought someone who wasn't your friend back to my home.

My home, I say quietly.

The lease explicitly states that you cannot do that. For the privacy of our family. My family. We can't have strangers wandering around at four a.m.

She leaves a silence hanging, a powerful I-have-you-now silence.

But I've nowhere else to go.

I think four weeks' notice is sufficient time to find somewhere else. If you find somewhere available before then, of course, please take it.

Becky, I say, in total shock. Please, I beg. I'll be a better tenant, I promise. I have to stay here. I need to stay. I'm working on something. I'm here for a reason. A very important reason.

Yes, working with the president of the Chamber of Commerce and the Minister for Justice, she says cattily. Pull the other one. I haven't even mentioned the police calling out to the house on not one but two occasions. The gardaí on duty believed you were acting strangely. I don't know what you're trying to do, break into my home when I'm out, but there won't be a repeat, and you certainly won't be allowed near my children again.

I look over at Cillín, hoping he hasn't heard her speaking to me like this. His head is buried in my phone, playing with the apps I downloaded for him.

I only did it once, I say feeling hysterical. The first time was the fox. Okay the second time it was me falling into the bins, and the third time it was a girl who is not my friend any more and who never will be. I'm sorry for all of it but I wasn't trying to break into your house. I could prove all of this to you, couldn't I, by showing you the CCTV footage, if you hadn't wiped it to cover your own arse. And honestly, I continue, my voice trembling, I think you just want me gone because I know what you did. You hate that I know and you're terrified I'm going to say something.

What did you say, she whispers.

Donnacha checked the camera footage. He told me it'd been wiped. Wonder who wiped it. But it doesn't matter, he doesn't need to see it, he believes me.

Oh I'm sure he does, Allegra. I'm sure you have your ways of making people believe you. You had me fooled for a while too. I found it, she whispers then. It's eerie. Her pretty face so twisted and creepy.

Found what. I'm so confused.

Your little secret, she whispers again.

Becky, I don't know what you're talking about, but I hear the lie in my voice. I do have a secret, a big one, one I've carried with me every day here. The one about my mam, but why it would make Becky angry, I've no idea. I'm trying to figure it out how it relates to Becky, when she stands up, moves quickly across the kitchen and suddenly reveals a canvas. Of me naked.

This. Little. Secret, she says, her voice a hiss now so that Cillín can't hear. I found it in Donnacha's studio. Hidden. Did you two think I wouldn't find it.

My mouth opens and closes with nothing coming out. I don't know where to begin with this.

Sex sounds coming from the couch area end our conversation. A man and woman in throes. I recognise it immediately. It takes Becky a split second longer than me. It's her in the video. Her and hairy hole. On my bed, or her bed, in my home, or her home. I'd forgotten to delete the video and Cillín is sitting there, face screwed up in confusion, watching. I race to him and grab the phone from his hand. Flustered, fingers shaking, I try to stop it, lower the volume, then delete it before Becky can see it. But it's too late. She's heard it, she knows what it is and that her son has seen it. Though there are no faces, just twisted bodies, he still saw something he shouldn't have. She's pale, stunned, then the colour returns, along with her anger.

You disgusting little freak.

I can't defend myself.

Get out of my house. Get out of my house, she screams, and I hop to it, to the back door. You better pack your things straight away and be gone by tomorrow. Silly Allegra, silly silly Allegra, I hear her say to Cillín in her shrill tone as she comforts him. What were her silly friends doing in that video. Do you want some cookies, sweetie, she asks and I hear the tremble in her voice.

I walk across the lawn, feeling dazed, disoriented, and in shock.

You pervert, she hisses at me finally, before the door slides over and bangs closed.

And now it's not just the freckles that connect me to Pops.

29

Paddy answers the door. I wasn't sure if he'd be home. I wasn't sure if he'd answer the door. I wasn't even sure if he'd let me in. He does all of these things.

He leads me to the TV room. He has *Come Dine with Me* paused. He looks at me, twiddling his thumbs.

Is your mam here, I ask.

No. She's in the home. I'll take her out for the day tomorrow.

I nod. Here. This is for you. I hand him the bag, so heavy it has almost pulled my arm from my socket on the walk from the bus stop. Happy belated birthday.

It's an olive oil hamper. It was expensive. A selection of infused organic olive oils.

You already got me the marinades, he says, taking it out of the bag. Ooh. White truffle, he says, running his fingers over the plastic that protects the hamper. Mint-infused, basil-infused. Hey, lime-infused. He grins, a real smile. Liquid gold. Thanks, Allegra.

Okay, maybe it's more of an apology present. I'm sorry, Paddy. You've been nothing but kind to me since I arrived in Dublin and I haven't been that back to you. I want you to know that I consider you a friend, whether you like me or not right now.

Thanks, Allegra. I appreciate it. Really, it's all water under the bridge now.

But it's still awkward. I've ruined it forever. I better go. I have some house-hunting to do. I have to be out of my flat by Monday. Hopefully I can stay in Malahide.

You should probably wait to see where you're relocated to.

Yeah. Have you heard anything yet, I ask, hopeful the whole system has miraculously changed.

I'm leaving Fingal.

What, why.

I got a new job as a parking patrol officer. In town. Rotating roster. Four ten-hour shifts per week. Possible overtime. I get to drive a brand-new van, new uniform, mobile phone and personal protective equipment. Forty k a year.

Wow, Paddy. Congratulations.

Yeah. Yeah, it's good for me. And I need it for Ma's bills you know.

Yeah. That's great. I'm surprised by how I feel the emotion swell in my throat. My feeling that this is the end. Everything's over or at least is finishing before I'm ready to go. Good luck, Paddy.

I'll be around for the next few weeks though. And I'm not dying. We can still keep in touch.

Of course. I smile. Okay see you Monday.

Good luck with the house-hunting.

I have no luck with the house-hunting. Everything in Malahide is too expensive. I've everything packed up, my whole world in two suitcases and I'm contemplating checking into a Premier Inn when Donnacha calls by.

I'm sorry, he says immediately. It's my fault.

I don't know if he knows about the video on my phone but I'm not bringing it up.

It's not as creepy as it seems, trust me, he says. He moves out of his position and reaches out of sight to retrieve the canvas. I bought it for you, he says. I was going to give it to you. Just didn't get around to it yet.

299

Was trying to figure out how to do it in a way that wouldn't be creepy. So much for that.

I have to laugh at that.

Becky thought I drew it . . . I have informed her of the facts.

He hands it to me.

I saw this at the gallery. I thought it captured you beautifully, that you should have it.

I take it from him and study it properly. It's pastel crayon. I never saw this one before. And he's right, it is me. I look into my eyes and it's like I'm trying to tell myself something. A kind of bemused tilt to my lips. My freckles, dotted all across the bridge of my nose and cheeks. Less so on my body, but it's as though the artist has captured each one perfectly. Mapped them out like the stars in the sky. My left arm shows the scars, the constellations I spent countless nights mapping out. An artist who noticed. It's better than beautiful. It's me.

Genevieve is the artist, he says. It wasn't for sale, and I had a hard time convincing her to sell it. But then I told her it was for you. First time I've ever seen Genevieve shy, but she wanted you to have it.

Thank you, I say, deeply touched.

Do you have somewhere to stay, he asks.

I shake my head, tears welling.

A friend you can call, he says, shifting from foot to foot nervously. He doesn't want me to be his problem and the more questions he asks, the higher the chance that I will be.

Again, I shake my head.

Well then we can't just chuck you out on the street. Legally. You've paid until the end of the month, he asks, and I nod. Stay until the end of the month. Find someplace else in the meantime. I'll tell Becky. And just maybe, for both your sakes, stay out of each other's way.

Thank you, I sigh with relief.

Everything's packed away and I'm exhausted. I can't find my pyjamas so I sleep in my underwear. I hug my portrait to my chest. Refreshing and refreshing my emails in the hope that the minister emails me back.

★ ★ ★

Hey there, Tristan says, appearing out of nowhere and sitting down on an electrical box. What are you doing.

Sometimes the worst parking offenders can be disabled badge owners thinking they can park anywhere for however long they like, I say.

He laughs.

And then there's people like this guy here — I point to the white minivan — who have a secret strategy. Or at least they think they do.

And what's that, he asks me, eyes on me, grinning, arms folded, always amused by my job, or of how seriously I take it. As if, between me and him, I have the most entertaining job.

He's hogging the temporary space, I explain. Once this van has exhausted the time in a free parking bay, he leaves and instantly returns to the same spot.

Ooh.

Yes ooh. So what I do is record the position of the wheel valve on my handheld computer so that later I can prove it's been reparked. I've been doing this all morning, actually. He's moved it three times already. Why are you looking at me like that.

You're fascinating, he says with a grin. Shut up.

I haven't told him I'm being relocated. Not because I don't think he'll be able to cope without me, but because I don't know if I can. I don't want to say it out loud, make my moving away real, though maybe when my plan plays out with Carmencita it won't matter if I don't work here or live here. We'll have formed our own new relationship. A healthier one where I'm not just an irritating parking warden to her. By then I'll be visiting her in Malahide. It won't be just a workplace. It'll be a happy place that I look forward to spending time in. Instead of patrolling, I'll be strolling with her. Maybe get an ice cream and sit on the beach like other people do. Maybe people won't give me ugly stares and run when they see me.

I'm on a break, he explains. I like to watch you work. It calms me. Your face goes all — he scrunches up his face — so intense like I have all the power. Mwa-ha-hahaha.

I laugh and finally lower the machine. He's lifted me out of my dark mood.

Want to have lunch in my office, he asks, I have something to show you.

I would if I could, but I can't. I'm meeting Carmencita to discuss the event next week.

Oh of course. Lunch with your mother. He turns serious. I preferred the goofy Tristan. When are you going to tell her who you are.

When the time is right.

Don't leave it too long.

I know, I know. Look, I'm nervous as it is. I know that I shouldn't drag it out any longer and I keep meaning to tell her every time we meet but she's so bloody excited about Minister Brasil coming to the event that I can't tell her now. Maybe on the night when I'm in her good books. When it's all worked out and I've proved myself. I gulp hard. Or after.

You don't have to prove yourself to her, he says.

I don't answer.

Is the minister really coming, he asks, and I hear the doubt in his tone.

You think I'd lie, that I'm some kind of con artist, I ask angrily, as Becky's accusations return to me.

No, not in a bad way, just like, maybe you're being hopeful and enjoying your time with her. Maybe you're caught in a promise that you can't keep. He studies me to see if he's right. I just don't want you digging yourself into anything you can't get out of.

You sound like my mother. She keeps checking and checking over and over. She keeps calling and meeting with me to go over the details, like she doesn't believe that I'm handling this.

She's not dealing with the minister's office directly, he asks, that suspicious tone entering his voice again.

No. I am. That way I get to act as a middle person. I get to talk to Carmencita more.

Allegra, he rubs his face. You're stressing me out.

A fella rushes towards us, keys out, as if this is the first time he's moved the van. Sorry sorry, moving it now, he says good-naturedly.

Another criminal off the streets, well done, Tristan says.

I don't rise to him.

He pauses. Looks at me for a while. Are you okay.

I have to find a new place to stay. My lease is up. I didn't get much sleep, I'm just . . . I sigh . . . tired.

Take a quick break then and let me show you something, it will cheer you up.

I can't.

As he's walking away, I give up.

Okay fine, I call after him, what do you want to show me.

★ ★ ★

We sit upstairs in his office. He hasn't claimed Tony's, even though it's empty.

The game starts. Warden Wipeout. No blood. No violent beginning. It's different.

He checks my face.

Don't worry, I've made changes, he says. The idea of the game is to get the errands done in time to get back to your parked car before your parking ticket expires.

The developed town centre looks like it's modelled on Malahide. A lone person walks the paths, dressed in navy blue and a high-vis vest. The music is upbeat and chirpy, unlike before. A map on the top right of the screen reveals the warden's whereabouts with a red dot. A timer counts down to the parking ticket's expiry.

He pulls down an errand list. He needs to go to the supermarket to purchase milk and bread, post a letter, buy a coffee, collect dry cleaning. That kind of thing, and it all needs to be done before a parking ticket is issued. He collects money after achieving each goal.

He achieves it all on time, and happy warden, happy music. A sprinkle of colour, a tinkly tune. A *wow* and a *good job*. He wins level one.

It gets more complicated in each level, he says. Less time, more errands. If I don't achieve it all I get a ticket and I lose money. Warden Wipeout. You can get

304

rewards based on performance, he explains. A parking angel is one. It tops you up and gives you more time.

I smile.

The warden is not evil. She's the hero of the game.

It doesn't have blood, guts and gore. It's the least complex game we've created but its simplicity is its magic. There's a clear objective, it's easy to navigate. It rewards you for your deeds and makes you feel good. Ideal for those who crave the instant gratification and sense of accomplishment that box ticking brings. It's going to be Cockadoodledoo's first game, he says. Launching in the app store next month.

I smile. Thank you.

30

The jewellery robbery is headline news. Two men attack the woman inside and take off with gold. I immediately recognise the white van that they describe and, knowing this is a way to prove that I'm not what they thought I was, I go straight to the garda station. I ask for Laura and I'm grateful to have a face-to-face with her, even if it's speaking to her through the hatch. I have to do my duty and I want to prove to her that I'm a good person, friend worthy. I tell her everything I know about the white van that was parked in the free parking bay all day. I show her the photographs I took of the wheel valve, how it was moved various times, clearly in an effort to do reconnaissance of the area, not that I was trying to lead her, or plant motive and whatever in her head. She listens and takes notes. I even explain the description of the guy I saw driving the van, as I got a clear look at him.

Thanks, Allegra, she says, we'll follow up on that. We'll be in touch with you if we need anything further.

Great. Cool. Oh and one other thing. I hand her a leaflet for the event. This is happening this week. It's a women in business event being organised by the president of the Malahide Chamber of Commerce. I'm helping to organise it. The Minister for Justice is coming. She's the guest speaker.

I've seen the posters all around the place. I didn't realise you were involved.

Well I know the minister. So . . .

She must be very busy with everything going on at

the moment.

Yes. She is. But she'll still be there. She's definitely coming.

Okay. Thanks, Allegra. I might see you then. She takes the leaflet and goes to close the hatch.

Good luck catching the man in the white van! I wink and exit the station feeling good. Coins collected. Level up. The parking warden is not a bad person.

★ ★ ★

The twenty-fourth of June has arrived. The day of Carmencita's big event.

My bags are packed, I move out tomorrow. Genevieve helped me find a room in a three-bedroom townhouse. I'll be sharing with a tech guy and a barber. I won't sleep with either of them. It's five hundred for the month. I don't have the same space and privacy that I have now, but at least it's where I need it to be, near my mam.

I haven't seen or spoken to Becky since she evicted me. I haven't even spoken to Donnacha. Everyone is giving one another a wide berth and the tension I feel when I step outside to walk through the secret garden and past the house is enough to convince me that it's time to leave. I've requested to Fingal County Council that I stay in Malahide, so I'm hoping they don't relocate me. I believe Becky will be at the event tonight and I'm hoping that when she sees Minister Brasil there, talking to me, she'll realise I'm not the lying freak she has convinced herself I am. Most importantly, I can tell my mother who I am and she can feel proud. I'm hopeful about it all. I really am.

Carmencita has offered to do my hair for the event.

307

We do our hair, our nails and have a glass of champagne before walking up the road to St Sylvester's GAA club along with her staff. I'm really in a bubble of bliss. Every moment spent with her, even with her not knowing who I am, feels like a gift. Everyone's excited, giddy and on a high.

Local and national journalists are inside, but outside TV crews and newspaper photographers are parked up on account of the big political drama that's playing out, hoping to get a statement from her on the current state of affairs. The minister is due to arrive at 8.30 and also be the guest speaker. Even though she's not a local business-woman, Genevieve is my plus one, here to support me. Tristan arrives and Carmencita fawns all over him.

Are men allowed in, he asks.

Of course you are, she says. My children absolutely adore you, my daughter in particular. Rooster, Rooster, Rooster, she laughs.

Is that so. He looks up at me, teasing.

I widen my eyes, afraid he'll give it away. Not that daughter. Not yet. Not yet. I need this night to be a success first.

Did you know that Rooster paid for all the wine tonight, Carmencita tells me before moving on.

No, I didn't know that, I study him, appreciatively . . . thanks, Tristan.

I wanted to help, he says, moving closer to me, but I look past him, my eyes on Carmencita.

Becky, who's dressed in her Prada power trouser suit, has been enjoying the attention as the room's top business-woman. I hadn't realised the excitement that surrounded her, as the founder and CEO of Compression, a global tech company. She has been surrounded by adoring business fans since she arrived, even Tristan was impressed. All but Genevieve, who throws angry glares her way while she sips her wine. Defensive on my behalf. Becky hasn't glanced in my direction once, but her deliberate avoidance of me and any direction that I'm in tells me she always knows exactly where I am in the room. At one point she seems to swoop down on Carmencita, says something close to her ear with a stern expression, and then they both start making their way away from the crowd towards the hallway.

I leave Tristan, who's still talking about something I wasn't listening to, and reach the hallway before they do. I step into the cloakroom area, out of their view.

You have organised a wonderful night, Becky is saying. We're all here to support you.

Thank you, and I do appreciate your support but you have me concerned, what is it that you want to discuss, Carmencita says.

I notice the minister hasn't arrived yet, Becky asks.

No not yet, but she should be very soon, Carmencita says. Eight thirty.

Allegra arranged it, Becky asks.

Allegra. Yes Allegra. Do you know her.

Yes I do, she says and her tone is less than flattering. Unfortunately I do, Carmencita. I would just be . . . careful.

Yes, yes. She's a little strange.

I feel sick.

I'm concerned she may have misled you. The news on the way here, Becky says, is that the Taoiseach has resigned. That Minister Brasil may be next in line. There will have to be an emergency vote within the party to elect her. I just can't imagine that she can be here tonight, with everything that's going on, or even this week, that her office wouldn't have had the foresight to inform you.

Do you think Allegra is lying.

Carmencita sounds angry. Very angry. I know I should jump out and defend myself but I'm shaking. I'm trembling at their tone, their accusation. They intimidate me, make me want to crawl inside my shell.

I'd hate to accuse somebody of such a thing, Becky says, but in my dealings with her I wasn't sure if Allegra was a con artist, delusional, or a little of both. Whatever she is, she clearly can't be trusted. She inserts herself into situations that she has no business being in. For attention, perhaps. I hope that tonight I'm wrong, but it would be remiss of me not to mention anything.

It is remiss of you to bring this up only now, Carmencita says, taking no prisoners. She lets out a slew of curse words. Excuse me, please, Becky, I must go find her.

My heart is pounding. I escape to the toilets and lock the cubicle door. I can't believe Becky would do that to me. Forehead against the door, I close my eyes and grab my left arm, run my finger over the scars from freckle to freckle, feeling the raised scarred skin through the silk of my dress. I try to breathe and calm myself.

She's coming of course, of course she's coming.

I regain my composure and rejoin the guests. The community is chattering happily, glasses of wine in everybody's hands, the journalists are looking around, nobody is showing any signs of concern. If anything there's an atmosphere of excitement. Of people with common loves and goals together in one room, raising each other up. It's a great thing, what my mam has done. She left me for a better life and I've found her and see that she found a rich life. I'm proud of her. I'm proud to be her daughter. I just hope that I can make her proud tonight.

Allegra, Garda Laura says, grabbing my attention.

You made it, I say happily, my mood lifting even more. Thank you for coming.

I'm not staying long, I'm still on my shift, she says, displaying her glass of water. I just wanted to pop in. To have a quiet word with you, actually. We looked into that van.

Yes, I ask, my heart soaring. This is it. I'm not a weirdo, in fact I'm helpful, in fact I'm the kind of person you'd like to have as a friend. Would I like to go out on Friday night with you, Laura, and the other female gardaí to Copper Face Jacks on Leeson Street. Oh thanks for asking, yes please.

It wasn't our guys, she says, sticking a pin in my bubble of excitement, and I'm so confused. We appreciate you helping but we wouldn't want you to deliberately hinder an investigation. The photographs and details you brought to the station are of course private, they are the property of the council, as soon as you take them and log them. I don't believe you had permission to print them and bring them to the station.

There's a hardness in her. I'm being told off.

But I'm so confused. It was exactly like the white van that was described in the report, I say. They must have made a mistake. I logged it. I spent the afternoon watching the van. It was parked right there. On a reconnaissance.

It was a white van, she says, nodding. You got that bit right. Allegra, I know you wanted to be a garda and we do appreciate help from the public, but we don't appreciate being deliberately misled.

The way she's looking at me. I can see she thinks I'd do this on purpose.

I don't even have time to drum up a response because I feel a pinch on my upper arm.

Excuse me to interrupt, Carmencita says. It's eight forty-five, where is the minister, she asks rudely.

Garda Laura steps aside.

I'll check now, I say, feeling the panic rising again.

No, I will. Give me your contact — now. I should have done it myself weeks ago, she says, but her attention is taken from me as yet another person takes her away for a conversation and congratulations, allowing me to move to the fire exit door which is open a crack to allow fresh air into the hot and stuffy room.

I refresh my emails over and over again to see if there's been anything from Minister Brasil's office. Nothing. I go back through my sent emails: 24 June, 8 p.m. Guest speaker at 8.30 p.m. St Sylvester's GAA. Yes, I have supplied the office with all the correct details.

Tristan joins me outside, a glass of wine in his hand. Genevieve is just inside the door, looking out at me. I feel like they've teamed up to check on me.

Everything okay.

Yeah. Yeah. I feel a trickle of sweat down my back.

You know, Allegra, we've been talking, Genevieve and I. We're here for you.

I appreciate that. Thank you. I refresh my emails again.

If you think that she's not coming, he says slowly, for any reason, you should probably tell somebody now. You should tell Carmencita before it's too late.

So that she can arrange something else.

My heart is pounding. I don't think I've ever been so nervous. Or confused.

But she has to come, I whisper. She has to. I've everything riding on this.

I know. He takes my hand to comfort me.

Excuse me, a voice says loudly and Carmencita bursts out past Genevieve and into the laneway. She pulls me away, roughly, from the open fire exit so that nobody can hear her.

Hey hey, gently now, Genevieve says protectively, trying to remove Carmencita's pinching grip from my arm.

Where is she, she practically spits in my face. Where is my special guest.

I swallow. Look down at my phone and refresh, refresh, refresh with a trembling hand.

And then I know it's over.

She's not coming is she, she shouts.

Tristan looks at me with a face so full of hope that I hate myself so much right now. It's finished.

I shake my head and finally speak, my voice shaky. I just got word now. The Taoiseach has resigned and uh —

She freaks out. She pushes me against the wall, and I feel a shooting pain in my back. Tristan dives forward and tries to separate us but he doesn't want to hurt a woman, I can see that.

Fooled me. Liar. Humiliation. Journalists. The whole village is here. Liar. I knew it.

These are the main words that I hear. I see lips. Big glossy lips. The gap in her teeth. Spitting words of hate. Eyes filled with hate. The tight hand on my arm twisting and twisting. I know I will be bruised in the

313

morning. Another hand on my scars. The scars that link my freckles, that link me to Pops, yet I left him to be here with her and I'm still not good enough. My eyes fill as she continues.

Okay okay, Tristan says, firmly now. Him and Genevieve pull her away. You're hurting her.

Hurting her, ha. I could pull her hair out, her eyes out, she says viciously, then mumbles at me in Spanish. Nothing good.

I'm sorry, Carmencita. I tried. I really did. I wanted you to be proud of me. I wanted you to like me.

So you lied. Like a crazy person. Why would I be proud of this.

No, I say, firmly. I never lied about anything. Let me explain. Please.

Genevieve nervously bites the skin from her nails. I look at Tristan and he nods at me encouragingly. Pull the Band-Aid off quickly. Do it. Tell her. I take a deep breath. It's now or never. I can't live with a life of never.

Carmencita, my name is Allegra Bird. I'm your daughter.

She freezes. Literally. She's not moving, not blinking. I wonder if I should say it again. The first time was difficult enough. I count. One, two, three . . .

What did you say, she asks, her voice quiet. Not angry. Not cold. It's encouraging.

My name, Carmencita, is Allegra . . . Bird. Bernard's daughter. I moved here to find you.

Nooooooooooooo.

She yells it so loudly a few heads peek out of the side exit and Genevieve closes the doors and stands there protectively. She screeches it a few more times, hands to her face, long nails, painted and polished

314

to perfection, like she's the Wicked Witch of the West melting.

Then she stands up straight and looks at me, dead in the eye. Not a friendly look. And she slaps me across the face. A sting that shocks me.

Hey, Tristan shouts, pulling her away from me, but she's finished with fighting with me. She only has words left. The slap was easier.

You listen here. Finger in my face. You should never have been born. I should have gotten rid of you. When I think of you, that is all I think about now. That I should have gotten rid of you . . . I went to him for help, to get rid of you, and he said he would keep you. The biggest mistake I ever made. He was supposed to keep you away from me, do you understand. That was the deal.

Stop, I cry.

Okay, stop now, Tristan says, hands coming across my shoulders, pulling me in. I don't think she needs to hear this right now.

Oh yes she does. She's a liar. She's made a fool of me. You disgust me. Go back to him. You deserve each other. Two crazy fools. You are just like him. I didn't want you then, I don't want you now.

I tune out the rest.

Stop, I hear Tristan saying to her, angry now. Stop it now. Calm down and go in and talk to your guests. Allegra, stay here, I'll be back in a minute.

But I can't stay here.

It's over.

★   ★   ★

315

I pull away from Genevieve, who's trying to keep me back, but she lets me go. I walk down the alleyway. The media are outside the entrance to the GAA club, awaiting the arrival of the special guest who will never arrive. I'm crying so much I can't see straight but I know I need to turn left, away from them. As I walk, I'm aware of the stares as people pass me by.

Are you okay, someone asks, concerned.

I stumble on.

Come here, love.

I feel an arm around me. Strong. Tight. An arm that has held me that way for so many years. Pops.

She didn't want me, I say, crying harder, wrapping my arms around him. I sound like a child. I hear it in my voice. The loss, the hurt, the pain. The little girl aching.

I know, love, I know. It's her loss. It's always been her loss. But you had to discover it, didn't you. You know now. You brave girl. You brave, brave girl, he says hugging me, his voice firm and strong, repeating it over and over, trying to make me believe it. I had to let you do it. I had to stand back and let you do it. My God, it almost killed me. But you've done it now. You're a brave girl, Allegra. Most of us would run away from a thing like that. He speaks to me in the familiar voice and tone, as if I'd fallen on a slippery mossy rock and hurt my knee. Rocking me, brushing my hair, mouth to my ear. Repetitive soothing sounds and words.

★ ★ ★

This is nice, he says, and I snap out of my zombified state and realise that we're sitting on my bench without any clear recollection of how we got here.

316

I have my lunch here every day, I say. Granary bread with cheese. An apple, walnuts, and a flask of tea.

Is that so. Very nice.

Tell me again how you're here, I look at him, suddenly seeing him properly.

I was up for the post office closure protest on the government, but I thought I'd swing by here, in case, you know . . .

That's convenient, I say, wiping my eyes.

Pauline told me to stay away, that you're an adult who can make her own decisions. He looks at me questioningly. Should I have stayed away.

I shake my head. I'm glad he's here. You knew what would happen, you knew better than I did, I say, fresh tears falling again. I wipe them roughly, angrily, annoyed with myself.

As a parent, we always consider worst-case scenarios. We've got to be prepared for all events, but we always hope we're wrong.

A sudden car horn gives me a fright. It rings out long and urgent.

Bernard, a voice yells. Bernard!

I wipe my eyes and look up. An attractive older woman, blonde with quirky squared glasses, sticks her head out of her car window, blocking traffic, hand on the horn, a tough but concerned look on her face. I must look a state because she takes one look at me and shouts, I'll park over here, and speeds away.

That's Bonnie, he says.

Despite everything, I can't help but smile. Then I laugh, a delirious kind of laugh.

What's wrong with you now, he says, all embarrassed.

Ohh, I say slowly.

317

Stop it now, Allegra.

It all becomes clear.

Stop it, he says, but he can't fight the smile that's breaking on to his face.

The post offices, I say, fingers up in inverted commas, winking at him and nudging him. We've got to save the post offices.

He's laughing now, at the teasing, and he doesn't want to.

How many people were at the protest today, I ask.

Ah.

Come on, tell me.

Two of us.

Did you even protest, I ask.

We had lunch in Stephen's Green.

We both laugh.

But we're serious about the post offices.

I believe you.

We're enjoying each other's company, he says finally.

Well that's good, I say, I'm happy for you.

Yes, well. He looks everywhere but at me, he's embarrassed.

I stop smiling, the penny dropping. Was there even a protest today, Pops, I ask.

I wanted to be here for you, he says. Bonnie said she'd drive.

Who needs four more when I've one like this.

I look out and mentally say goodbye to the view, to this place, that accommodated me and my hopes. Time to check out.

31

I'm sitting with Pops at home in Valentia drinking his much-improved home brew. It's a Friday night and we're watching the aptly named *Friday Night Show*, the highest viewed live Friday-night entertainment talk show in the country.

The next guest gets my full attention.

This week has been a tumultuous week for the country, says the presenter Jasmine Chu, and especially so for my next guest. Ladies and gentlemen, please welcome our new Taoiseach, Ruth Brasil.

Pops looks at me in surprise. He sits up, turns the TV up.

Thank you, Jasmine, she says sitting down.

Taoiseach, how's your week been, she asks.

The audience laugh. So does she.

Jasmine, it's been a wild and wonderful week in many ways. I think what is most important is ensuring that there is stability and contentment within the people of this country. While everything has been going on behind the scenes, I suppose it's very important to keep the calm and the balance for this country, for us to continue to prosper and move forward . . . I zone out a bit as she continues the politician-speak about how everything has changed but nothing has changed.

So can you tell us how it felt for you personally, when you heard you were to become the next Taoiseach of this great country.

I was on my way to an event actually. A business

319

event in Malahide organised by the president of the Chamber of Commerce, where I was to speak to the attendees about women in business. So I must apologise to all those who had gathered at the event to hear me speak and to those who I let down. I received the phone call from the Taoiseach to say that he was stepping down, that he was putting me forward and that I was to go to the party immediately for a vote.

Pops looks at me, fist in the air proudly. They'll know now, Allegra. I hope they're all watching.

My heart is pounding. I feel vindicated. I hope that Carmencita is watching. If she isn't, she'll hear about it. Of course she will. She was mentioned. She'll be delighted. Everyone who was at the party, Becky, Garda Laura, all those who thought I'd lied about securing the minister as a guest speaker, will believe me now. Even Tristan and Genevieve, who said they believed me but probably doubted me, will have proof. And yet it doesn't make me feel better. It's too little too late. Nothing can change what transpired.

They talk about the Taoiseach, her inspirations growing up, and her aspirations for politics.

A young woman from Valentia Island said to me recently — and thank you, Allegra Bird, if you're watching — that you are the average of the five people you spend the most time with. And I have to say when I heard the expression it gave me pause. It made me take stock of who was around me, who I want to be, and the traits of those great people I have been surrounded by, as a result of which I have been able to flourish. Because I think that's what great support does, great mentors and friends, support and guidance, it helps you flourish. I would not be in the position I am in now if it weren't for those very special five. I want the same for this country. I want this country to be surrounded by the best so that it too can flourish.

Pops reaches out and grabs my hand. And that's really all I need.

He's my one. He's always been my one. The most powerful, my everything. My five people all in one.

★ ★ ★

Look, Allegra, look, Pops says, pointing to a creature moving on the beach.

What is it, I ask, wriggling my toes in my Wellington boots. My socks are wet. I jumped too much, splashed too hard, I don't like the feeling of wet feet in my boots. But I like my boots. They're new. They're yellow with fish on them and Pops gave them to me this morning as a present because I am five years old today.

Let me tell you about the hermit crab, Pops says, hunkering down close to the crab. Come closer, pet, don't be afraid, he says, taking me by the hand and leading me from my rock to the sand. He knows I don't like to touch these things like he does, but he always tells me not to be afraid and I try not to be. I hunker down beside him.

The hermit crab has a soft abdomen, a soft body here, he points, so it needs to be protected by its shell.

Like a snail.

Yes, like a snail. That's also a gastropod. But different to the snail, Allegra, because as the crab grows, it requires a larger shell. Sometimes they swap shells with other crabs, the bigger crabs leave their shells for the smaller crabs, and so on, like a chain. But sometimes there aren't enough shells to share and the hermit crabs argue over it. But they usually try to be fair and so they line up, and they wait for the right shell to come along. They're very picky about their shells, they need them to be just right, but they never keep the same shell forever, they're always growing and finding new shells to fit them.

We watch as the hermit crab tries to crawl into its new shell.

Later that evening I'm crawling around the living room with the shoebox from my new Wellington boots over my head.

I'm a hermit crab, Pops. I've grown and this is my new shell.

Pops chuckles as I crawl on all fours around the living room. Oh you're a big girl now, pet, aren't you. You're going to need a much bigger shell than that.

★　★　★

I remember this now as Pops and I sit in the living room together twenty years later. The year that I've had was one of those years, when I grew, when I had to leave my shell and scrambled to find another. I've crawled around, on hands and knees, going sideways to move forward, with a cardboard box over my head, trying to find a place to fit.

32

It's one of the last boat trips of the day, close to 10 p.m. We're heading to Reenard's Point on the car ferry for the final run. I've been back working on the ferry for the past few days and it's not been bad coming back because nothing is the same. Nothing can ever be the same when all the time we're changing. I stand at the edge after going from window to window, from car to car, taking the payments, and I watch the red clock tower of Knightstown get further away. The evening sky is still light, will be until eleven or so. The great stars will shine brightly soon, Saturn and Jupiter are in line with the moon tonight. Next week I begin a new job as a tour guide for the International Dark Sky Reserve, using laser aids, telescopes and high-powered binoculars to show groups the special sights that have guided me all my life. Like turning over a rock on the beach, I'll help reveal what's hidden by day. I can't wait to start. I realise now that the same stars and constellations have always been above me no matter where I travel, but there's only one place where I can see it all clearly, and that's here. Home.

I hear a sound that makes me spin on my heels. It's coming from Reenard's Point. An engine. Distinctive. I don't need to concentrate hard to see, it's popping out from the landscape, the bright yellow Ferrari amidst the dark, drab fish factory buildings lining Reenard's Point. As we get closer the car door opens and Tristan gets out. He grins at me. He beeps his car.

What are you doing, I shout across the water as soon as we're close enough for him to hear. He grins and gets back into his car, preparing to drive on after the ferry has unloaded. I step back and watch in shock as he drives on first, slowly and carefully being the vehicle that it is, followed by the remaining cars in the queue that I ignore and am too stunned to guide to their places. He turns off the engine and gets out of the car with a cheeky grin, loving my absolute state of surprise and confusion. The passenger door opens and Pops climbs out.

Well it's the first time I've been in a Ferrari, Allegra, and my my, that's what brings the wild to the Wild Atlantic Way, Pops says, grinning at me.

Your dad drives very fast, Tristan says, eyes wide and faux scared.

I know, he drives very . . . what the . . . what are you doing, I stammer as I try to compute the vision. Why are you two, how are you . . . what the . . .

You left your notebook behind, Tristan says, holding up my gold notebook.

I'd left it behind on purpose. I'd thrown it in the bin at Becky and Donnacha's. I should have ripped the pages out too, but I'd discarded it because nothing in it meant anything to me any more.

Becky, your landlord, came by my office to give it to me. After she saw the *Friday Night Show*, by the way.

I do feel a small sense of satisfaction. Quite regularly I like to imagine her expression when she heard my name from the mouth of our new prime minister. I like to imagine Carmencita's reaction too, but I don't think anything I do or say could ever win her over and I can't imagine that will ever stop hurting. That's a crack that may always remain in my shell.

324

I'm sorry but I read it, Tristan says.

It doesn't matter, it wasn't a diary. Half-written notes to Katie, Amal, and the now Taoiseach. My practised letter to Carmencita. He knew what was in those letters anyway.

There was one page that caught my eye, he says, and he opens it up to show me.

The title was my five people and beneath it, the constellation w-shaped list I'd compiled of the five people I actually spent the most time with.

Number one, he reads aloud and my heart starts banging in my chest. Pops, he says, because he loves me. Number two: Spanner, because he sees me. Number three: Paddy, because he teaches me. Number four: Tristan, because he inspires me. Number five: Genevieve, because she knows every inch of me, warts and all.

The driver's door opens in the vehicle behind.

Hi Allegra, Genevieve sings. My God, my legs are stiff, wow, this is beautiful. Jasper's minding the gallery, I'm here for the week, she grins.

Paddy emerges from the car next in line with a wave, and finally Spanner, with little Ariana who bounces around, excited to be on a boat.

Got custody for the holliers, Spanner says with a wink, taking off after her.

I look at them all, totally confused and stunned to see them, this mix of people, all together, here, on Valentia Island. They all gather together, around Pops and Tristan, looking at me with grins on their faces, proud of themselves for pulling off the big secret.

Go on, Spanner says, nudging Tristan roughly.

So I guess I'll do the talking then, Tristan says, sounding more nervous than I've ever heard him. We

325

are all here because, we're your five. But most importantly we all have something in common which is that you, Allegra Bird, are one of our five. I'll go first.

He clears his throat.

Apart from my parents, he says nervously, you're the only one who lets me be Tristan. Everyone else has me on their list as Rooster. And of all the mentors I've had and searched for, you're one of the most inspiring people I know.

Because you're beautiful inside and out, Genevieve says loudly and confidently, the sentence like a song.

Because you show up every day, shouts Spanner.

Because you're my friend, says Paddy, delivering it with such duty and honour.

I look at Pops. His voice trembles and it's the undoing of me. Because you're my daughter, he says. My one and only.

Pops' lopsided smile and trembling lips. Tristan's nervous, embarrassed face, his puppy dog eyes. I'm in shock. I look at them all. Feel utterly speechless but so happy, so very bloody deliriously happy.

And if it makes any difference, Tristan adds, you're my number one.

I might have to battle you for that one, Pops says to Tristan, then winks at me. His wink forces a tear down his cheek, which he wipes away with the back of his hand.

Acknowledgements

Thank you, Lynne Drew, Lara Stevenson, Kate Elton, Charlie Redmayne, Elizabeth Dawson, Anna Derkacz, Hannah O'Brien, Abbie Salter, Kimberley Young, Isabel Coburn, Alice Gomer, Tony Purdue, Patricia McVeigh, Ciara Swift, Jacq Murphy and all the innovative team at HarperCollins UK. I feel honoured to be working with you, to be published by you, and to have a seat at your table, even if it was a virtual room this year.

Thanks to my literary representatives at Park & Fine Literary and Media Agency. In particular, Theresa Park, Abby Koons, Ema Barnes, Andrea Mai, Emily Sweet and Alex Greene. A super team of superwomen. Thanks to Howie Sanders at Anonymous Content, Anita Kissane and Sarah Kelly.

Thanks without end to booksellers and readers for your support.

Thanks to my tribe — my friends, my family, my David, my Robin, my Sonny, my Blossom . . . my everythings.

F/AHE   25/11/21